Praise for works by

JUDITH JAMES

"Fueled by sizzling sensuality and sharp wit,
James' refreshingly different historical deftly re-creates
the glittering, colorful court of Charles II while also
delivering an unforgettable love story."
—*Booklist,* starred review, on *Libertine's Kiss*

"James' unusual love story is one of emotional impact….
Readers will find this poignant love story
enthralling and unforgettable."
—*RT Book Reviews* on *Libertine's Kiss*

"Judith James fearlessly bursts through the ceiling of
the historical romance genre and soars to astounding
heights. Her writing is intriguing, daring, exquisitely
dark, and emotionally riveting."
—*USA TODAY* bestselling author Julianne MacLean

"Sarah and Gabriel's heart-wrenching struggle to
keep their love alive…will really keep readers entranced
throughout this epic read."
—*Publishers Weekly* on *Broken Wing*

Also available from
Judith James
and HQN Books

Libertine's Kiss

the King's Courtesan

JUDITH JAMES

Recycling programs
for this product may
not exist in your area.

ISBN-13: 978-0-373-77559-0

THE KING'S COURTESAN

Copyright © 2011 by Judith James

This edition published by arrangement with Harlequin Books S.A.

For questions and comments about the quality of this book please contact us at Customer_eCare@Harlequin.ca.

www.HQNBooks.com

Printed in U.S.A.

Acknowledgments

My thanks go to my editor, Ann Leslie Tuttle, for bringing calm during the storm (literally) and for bending over backward to give me the time so I could do what needed to be done. I would have been lost without her.

Thanks also to Bob, for helping me navigate the peaks and valleys, and for thinking to take and send a special picture. That was so thoughtful and sweet.

And to my wonderful friends Anne, Bev, Cheryl and Nick, thanks for your patience and support when I disappear into my cave to write for months on end.

Last but not least, to all those wonderful readers. Your support and good wishes make it all worthwhile.

This book is for my mom, who faces life's challenges with courage, grace and humor no matter how tough it gets, and still takes the time to go on helicopter rides. And for my dad, who lives life to the fullest, enjoying every moment of the ride. When I grow up, I want to be just like them.

the King's Courtesan

PROLOGUE

London, 1651

THE DAY HOPE MATHEWS'S life changed forever dawned crisp and clear. She awoke, clutching her kitten, lying on a cot in a corner garret of a steep-gabled four-story building. Her home, a substantial structure comprised of three linked houses, all of them leaning drunkenly over the street below, was at the center of a zigzag web of side streets and alleys, some barely wide enough for two pedestrians to pass. It was late autumn. The metallic bite of winter was in the air and frost patterned the rooftops, making the city beyond her windows shimmer like some alabaster-and-diamond fairy land. She imagined she was a princess, trapped high in a tower, waiting for a handsome rescuer to charge the battlements and take her away.

The bells started ringing well before dawn, invading the gloomy quiet generally reserved for bakers starting their day and link boys ending theirs. The sleepy city was stirring, and there was already a bustle in the streets below. The Lord Protector and his army had been sighted. Fresh from victories in Ireland and Scotland, the young Charles Stuart driven from England's shores, they were returning home. Despite the Protector's edicts against gambling, roistering and drink, soldiers did as they had always done. As the good people of London, deprived of any spectacle since the beheading of their former king, set out early to secure a place along the route to watch the coming parade, every shopkeeper, wine maker, tavern worker and whore were making preparations for what promised to be a very lucrative day.

Drury Lane, on the eastern edge of Covent Garden, was one of the most colorful areas in London even in these drab times. Brightly painted sign boards hung from every house and business. Her own home was marked by a proud fighting cock, strutting past a golden-haired siren with wide blue eyes and crimson lips. Her mother boasted to one and all that the Merry Strumpet was listed in *The Wandering Whore,* and as its proprietor, she was noted therein as one of London's best known bawds. It was one of the establishments counting on profits this day, and Hope knew she needed to escape immediately or be trapped running errands, raking cinders and cleaning floors, missing the spectacle entirely.

She slipped down the stairs and ducked through an alley, joining a laughing band of urchins who greeted her as one of their own. The sun had risen, the throng was thickening and they weaved in and out of jostling crowds, nimbly dodging carts and angry merchants as they stuffed their pockets with filched fruit and biscuits. She lost her companions as she approached the city center, their loose-knit brotherhood disbanding as each sought a perch from which to watch the show.

The steady drumming in the distance was getting louder by the minute and she jumped up and down, trying to see past the people in front of her. Spying a low-hung balcony, she forced her way through a river of people and pulled herself up, kicking and squirming, wrapping her arms around a beam. Ignoring the protests of its already cramped inhabitants, she positioned herself so she had a bird's-eye view of the street below.

First came a vast army of grim-faced pikemen in their shining breastplates, pot helmets and buff leather coats, marching in rigid formation, their weapons bristling as the air rang with the tramping of booted feet. Then came Cromwell himself at the head of the Ironsides, his famous company of horse, but there was none of the pageantry and color, the smiles and waves and dashing displays of a royalist parade. They passed by, row upon row, a faceless army with nothing to distinguish one from another, and the cheers that greeted them were dutiful rather than spontaneous. It was clearly a display of might and power. Veiled threat and stark reminder more than celebration, but any kind of public gathering was scarce in the city these days and any spectacle was preferable to none at all.

She was beginning to wonder if the adventure had been worth the bother when a prancing black horse caught her attention. It frothed and fretted, tossing its head and stepping sideways, breaking an otherwise perfect formation, yet its rider did not seem inclined to curb it. Unlike his fellows, who looked straight ahead, he seemed to scan the crowd with interest. Tall and broad-shouldered, he managed the beast with ease. He wore no uniform and looked more like a cavalier than a Puritan. He must be an officer, and a wellborn one at that. Her heart thudded with girlish excitement. From a distance he appeared to be young and handsome, and much like the gallant rescuer she imagined in her daydreams. It was hard to get a good look at him, though, with his wide-brimmed hat pulled low, obscuring his features.

Interest piqued, she leaned out further, trying to get a better look, when a sudden scuffle behind her knocked her off balance and sent her tumbling to the street below. She lurched to her feet a moment before a shod hoof would have crushed her fingers, only to back into the hindquarters of a startled horse. When it shied away from her, its rider cursing, she slipped and almost fell again. Surrounded on all sides she dodged and darted, wooden shoes slipping on the muddy cobbles, trying to remain upright as she was buffeted from beast to beast. As her panic grew someone snarled and cuffed her and one man kicked her between the shoulders, growling for her to get out of the way. People were trampled to death in London every day and if she fell again—

A strong hand gripped the back of her dress and swung her up and into the air as easily as if she were a small child. Her rescuer deposited her in his lap, holding her tight with one arm, apparently heedless of his fine clothes and her muddy form.

"Apologies, my lady, for the rough handling and the loss of your shoes, but you seemed in imminent danger of being trampled."

It was him! The man she'd watched but moments before. The man from her daydreams. He was real. He had come to her rescue. She had never been at a loss for words before, but now, when she desperately wanted to say something witty, charming, memorable, she was tongue-tied. "I…I…I…"

"There now, lass. Take a deep breath and don't worry. You've had a scare and need some time to gather your wits."

She almost moaned in frustration. He thought her a witless fool!

"You're shivering. Sit close now, and share my warmth." She *was* cold and she had nearly died. She sank against him, her arms wrapped tight around his waist, enjoying the feeling of comfort and safety, the strength she felt in his arms and chest, and the sound of another heart beating, just inches from her own. As he tucked his cloak around her she heard cheering from the crowd. She'd had no idea anyone was aware of her plight or cared if they were. Now she beamed and waved to them and they roared their approval.

Her companion chuckled. "I think we have brought some entertainment to an otherwise dull morning. I'm afraid you'll have to ride it out with me the rest of the way. There's no place to put you down safely until we reach the palace gates. Will that suit?"

She nodded, shy for the first time in her life.

"Excellent! You're safe now, lass. And you've the best seat in the house. Relax and enjoy the view."

She felt like a princess in his arms, and as unlikely as it might seem, she decided he was her prince. Why else had he passed her way this day? Why had she noticed him right away? How was it she had fallen just as he was passing and what made him save her when no one else had even tried? It didn't matter if she found nothing to say this moment, for fate had brought him to her and he was destined to be hers.

Even so, she still wasn't sure what he looked like. His hat was pulled low, keeping his face in shadow. She could tell he was young. She could tell he was handsome from his strong chin, firm mouth and white smile, but she couldn't see his eyes.

When they reached the courtyard outside the palace gates, he used his horse as a bulwark against the crowd, making a little island in a corner by the wall. He dismounted first, then lifted her from the saddle as if she were light as air. He grinned and wiped a speck of dirt from her nose. Her face blazed with embarrassment, but his smile was kind and amused. "You're hard to see, lass, under all of this." He rubbed a dab of mud from her cheek with one finger. "But if you're half as lovely as those eyes, you must be a vision." He took her hand and bowed, as though she were a great lady, then slipped half a crown in her palm. "To replace your shoes, my lady."

"Thank you, my lord. For saving my life." They were the only words she could find. Her heart was pounding so loud it was a wonder he didn't hear it.

"No lord I, lass. Just a humble soldier who stumbled upon a pixie on the way home. To catch one must mean luck of some kind. Stay safe, girl, and wish me well."

She watched as he rode away. She didn't know his eyes, she didn't know his name, but she knew he was hers and she'd see him again. She caught one last glimpse of him as he passed through the castle gates. As if sensing her gaze upon him, he looked back at her and waved.

She started home with frozen toes, a smile she was sure would never go away, and the feeling she was walking on air. When she wasn't humming to herself she broke into laughter or sudden bursts of song. Halfway there, she met two of her mother's ladies accompanied by a burly doorman. They hurried over, breathless. They had been searching for her all morning. Her mother needed her at once.

The brothel was always humming with energy and noise. It rang with the sound of song and laughter, though the singing was drunken and off-key and the laughter often shrill. It smelled of braised beef, brandy and ale, stale perfume and stale sex. Silks and petticoats rustled up and down the stairs and in and out of the secret exit for those guests who preferred anonymity, and well-dressed gentlemen and partly dressed ladies wandered its halls.

Several of those who lived there were her friends. Her mother's ladies often told her stories as they taught her how to mix perfume from oils and flowers, and how to paint her face and fix her hair. She wasn't terribly interested in those lessons, but many of them were country girls and she loved their tales of princes and princesses, magical folk who granted wishes and careless girls who got lost in the wild. *And now I have a story all my own.*

They had told her other things, too, over the years. Things about men, though her mother had been careful to keep her away from the customers. How to soothe them, how to excite them and how to give them pleasure. How to use a beeswax cap or silk-covered sponge to prevent an unwanted baby, and a sheath to protect against a man who appeared diseased. Between their frank talk and what she'd witnessed through open doors, around corners and in supposedly quiet corridors she'd seen enough of naked husbands and great lords, callow young men and randy soldiers, to feel she didn't need or want to learn any more. *That's not love.* Love was what *she* wanted. And she'd found her true love today.

Not that her mother would approve. From early on, her mother tried to instill in her the importance of wise commerce. It was how she herself rose from the ranks of drabs prowling London's streets, working in alleys with their backs against a wall, to become a prosperous woman of affairs. *But I don't have to be like her. I don't and I won't.*

She was hurried up to her room with a great deal of fussing and clucking, only to find her mother waiting with a warm smile and a cup of hot chocolate. She eyed her warily and clutched her kitten defensively. Her mother was not one for kind gestures or maternal concern.

"Well, here you are, lovey. And just in time. Today's a very special day for you indeed."

Hope blinked, confused. "What do you mean? I don't understand."

"You've grown up within these walls, girl. You understand. Today you take up your duties as a woman. You've had a roof over your head all these years and plenty to eat, too. That's more than many a poor lamb in London can say. But you *are* a woman now. Your courses started last month. Your greatest possession besides beauty is your maidenhead. A jewel that is. A thing of great value. Something a woman can give only once, despite what certain lying sluts might do or say. But it needs proper management. Just like arranging a good marriage. Don't look so shocked, child!" She reached out a gnarled hand to pat her shoulder in an awkward and unconvincing display of motherly concern.

"You're a whore, my dear. Born into it right and proper, though I was married to your father for all that. You'd best get used to the idea because you can never be aught else. You've no breeding, no property, and there's no chance any decent man will have you. A girl like you won't ever be married and who would want it? Your own father was a useless bastard. But for all that you're a rare beauty, with his raven hair and very fine eyes indeed. And you've charm and a quick wit. Such gifts are wasted on a wife. She's no need of them to catch a man, provided she has money, and she's nay allowed to make use of them once she's married. Property she is. Broodmare and slave."

Hope was too shocked to speak. It was the longest conversation she'd ever had with this stranger who'd once been her mother, and it was not the awkward declaration of love she'd both dreaded and longed for. She blinked back tears, feeling like the world's biggest fool. *She didn't keep me safe to protect me, but to add to my value.* She wanted to feel contempt and hatred but she couldn't move past a soul-killing pain. *I should have known. I should have known.*

Her mother stroked her hair as she spoke, taking no notice of how it made her flinch. *Is this how she recruits new girls? Stroking and cooing like a beady-eyed pigeon? Is this all I am to her?*

"Now look here, at the pretty dress his lordship has sent you!"

The dress, with its white satin underskirt and sleeves shot through with silver braid, looked like a wedding dress but for the indecently low-cut bodice. She knew what it meant. There would be no prince for her. No choice. No happy ending.

"Which lord?" Her voice was barely a whisper.

"Let's leave that as a surprise for now. It will add authenticity to the undertaking." Taking her silence for acceptance, her mother rubbed her hands together and nodded briskly. "Good girl! The anticipation is building, child. We're to have an auction tonight and you are the prize. There's naught to fear. You've seen enough of what happens here to know that, and only my best gentlemen will take part. Remember what all the other girls have told you and use it well. You'll fetch a fine price, my dear. Half to you and half to the house. You'll be off to a grand start in life. No daughter of mine will be a common whore. You'll be a rich man's mistress. You're a lovely girl. Sharp and lively, too. You'll climb higher than I ever dreamed or dared."

There must have been something—a flash in her eyes, the stubborn tilt of her chin that hinted at rebellion—because when her mother left she locked the door behind her and positioned a doorman in the corridor.

They bathed and perfumed her, and then tamed and combed her unruly hair so it fell like a dark silken river to her waist. They ushered her into a paneled room where her mother and two of her "ladies" sat in attendance, as if she were a bride. There were at least five gentlemen present, though all she could see were their boots. She kept her eyes on the floor, willing them all to disappear, imagining if she but closed her eyes and opened them again the day would start anew.

But it didn't, and she stood red-faced and mute as they joked and murmured, waiting for the bidding to begin. There was no doubt as to the outcome. Sir Charles Edgemont would have her. 'Twas he who'd provided the dress. Nevertheless, her mother knew an auction would raise the price he paid for her "dowry" and had refused to spare her the humiliation when several hundred pounds might be at stake. Two of the ladies stripped her of her bodice and overskirt as the bidding heated up, leaving her tearstained and trembling, standing in her shift.

Inflamed by the sight of her and determined no other man should see naked what was meant to be his, Edgemont rose and bid two thousand pounds, raising howls of protest from the other gentlemen but effectively quelling the game. She looked at him then, from under her lashes. His hair was dark and close-cropped, interspersed here and there with flecks of grey. His eyes were cold, his face harsh, his jaw square.

Furious at being duped when he'd expected a private negotiation, but too proud to back out in front of his friends, Sir Charles took her wrist in a cruel grip and jerked her toward the door, stopping before he left to toss a heavy purse on the table. "This will have to do for now, madam. I had not expected the price to soar so high. My man will bring you the rest tomorrow."

"But of course, my lord. You are known throughout London as a man who pays his debts. I shall await your pleasure. In the meantime, take the girl and enjoy her."

It was clear the auction had raised far more than even she had anticipated, and the poorly concealed smirk on her face and hard-edged gleam of avarice in her eyes almost made Hope retch. Instead, she placed a delicate hand on Sir Charles's chest and leaned into him, shivering, tucking her head against his shoulder. His lips twisted in annoyance, but he released his grip on her wrist and removed his coat, wrapping it around her. She spoke for the first time since entering the room.

"You must only give her one half of it, my lord. For the rest was promised to me."

"You're as greedy and canny as your mother, girl," he growled. "If you're a virgin still, I'm Archbishop of Canterbury. But I'll have my money's worth from you nonetheless."

"Of course, Your Grace," she said with a curtsy. Amidst her mother's furious squawking and the laughter of the other men, a grim-faced Sir Charles bit back a reluctant chuckle and bundled her out the door and into his waiting coach.

The day she met her own true love was the day her mother sold her. It was the day she lost all hope of him. The day her childhood ended. She never saw him again. She never spoke to her mother again, and she stopped believing in happy ever after. Her mother had named her Hope. It seemed a cruel jest, but she did the only thing she could do. She took the name and made it a talisman. She did what she needed to keep her own hopes alive. The day she left her mother's doorstep she stopped dreaming about what couldn't be, and started planning for what might. The only thing she couldn't stop was asking herself one question. *What kind of parent puts a price on innocence and sells their child like a slave?* It still had the power to steal her breath.

Nevertheless, what started as a cruel betrayal and felt like the end of the world was the start of a journey that transformed her into a well-spoken, smartly dressed, well-educated young woman. An accomplished dancer with a smattering of French and the attention of a monarch. *How dramatic and short-sighted we are as children.* Along the way she let go of her fantasies of true love and imaginary princes, and found herself a real one, with all his flaws and imperfections. If from time to time her heart ached for something more, for someone else, no one knew it but her.

CHAPTER ONE

Cressly Manor, Nottinghamshire, 1662

HE DARTED AROUND *a corner, his pursuers snarling at his heels. It was dark, the sky an impenetrable blanket smothering a ruined town blackened and seared by fire. Pockets of angry flames licked the sky and bodies littered the street. Those who'd survived the inferno and escaped the sword huddled in cellars, wells and ditches, hushed and trembling, waiting for the storming of booted feet to pass them by.*

He sprinted toward the town center and ducked down a secluded street that was little more than an alley. There was no moon and no illumination other than the reddish glow of torchlight. The path he'd chosen led nowhere but a wall too high to climb. He'd reached a dead end.

Straightening, he turned to face his pursuers. They slowed and stopped, suddenly wary, something in his face, his stance, turning anticipation into confusion and fear. He growled low in his throat. Ferocious. Triumphant. This was the moment he'd been training for, waiting for, living for. They stumbled over each other, slowly backing away; all but their leader, who seemed oddly bemused. They'd understood too late. They were the prey.

He might have got off two shots with his pistols in those first moments of stunned surprise, but this wasn't an act of war. This required intimacy. This was personal. His eyes flashed and metal sparked as he drew a gleaming sword, attacking with a lightning-quick savagery fueled by hatred, fanned by a lust for vengeance and nursed over the course of several years. One man took the blade to the throat before he could ready his weapon. Another fumbled with a pistol only to stagger backward, ashen-faced with shock, before falling.

Their leader hadn't moved. A handsome man with graying hair, he stood waiting, sword at the ready, curiosity rather than fear in his eyes. "We have met before. How do I know you?"

"Cressly," he hissed, leaping forward, slamming him hard against the wall. He pinioned him by the throat with one arm as the longsword drove under his guard between breast and back plate and thick buff coat, cutting through leather, skin and bone. The man's eyes showed shock and bewilderment but it wasn't enough. He leaned into him, turning and twisting the hilt of his sword with sadistic force, not bothering to stifle the man's shrill scream of agony.

"'Twas Cressly in Nottinghamshire we met, Lord Stanley," he growled against his cheek. "My name

is Robert Nichols and this is how I want to be re-membered. Her name was Caroline...and this," he said as he twisted again, "is for her." He saw it then, the startled flash of recognition. He gave one final thrust, jerking the earl's body up and nearly off the ground before pulling out his sword and stepping back, letting the lifeless corpse slide down the wall to join the refuse that littered the blood-slick pavement. He felt strangely empty. There was no satisfaction. No thrill of righteous retribution or sense of justice done. But Stanley was just the first. There were three more yet to go. Perhaps then she'd let him be.

He regarded his handiwork, face impassive, before turning to look at a huddled form, mewling in the corner. Off in the distance, Prince Rupert's forces were still hard at work, fanning through the town, routing out those who had run too late, stayed too long, or hadn't found a place deep enough to hide. The night echoed with sporadic musket fire, shrill screams, drunken laughter and desperate cries of "sauve qui peut." The rumble of cannon fire rever-berated through the city. Strange now the walls were breeched and the battle done but for the looting. He cocked his head to one side, assessing, and then he spoke. "Run!" Somewhere, impossibly far away, a young girl cried....

Robert Nichols jerked awake, heart pounding, his body bathed in a cold sweat. Thunder growled in the distance. A steady rain tapped on the windows and pattered against the roof. He groaned. Another damned storm. They'd been rolling across the county for weeks. Soon the river would flood its banks.

Vestiges of his dream still lingered. No surprise there. He'd had the same one over and over through the years. It clung to him like a burr. Bolton. The first massacre of the civil war and he all of seventeen years old. Over three quarters of the town murdered, perpetrated by Price Rupert and the Earl of Derby in the royalist cause. He'd witnessed atrocities aplenty on both sides since then. The Lord Protector had been a pitiless man, too.

He rolled out of bed and pulled on his boots and a robe, his nerves frayed. The girl's sobbing still resonated, wrapped within the wail and sigh of the wind. *Caroline*. She wouldn't leave him alone. And why should she? Wasn't this her home, too? Didn't she have the right to demand retribution? And who to avenge her but him? Bolton had given him the opportunity to dispatch James Stanley, the first of her murderers. George Stanhope followed soon after, cut down in another bloody engagement, though he'd almost lost him to a Yorkshire pikeman during the melee.

Chisholm had been harder. He was a superior officer, an ex-cavalier who'd switched allegiance with the bloody-minded zeal of the newly converted. Now there was just the one remaining. But she must be getting impatient. After all, she had been waiting for over ten years.

He poured himself a tumbler of whiskey, something he'd developed a taste for while on campaign in Ireland. Sleep had deserted him and he was as wound and ready as if he'd only just stepped from the field of battle. He supposed in a way he had.

In his youth life had been simple. He'd believed in family, king and country. He'd believed in himself. A thing was right, or it was wrong. A man honored his word, protected the weak and defended his sovereign and his homeland, but Caro's death changed everything. When politics and religion tore his homeland in two, it gave him an outlet for the grief and fury he had no other way to express. The civil war became his private one, and he'd used the field of battle to exact his vengeance and focus his rage.

General Walters, his commander and mentor in matters of politics and war, replaced the father who blamed him for his sister's death, and the idea of an English Republic, with no man above the law, allowed him to pretend he fought for a greater good, easing his guilt and pain. In a strange way, the war, at first at least, had brought him peace. But ten years of fierce fighting had taught him the horrors men justified in the name of some greater good. He had witnessed unspeakable cruelties and been powerless to stop them. He had done things he had once thought unthinkable. Surrounded by cold-blooded men and ideologues, he'd realized he was neither, and the only things he could control were his own actions and his own small company of men.

By the time he'd walked in on some of them assaulting Elizabeth Walters, he'd begun to doubt if even that were true. They'd been hot on the trail of William de Veres, a royalist cavalier who played at highwayman and spy for the exiled Stuart king. The Irish campaigns had left his precious honor so sullied that all that mattered was protecting an old friend's daughter. He made it his duty to help her, and for a while he'd felt clean again. Those who knew him thought him cold, capable and straight as an arrow. None of them had any idea of the dark forces tearing him apart inside. He'd learned long ago to guard his secrets and keep his true thoughts to himself.

Now the wars were over and the king restored. All was forgiven. Men no longer proclaimed themselves for crown or parliament. They were all Englishmen now. He was ready to retire at the ripe old age of thirty-five and settle down to the quiet life of a country gentleman, hoping for some semblance of a normal life and perhaps a little peace.

Yet things were left undone, and he hadn't earned the right. *There is one who remains.* Passion had deserted him but duty had not. But to find and kill a man on the field of battle or during a campaign was one thing. To find and kill a man who'd fled the country and spent the past ten years in exile was difficult indeed. He wasn't even sure he had the stomach for it anymore.

For Caroline you do. You must.

He paced the halls, his footsteps echoing behind him like some damn ghost. *Cressly.* Once it rang with children's laughter. He had raced her through these halls. At times he imagined he could hear her still. Her merry laughter and the patter of running feet. That was before a group of drunken cavaliers had come and woken something savage. All that chased him now were the far distant sounds of hoarse shouting, artillery fire and the stomping of booted feet; the hollow remnants of troubling dreams. Cressly was all he had left to hold on to, though, even if it was as bare and haunted as he was. *I failed you then, Caroline. But I won't fail you again. I haven't forgotten. I promise you he'll pay.*

He tossed back what remained of his drink, surprised to note he'd wandered all the way to the library. Flashes of lightning illuminated the room in flickers of silvery light, painting the furniture, fireplace and rows of books in hues of bluish grey and black. They jumped out in stark relief, transforming what was once familiar into a harsh and alien landscape. His image flickered before him, reflected in the window. His sandy hair looked white, his eyes bruised and hollow, like one of the unseen things his staff believed walked Cressly late at night. *Christ, I even scare myself!*

Tossing a log into the fire, he kicked it with a booted foot, waiting for the coals to spark and flame before pouring another tot of whisky and settling into an overstuffed chair. The fire gave him just enough light to read by. He picked through the mail listlessly, but his gaze sharpened as he neared the bottom of the pile. There were two letters, both notable for the quality of paper and their ornate seals. One was addressed in a fine cursive script, while the other bore the king's seal. His hand hovered a moment before picking one up. The letter was from Elizabeth Walters.

Elizabeth. Hugh's daughter. Many had been the time he'd watched her from afar when he'd been to visit her father. A solemn-faced, shy little girl, motherless and always alone. He had made it his mission to draw her out, engaging her in conversation and bringing her little gifts. Her father had not disapproved and it brought him pleasure to make her smile. She'd even laughed for him the day he'd set her on his horse. He'd offered her marriage after Cromwell took her lands. He'd owed that much to her father. But she'd refused him, choosing the company of a noted rake and libertine instead, even following him when he was banished from England in disgrace.

He understood why. He was all but hollow inside.

His passion gone. No doubt she had sensed the flaws deep within him; the violence, the coldness, the dark. She had been right to refuse, and he had been wrong to ask.

He wondered why she wrote him now. Had her lover deserted her? Did she need his aid? Would he help her if she did? *Yes. It's what I promised.* Interest sparked, curious to see what she wanted and how she fared, he broke the seal.

She was happy, healthy and well, and she wished him the same. She wanted him to be among the first to hear the happy news. Just two months past she'd married William de Veres in a quiet ceremony in a small chapel in Maidstone, with only their servants present. They had thought it best to be circumspect, given her new husband's delicate situation in regards to the king. Things had improved in that regard, however, and she had every reason to expect they'd be free to travel shortly. She thought of her dear friend and rescuer often, and hoped they might visit him at Cressly soon.

He was surprised she had thought to write him, though she had claimed him as a friend, and surprised most of all at how her news stung. He fingered the remaining packet, tracing his thumb back and forth across the royal seal, at a loss as to what it might contain. He was a country gentleman, a minor baronet, hardly the sort to be called to court. Life as a soldier had taught him to be wary of surprises. They seldom resulted in anything good. He broke the seal. Although he steeled himself, nothing could have prepared him for what lay within.

To Captain Sir Robert Nichols, Baronet:
Notwithstanding the general amnesty offered by his most gracious Majesty Charles II to those who took up arms against his Father and himself, it has recently come to our attention that the aid and comfort you provided the traitor Oliver Cromwell and other enemies of the Crown were of a more serious nature than originally known. As such, your title and properties, including but not restricted to the estate and manor known as Cressly, are herewith forfeit to the Crown. In the spirit of reconciliation in which the amnesty was first proclaimed, you are hereby allowed to keep your commission and any monies derived thereby, as well as any personal possessions of sentimental value, including horse and weapons, not to exceed in total worth the sum of two thousand pounds. You are herewith given one month to vacate, or be held in contempt of King and Crown.
Signed this third day of April, 1662, by Chancellor Hyde, Earl of Clarendon, for His Majesty Charles II, King of England, Ireland, Scotland and France.

It felt as though the earth had just given way beneath him. He struggled to contain a dizzying wave of anger and a sickening sense of loss. He knew exactly what had happened. He was on the wrong side of history, and the very things he thought would keep him safe were about to cost him Caroline's home.

He tossed the chancellor's letter into the fire, watching as its edges bent and curled. Rivulets of flame reached melting wax and a moment later the paper burst into a molten flower and was gone. Just like that. *Just like Cressly. There is nothing left.* The storm continued to rage outside. He sat where he was, cold and still, till dawn.

CHAPTER TWO

Whitehall Palace, London

MILES TO THE SOUTH, in a luxurious chamber overlooking the mighty Thames, a sharp crack of lightning jolted Hope Mathews from a troubled sleep. She pulled back the gold-embroidered bedspread and sat upright, heart pounding, and looked toward the open casement window. There was no rain yet, but it was close. The air had a metallic taste, and a low rumble echoed in the distance, approaching from the east.

The fine hairs on the back of her arms stood on end and her breath quickened with excitement. Ever since she could remember, she had loved storms.

She glanced at her royal lover, slumbering peacefully at her side. It amazed her still that England's king had reached so far to find her and place her by his side. Her face softened as he stirred in his sleep, and a deep sadness tore at her heart. Despite his unrepentant promiscuity, it was almost impossible not to fall under his spell. He was her third protecter, but the first one she'd had any real feelings for. She was half in love with him, which she knew was foolish and forbidden, and she knew he was not in love with her. It hurt, but life was full of pain and she had survived other wounds. The path that had brought her to the bed of a king was a harsh one, strewn with heartache and bitter betrayal, dashed hopes and danger, and any feelings she had for Charles were not what mattered now.

She was not so foolish anymore as to dream of gallant knights or trust in anything as fickle and insubstantial as love…but security, independence, freedom…these might be in reach. The king would be married soon. His new queen would arrive on England's shores any day.

Her world and his were about to change. She had fine clothes and rich jewels, a carriage and servants and a beautiful home on Pall Mall. The problem was, none of it was official and very little of it was hers. It was his money that paid the bills. She had no suite at the palace, despite the many hours she spent wandering its halls, no lands or titles, and her beautiful home and servants were lent to her, not given.

The truth was, she was ushered up the river stairs whenever she came to see him, and at the end of her visits, she was sent home the same way. As much as he treated her as friend and confidante in private, her lowly background meant that in public she would always be treated not as a mistress, but as a whore, and what had been so easily given could just as easily be taken away. She needed to ask for what she wanted, no matter her fears of how it might affect what lay between them.

It took her a moment to notice that everything around her had gone quiet. *The calm before the storm.* A lightning bolt flashed, silent in the distance, and a dog barked far away. She plucked a luxurious oversize robe from the edge of the bed. Lost in its folds, with sleeves rolled up and hem trailing on the floor behind her, she went to stand by the casement. The rain came in a sudden hiss, sweeping in great sheets from off the Thames, accompanied by a jagged bolt of lightning that lit the sky, bathing her face and the room in a ghostly glow. Fanciful as a child, eyes sparking with excitement, she loosened her grip on the robe and spread her arms wide, waiting for the clap of thunder she knew would come. The wind whipped her unbound hair and the silken robe billowed behind her like blue-and-gold embroidered wings.

She imagined herself a magical creature, a goddess perhaps, mistress of an ancient force much larger than herself. One who could bid the rain to rise to her command, and control the ferocity and direction of the wind with a sweep of her arm. One who could effortlessly set the course of her own life, and influence the decisions of a king. Perhaps this feeling was why she greeted storms with such anticipation. Because she was always remaking herself. Always aching to be reborn as something new.

"God's blood, woman! What madness are you about now? I swear you traipse about my palace opening every bloody window in your path. A storm is upon us. Climb back into bed before we are awash."

She tumbled in an instant, from mighty goddess to lowly mortal. *But not so low as that. I am a royal courtesan. And there is power in that, too.* Though she turned to look at him, she made no move to obey. He had flung off the covers and lay stretched in all his glory. Her lips pursed in a half smile and she absently twirled a strand of hair as her eyes boldly traveled his length. *There are far worse things than being mistress to Charles Stuart.*

Her eyes widened and she gave an exaggerated gasp as he leapt from the bed and strode purposely in her direction.

"Ods fish, you've even pilfered my clothes! And what are you grinning at, eh? If you'll not mind me, my dear. I shall have to take you forcibly in hand." Growling, he reached for her but she screamed and ducked, eluding his grasp, circling to the far side of the bed, agile and quick as a cat. It was his robe that tripped her up, stopping her short when she stepped on a trailing hem. As she careened sideways he caught her firmly by the front of the oversize garment and set her back on her feet. A sudden gust swirled through the chamber and the fire danced to life, casting wild shadows on paneled walls and bathing them both in an earthen glow. He jerked her hard against him.

She elbowed his ribs, making him grunt, and tried to pull herself free. This was not a man who valued easy conquests. He chuckled against her mouth, walking backward with her lodged firmly against him, one hand anchoring her in place as the other reached behind him, searching for the window latch.

"No, Charlie, don't," she murmured against his throat. "Leave it as it is. Please. I love storms."

"Ah, yes. So I recollect. You were born in a tempest as your rickety house swayed like a yardarm in the wind. Doubtless you gurgled and cooed in delight. You must be Electra in disguise. She who calls the storm clouds that move in from the sea."

"Really? There truly is a goddess of the storm?"

"But of course there is! Am I not holding her in my arms right now?" He twirled her around until she was dizzy, stopping at the foot of the bed. "You see what a mighty king I am? I have captured the whirlwind. Good Christ, but you're a bounteous handful for any man, my pet. You are truly a meal fit for a king." He dropped her in a tangle of multihued sheets and pillows and followed her down. "What am I to do with you, Hope Mathews?"

She gathered her courage. "What *are* you to do with me, Charlie?"

"Well…several ideas spring to mind."

His fingers traced the contours of her breast, but

she brushed them away. "You are a king, and I a girl from Drury Lane. We are very ill-suited."

"Nonsense. We are comfortable together and understand each other well," he said, settling comfortably beside her. "We have both been hungry and poor. We are both survivors. In fact, we are two peas in a pod, Hope Mathews, are we not? Outsiders who have fought our way in. We are in the palace, but not of it, and thus uniquely positioned to appreciate the joke."

"Yet your father was a king and my mother a brandy-swilling bawd. In this matter I believe I outrank you."

Charles laughed in delight. "I think I should have liked it better were my mother more like yours. She was a cold and angry woman, and every word, thought or deed was deliberate and controlled. She was much like Lady Castlemaine that way. I do believe she loved my father, though not as much as she loved God. After his murder she married religion, you know. He was a cold, demanding stepfather and I've had nothing to do with him, except, like Oedipus, to bury him. Now I make merry and dance on his grave."

"Oedipus?"

"You're such an innocent little strumpet. Half angel, I think. Pay me no mind. Tell me what dark worries have been plaguing you."

"I…"

"Yes?"

She shivered. His restless fingers had begun to explore again, tracing her collarbone with a delicate touch. "It's nothing that cannot wait for another time."

"You've been about to say something for over a month now, Hope. Don't you think it's waited long enough?" His knuckles stroked her jaw.

She took a deep breath. "Your…your queen will soon be on English soil. She'll be in London within a month."

His fingers stilled. He'd been waiting for her to bring it up for some weeks now. Barbara, Lady Castlemaine, had already made her demands. She would be named maid of honor to his Portuguese queen. The idea sat ill with him, but so did the thought of open warfare with his ever more strident *maîtresse-en-titre,* and in any case, it was better to begin a thing as one meant to continue. Catherine of Braganza had surely been raised to understand the duties and expectations of a royal spouse. She would adjust.

What did Hope want? A title? Jewels? An acknowledged place at court? It would be wildly inappropriate and an affront to his new queen. Barbara was bad enough, but at least she was a countess. He could hardly parade an overdressed street urchin under his new queen's nose, no matter how charming she was. But he wasn't ready to part with her yet. A luscious raven-haired vision with stunning eyes, she'd been an unexpected find, and rather than bore him, she'd grown on him steadily over time. Enchanting, intelligent and touchingly idealistic despite her tarnished past, she'd been just the tonic he'd needed as he dealt with increasingly burdensome affairs of state, a difficult and temperamental senior mistress, and the unexpected void left by the departure of Elizabeth Walters and that entertaining and annoying ingrate, de Veres.

He tapped her nose and then kissed it. "There's no need for you to worry about matters of state, my dear. Have faith. I promise you there is naught to fear. I will always see you well cared for."

She wrinkled her face in protest, and at the risk of annoying him, pressed on. "Your new wife won't like my being here at court. I shouldn't want to upset her."

He tilted her chin with a finger, so she looked him straight in the eye. "I have told you that you needn't concern yourself with it. Your concern should be pleasing me." His smile was gentle, but there was a coolness to his voice that hadn't been there a moment ago.

"Charlie, if I don't leave before she comes I shall be sent packing soon after. I am no lady to grace your court. I have no husband to give me any hint of respectability. She will think me a common whore and be mightily offended."

"Hush, love!" His look of annoyance changed to a rueful grin. "You are a most uncommon wench."

"It's close enough to the truth, Charles. You know I cannot stay."

"I know no such thing. I am master here and I won't be dictated to by ministers, mistress *or* wife. You have never asked me for anything for yourself, Hope. Should I send you back to the slums of London? Marry you off to some fat merchant? Or drop you by the theater to sell oranges and whatever else you fancy to every young gallant that comes to town?"

She bit back an angry retort. Did he think those were her only choices? She had saved her money and jewelry. She didn't gamble and she was no spendthrift. She had been preparing for some time for a day like this. "You could help me find a modest property, perhaps. A town house or small cottage where I might retire quietly from court." She was offering him an easy choice. One that should be a relief. She held her breath. Her future lay in his hands. With one word he could grant her independence and freedom. One gesture could make her dreams come true.

"So…the price to be rid of you is a modest one. I wonder…what is the price to make you stay?"

She slapped him, her palm leaving a red stain on his cheek. He grabbed her wrist and held it cruelly, denying her the chance to strike again. "Don't try Barbara's tricks on me. It only cheapens you."

"You *were* the only man who never made me feel like a whore."

"And you were the only woman who never set a price on her...friendship. It seems we are both disappointed."

She yanked her wrist from his grasp and sat up. "I am sorry. I should not have hit you," she said dully.

"And I should not have offered insult." He took her arm, gently this time, and raised her bruised wrist to his lips to kiss. "Damn, but you're cold as a corpse. If you'll not let me close the blasted window, at least let me warm you under the covers."

She let him pull her back into the bedding and cover them both beneath heavy blankets. Charles was seldom cruel, and his bursts of anger were fleeting and rare. But it hurt to be compared to the voracious and greedy Barbara Palmer. "I was not setting a price on my friendship. I was—"

"I know exactly what you were doing, my dear. I take no offense. Everyone does it. You are more subtle than most. You wish me to convince you to stay. To entice you...with what? I would prefer it did you just tell me."

"You don't understand at all."

"What don't I understand?"

"Soon it will be beyond my control. Your new lady wife will come. She will tolerate Lady Palmer because she must. Because she belongs at court and is married. But she will not tolerate me. I will be the sacrifice you make to show that you cede her something. I will be banished and shamed in front of the court. You know this is true, Charles."

"You truly think me so cruel as to abandon you?"

"You have never abandoned your children, Charles. But I have given you none. I won't be the first royal courtesan to become a nuisance. And I do not want to offend your wife. She has done me no harm. I should not be pleased as a wife to find my new husband surrounded by his harem."

"I repeat. What do you want?"

She whirled around to face him. "I want you to let me go on my own terms. Before she arrives. Let me leave court, Charles. I ask for nothing more than your permission to go. I am not without funds. I have some jewelry and some small investments. I would live quietly away from London. I only asked for your help because a woman like myself, with no brother, father or husband, cannot easily enter into contract to purchase property. I had hoped you might act as guarantee, but if the thought offends you I will mange on my own."

Hope wasn't sure how things had turned into an argument with the man who controlled her fate. She knew better, but her anger and hurt made her reckless. "Can you not at least grant me a dignified withdrawal? Surely you owe me that."

She felt him stiffen. She must not lose his goodwill at such a critical juncture. It was not the time to let her feelings show. Perhaps such things were never wise. Another lesson learned. She swallowed her anger.

"Forget what I said, Charles." Her voice was contrite. "I am a foolish woman. I am frightened, but I know all will be well if you say so. 'Tis but the storm, and a little jealousy perhaps. They have put me on edge."

Mollified, he patted her hand. "You have but to trust me, Hope, and all will be well."

BEYOND THE PRIVATE CONFINES of drawn bed curtains, the smell of coffee and the soft clatter of silverware, England's king opened his eyes and stretched. A thin sliver of sunlight crept in through jewel-encrusted hangings, warning him he'd overslept. If he didn't want to be overrun by functionaries before he reached the stables for his morning ride, he needed to escape his bedchamber soon, but a moment longer wouldn't hurt. He stretched and turned on his side, reaching for the soft warmth and comfortable weight of a sleeping woman, only to find an empty space and a stack of pillows. *Damn the impertinence!* She had left him without so much as a by-your-leave.

It was unusual for him to have angry words with a woman. There were so many better ways to converse, and Hope was as captivating a woman as he'd ever met. He chuckled to remember their first meeting. Her spontaneity, warmth and wit had made her stand out, and she was such a delicious morsel. As small and fine-boned as a nymph, her sultry looks, her throaty voice, her seductive smile and those knowing eyes kept a man on the constant edge of excitement. Yet she could talk and joke and carouse like a man, and a fellow felt at ease in her company, too. It was amazing, really, how she'd emerged from the bowels of London with a spirit so fresh and unscathed.

She imagined herself jaded and hardened, he knew, but he was a student of human nature, a master at reading others. He'd had to be to survive. It was the things people did when they thought themselves unobserved that told you the most about them. Most schemed for advantage and plotted against those whose demise might speed their own advance, but Hope... She was kind, a virtue usually lost within months of coming to court, and a weakness much coveted by those who would take advantage and abuse.

She gave clothes and coppers and many of the gifts he gave her to beggars and whores, anyone with a sad tale to tell. She had her own sense of honor. He knew her to be faithful, a thing he found both amusing and endearing, and she was a spirited little warrior, meeting the snubs and jibes of many of his courtiers with head held high and a witty retort of her own. And alone in the dark, when the winds blew wild, she raised her arms to the heavens and danced in the rain. He found her utterly enchanting.

She's been my mistress for almost a year and yet my fascination grows. The way she'd danced in the storm last night, her arms flung wide, naked but for his billowing gown, playful child and elemental seductress, whore and innocent and ancient power; *what more can a man want from any woman?* But now *she* wanted something, and it was not at all what he had expected. It seemed she wanted to be free of him. It was a most unsettling development. First denied by Elizabeth Walters in favour of that rogue William, and now spurned by Hope herself. A lesser man might question his own prowess.

He smiled to recall the night Elizabeth spent in his bed chatting, and the kiss he had given her in the palace gardens, and snorted to think of de Veres. The wench had taken aim and the court's second most notorious libertine had fallen like an ensorcelled stag struck down by Diana herself. Well, good for them both, but damned if the place wasn't dull without them. Their interactions and courtship, writ large on the stage of Whitehall with all of London watching, had been fine entertainment indeed. *Better than a play.* It was high time he called them back to court.

As for his stormy nymph…she was right, of course. Even he could not keep an unmarried woman of low birth and highly questionable background. It was one thing in a bachelor court, and quite another as a married man. The Portuguese were sophisticated. They would wink at a mistress of Barbara's stature, but to elevate a lowly street urchin to the company of his queen would be an insult they could not ignore.

So why had her request offended him? Under the circumstances it was convenient, even considerate, and perfectly reasonable. Was it the fact she had brought it up before he did that rankled so? That she seemed ready, even eager to move on? Ungrateful wench!

I expect I shall keep her awhile yet. Besides…she has no idea what she asks. She needs a man to take care of her. If I helped her out of the palace and onto her own she'd be defenseless amongst my courtiers. An unmarried commoner. A succulent lamb let loose amongst the wolves.

Unmarried commoner. That was the bar, and in it lay the solution. It was simple and elegant. The girl needed a suitable husband. A gentleman of rank, but not too proud to take a commoner as his lady. Someone indulgent, grateful and quick to understand he was set to guard a treasure. A country gentleman would be ideal. Suitably rewarded to remain discreet when the lady returned to court. Her stint in the country would allow him time to settle things between Catherine and Barbara, and allow her to reflect upon where her best interests lay. Then, like the phoenix, she might return, reborn as a noble married lady. All that was needed was to find the right man.

CHAPTER THREE

Maidstone County, Kent

ELIZABETH DE VERES SPUN AROUND in a circle, faster and faster, her arms stretched wide as azure sky and spring green meadow, leafy canopy and silvery stream, joined in a riotous whirl of color around her. When she tumbled to the ground laughing, her skirts billowing about her, her husband caught her safely in his arms and settled her back against him.

"Bedlam has many mansions, Lizzy. Have a care."

She chuckled and reached for his hand, finding it and clutching it tight to her chest. The sun was warm on her face and, even as the sky still spun above her, she imagined she could feel the slow turning of the earth below. She closed her eyes and listened…the shiver of leaves dancing on the late afternoon breeze, the soft babble of shallow water meandering lazily over smooth stone, the insistent calls and soft warbles of unseen courting birds, and underneath it all, the steady beat of his heart and the soothing rise and fall of his breath. "It makes me feel like I'm flying."

He tightened an arm around her waist. "I shall

have to anchor you tight, then, so you don't float away."

"You should really give it a try, Will. It's great fun."

He leaned over to nip her ear. "I have tried it in my youth, with you as I recall, and it gave me much the same feeling as overindulgence in very bad sack. The same tottering walk. The same sense that at any moment one's feet might leave the ground, which I assume is what you mean by flying, *and* an unfortunate and unpleasant urge to spew."

"Pfft! I must be married to the least romantic poet in all of England."

"Think you so?" He kissed the top of her head. "I'm fair certain I can show you other ways to fly." Easing his fingers from her grasp, he hooked them under the edge of her bodice, tugging gently but insistently as his knuckles slid up the soft outer curve of her breast. He lingered there a moment, caressing the sensitive skin from collarbone to ear, before deftly slipping her gown off her shoulder.

"William. It's full daylight. What if someone comes?" She spoke in an urgent whisper laced with excitement and alarm.

"I warned you if you married me I'd keep you very busy."

And so he had. Since Will's banishment from court for the scandalous poem he left nailed to the palace gates she had never been happier. They lived in their own charmed world here in Kent along with their little family of retainers. Samuel ruled the grounds and had a worthy garden at last. Thomas had learned his sums, been promoted to steward and married his Jeanine, and Mary and Marjory ruled house and kitchen as well as a baked goods stall at the local weekly market. William's writing was prolific and had never been better, and neither had his sleep. They had remodeled the house from top to bottom and it had become a joyous place where dark memories held no sway. He still had his cravings, but she shared them, too, and they delighted in indulging one another indoors, outdoors, day or night.

She turned into his touch with a soft sigh and he blazed a trail of molten kisses from her shoulder to her throat as his hand fondled her waist, then edged down her thigh to pluck at her skirt, slowly inching it up her legs. "Have I told you how very lovely you are? How trim your ankles and shapely your calves? How proud your breasts?" His voice, warm against her ear, sent shivers up her spine.

His hands caressed the bare flesh beneath her skirts, his palm hot against her thigh, and she yielded to his expert touch with a soft sigh. He shifted position so that she lay beneath him and claimed her mouth in a luscious kiss, his tongue stroking and teasing, coaxing her to open. She did so with a low moan, her body sinking pliant into the silky grass as his clever fingers reached higher, seeking the soft juncture between her thighs.

"Sweet Christ, Lizzy, but I am fortunate to have—"

"Praise God I've found you, my lord!"

Elizabeth's startled yelp was drowned by William's cursing as a flushed and panting Thomas wriggled, half crouching, through a narrow gap in the hedge. Hastily withdrawing his hand and using his body to shield her from view, William straightened Elizabeth's skirts and bodice before jumping to his feet and rounding on his man.

"God's blood, Tom! Is a little privacy on my own demesne too much to ask? The manor house had best be on fire or the Lord himself come to call."

Thomas brushed twigs and leaves from his coat and hair, and collected his dignity. "Your pardon, my lord, my lady, if I interrupted a private conversation. The manor house is *not* on fire, but the king, in a manner of speaking, *has* come to call. His messenger is here and he says it is most urgent he speak with you in person. I—"

"The king is *a* lord, not *the* Lord, Tom. And have you ever seen me brought to heel by a snap of His Majesty's fingers?"

"Never…Master William," Tom said with a tired sigh.

"Just so." William clapped Tom on the back and leaned close so only he could hear. "Few ever have reason to climb this hill, Tom. You have stumbled upon a private retreat. One my lady and I have shared since childhood. Unless we are under attack, in imminent danger, or the house *is* on fire, I should like it to stay that way. I know I can trust you to guard our secret."

"With my life, my lord."

"Excellent! Off you go, then. Make our visitor comfortable and tell him we'll be along in due time."

"Oh, William. Do you think he saw?" Elizabeth asked in a breathless whisper after he had left. "What he must have thought!"

"Does it excite you? Your eyes are alight and your cheeks are apple-red. It's very becoming."

"I was embarrassed," she said with a sniff.

"Were you?" he inquired playfully. He was stretched out on his side, his head resting on his bent arm, tickling the delicious mounds cunningly displayed by her décolletage with a long blade of grass.

"'As Chloris full of harmless thought
Beneath the Willows lay,
Kind Love a comely Shepherd brought
To pass the time away:
She blusht to be encounter'd so
And chid the amorous Swain;
But as she strove to rise and go
He pull'd her down again.
A sudden passion seiz'd her heart
In spight of her disdain,

She found a pulse in e'ry part
And love in e'ry Vein.'"

His fingers skimmed the soft skin between her wrist and elbow and her shiver was not from embarrassment or cold.

"I suppose he must have seen a great deal more, living with you in London."

"Hush, my sweet, I prefer not to revisit it." His thumb parted her lips and he kissed the bottom curve. "The only fond remembrances I have from then are of you."

"But London has come to us, Will. What do you think Charles wants?"

He groaned in exasperation, giving up. "I would expect His Majesty grows bored, little bird, as he always does. He will call us back to court. He is eager to see if you have turned from a lovely brown wren to a plump little partridge now you're married. He will want to see if I still bite and you still resist him. He will invite us to come for his wedding."

Elizabeth shifted position, laying her head against his chest, listening to the steady beat of his heart. "I have been so blissfully happy this past year, Will. If that's what he wants of us, is there some way we can refuse?"

"I've no great desire to return to court, love. The country air agrees with me and I have all I need right here." He smiled as her stroked her hair. "I can make some excuse or another. Charlie rarely maintains a grudge. It's too much work. We shall write him and thank him and send a nice gift. A fine mare for his breeding stock. And if he presses the thing, one or the other of us shall fall deathly ill."

"Do what you think best, William. You know him better than I. But shouldn't we hear the message before crafting a reply?"

"Saucy chit!" He snatched her stockings from where they lay discarded on the ground and set off across the meadow with them flung over his shoulder, trailing behind him like a scarf.

"William de Veres, you give those back!" Barefoot, Elizabeth chased after him.

CHARLES HAD INDEED RECALLED THEM to court to attend his impending wedding. It was both command and invitation. The haughty messenger in his royal livery was accustomed to fawning and deference. He was not accustomed to being made to wait, particularly by a country gentleman who dressed like a farmer, and his barefoot hoydenish wife. "I say again, sir. I am His Majesty's representative and you have kept me waiting half the day. I require a response. I require it now, so I may be about my duties."

"You've received your response. Thank His Majesty for his kind invitation and tell him I will write."

Two minutes later His Majesty's fuming courier was escorted out the back door like a menial by Tom and one of the footmen.

"Was that really necessary, William?"

"Feeding hubris only makes it grow, love." He poured them both a drink and sat down on an over-size upholstered couch. Elizabeth picked up the mail and came to lie with her head against the far bolster and her feet in his lap. "Poor little shepherdess. Your feet are roughened and bruised."

"Whose fault is that?" She wiggled her toes in his lap and he took a dainty foot and began massaging it.

"Mmm. That's heavenly." She could feel his interest growing, quite literally under her feet, but a familiar heavy scrawl had caught her eye. It was a reply from Robert at last. She had just about given up on him. He had been her only friend through some difficult years and she didn't want to lose him. She knew he would be hurt, possibly angry at the news of her marriage, but it was hardly something she could keep from him, any more than she could have kept it from Charles. Her cheeks flushed and she gave William a guilty look from underneath her lashes.

"What have you there, love? A *billet doux* from a secret admirer?"

"It is a letter from Robert."

"Robert?"

"Yes. You remember. Captain Nichols."

"Ah, yes! Marjorie's nice young man. The one who wanted to marry you. How did a little wren gain so many admirers? Poets, captains and kings. I was lucky I kidnapped you when I did."

"Yes, you were."

"Did I ever meet him? I think not. Some stuffed country Puritan, wasn't he?

"No. He's very elegant and handsome, if somewhat private and intense. A military man. He had his own company of horse. I am hoping you will get to meet him soon. I rather invited us to his home. I believe you would like each other." He chuckled and she made a face at him. "That's an evil laugh."

"He'll not like me, my dear. You know so little of men. No man likes the fellow who stole the woman he'd marked as his. Doubtless he judges me an immoral libertine and a terrible danger to your sweet soul."

"Which you were." She put down the letter. "You know it's strange. When last we met he told me he had wanted to marry me when I was a girl, but I never had any idea. He doesn't show his emotions. I thought at first he didn't have any. He has always seemed so lacking in passion and so very correct."

William shrugged, and moved his attentions from her heel to her arch. "That's true of many who've seen too much of war. People deal with it in different ways. It's not a thing one tends to share in conversation. 'Pass the biscuits, a lump of sugar if you please, oh, and did I ever tell you about the poor bastard who had his legs blown off as he stood beside me?' It's no surprise some develop the habit of silence."

"Did that happen to you?"

"Obviously not," he said with a grin. "I am the

type for whom little things take more meaning when larger ones disappoint. A fine wine, a lovely painting, a heated kiss replace glory, honor and duty. Perhaps for your Robert, it is the reverse."

She wanted to ask him about the lust and cruelty she'd seen in the eyes of some soldiers. Whether that was a thing men took with them into battle, or something they brought from it, but he had let loose her feet and was bent over a side table, penning a response to the king. She opened Robert's letter and began to read.

My dearest Elizabeth,
How kind of you to write and share your happy
news. I can scarcely credit that any woman
managed to bring de Veres to heel. It is an act
of superb generalship worthy of your father
and congratulations are due. I am delighted for
you, my dear, so long as he treats you well. It
is kind of you to offer to visit. I, too, value our
friendship, but I very much regret it is not pos-
sible at this time. It seems the king has found
a higher purpose for Cressly, and thus I must
find one for myself. I will be gone from it by the
end of next month.

Her gasp of outrage made William looked up from his writing. "Elizabeth? What does he write?" She raised a hand for him to wait as she finished.

I am been better suited to soldiering than farm-ing, I suspect, so it should prove no great hard-ship. It may be that I shall rent a suitable house in town. Once I am settled I will of course look forward to your visit.
Your servant, Captain Robert Nichols

"Oh, William, how could he? He is taking Robert's lands!"

William shrugged. "These things happen. He is a lesser gentleman who was on the wrong side of the war. It costs Charles nothing to displace him. There must be someone he needs to please and your friend's lands are the most convenient way to do so."

"Well, I have changed my mind. We *must* go to London now. Captain Nichols rescued me from Cromwell's soldiers, Will. It was he who intervened the day after you left. He spoke for me when I was judged and facing transportation or worse, and he helped me get settled in London. Perhaps if I speak with Charles I can change his mind. I must at least try. I owe him so much."

THEIR ARRIVAL AT COURT a week later was greeted with a great deal of excitement and as they made their way through the great hall to the privy chamber, the crowded room became a sea of craning necks. The court had been a duller place since the scandalous earl had left it. People still whispered and chuckled about his farewell gift to the king. They were shocked at the rumors he had married his mistress, except for the Duke of Monmouth, who'd made a fortune wagering on it and still maintained that Elizabeth Walters had been the earl's childhood friend.

"They look at me as if I was a tame bear," William growled to Elizabeth. He reached for her and pulled her close. "Why are we here again? Ah, yes. We must arrange another meeting for you with our gracious king, your old beau, so we might save your heroic captain. I swear, little bird, you delight in giving me competition. Look. There he is now."

"William! Elizabeth! How are you, my dears? What a pleasure to have you returned to the fold. I expect things to be much more entertaining now the two of you have joined us." Stepping between them, Charles Stuart clapped his arms about their shoulders and gave them both an enthusiastic hug.

"Come. I've been eager to show you some of the wedding preparations. You in particular, Elizabeth. I remember how taken you were by our last grand masque. My bride arrives at Portsmouth and we will sail down the Thames on a magnificent barge. Some of the decorations are being readied here on the palace grounds."

His enthusiasm and long stride swept them through a crowd of courtiers before either had a chance to respond. He ushered them into a bustling workshop where a swarm of busy artisans and work-

ers were carving and gilding, painting and brazing.
There were giant thrones and arches, water-spouting
seahorses and Poseidons, and magnificent mechanical unicorns and lions that reared and roared.

"What do you think of it, William?"

It took him a moment to respond. "If your bride
tends to garishness and excess she'll be transported."

"All of England will be transported. The barge
will be the centerpiece of a grand flotilla. It will
herald a new era for England. We make great gains
through this marriage. A fresh start, William,
yes? You have had yours it seems." Charles smiled
warmly at Elizabeth, and she gave him a brilliant
smile in return. He tore his gaze away and turned
back to William. "Do you remember all our dreams,
Will?"

His voice sounded wistful, and William bit back a
pointed reply. "I do, Your Majesty. I hope this marriage brings you more than lands and access to the
Mediterranean. I hope it brings you some of the joy
Lizzy and I have found."

"Thank you. I am delighted you both came. One
wants his friends around him on occasions such as
this."

"There is also a matter Elizabeth would like to
discuss, Charles."

"Yes, of course, my dears. People always have
something to discuss."

Elizabeth sat on His Majesty's bed, her back comfortably settled against a mound of gold-braided cushions, with a spaniel asleep on her lap. Charles's penchant for conducting most of his audiences in his bedchamber had at first shocked her, but now it felt comfortable, like visiting an old friend.

He poured her a glass of wine and one for himself. "So, Elizabeth, my dear. What did you come to discuss? One or another of my ladies is always annoyed with me, though I'm such a sunny fellow. I recognize the look. Out with it, madam."

"Very well. You have taken away the holdings of my dear friend, Captain Robert Nichols, despite your general amnesty and the fact he has been living there peacefully since your restoration. I can't believe he has done anything to deserve it. He is a reserved and honorable man. Gallant, kind and brave."

Charles held up a hand to stop her. "Robert Nichols…Robert Nichols. The name is familiar. Does he have property in Nottinghamshire?"

"Yes, he does."

"I did ask Clarendon to find some land for a fellow whose fundraising and…other connections have been vital to the crown. He told me the man specifically mentioned the lands in question. Does your captain have any useful relatives or connections at court? Besides you?"

"Not that I'm aware of, Charles. He was a parlia-

mentarian soldier and country gentleman. A baronet,
I believe.

"And what concern is he to you?"

"He intervened with Cromwell when I was arrested, and argued for me on my behalf. Without his
help I would have been transported or hanged."

"The devil you say! You have quite the knack for
landing in deep waters, haven't you, Elizabeth? But
what a pretty tale. Quite diverting. A modest gentleman of chivalrous character on a country estate, desperate to keep his lands. Is he handsome?"

"Well…yes. Quite," Elizabeth answered, rather
flustered. "But, Charles, that has nothing to do with
why I'm asking."

"No, no. Of course not. If you were the type to be
turned by a pretty face you would have surely chosen
me."

They both laughed and Elizabeth's eyes sparkled
with affection. "You are in truth a very attractive
man, Charles Stuart, and you know it well."

He grinned and raised his glass to her in salute.
"But not quite as attractive as that damned impertinent poet. You've ruined him, you know. He'll be
spouting love verses soon." She blushed and hid her
face against the spaniel's silky coat.

"Tell me more about him. Your captain friend. Is
he married? If he's not too proud, I might have a use
for him."

"Well, no, he isn't married, but he *is* rather proud—"

"Excellent! This is good news indeed, Elizabeth. I thank you for bringing it to my attention. Now if you'll forgive me I must speak with Clarendon at once. There's little time, you see. I look forward to seeing you and William at the ball tonight."

Charles hurried his stunned and sputtering guest from the room and called for his chief minister. He was delighted. With Elizabeth's help he had hit on the perfect solution. He would grant her request. The honorable captain of whom she spoke so highly would keep his lands, see his holdings doubled and be made an earl besides, provided he marry Hope Mathews. He had only to remove her to the country, treat her with all courtesy and comfort befitting a special friend of the king and return her to court when the time was right.

The message went out shortly after the chancellor entered his chambers. Captain Robert Nichols was ordered to present himself at court at once.

CHAPTER FOUR

Cressly

HE APPROACHED *the manor house across a pristine field veiled by a thin dusting of snow. The air was cold and sharp to breathe, but Kate Bishop, the dairy maid, had kissed him, and he didn't feel the cold.*

The moment his parents left to visit his uncle, he'd hurried to the village to stand vigil by her door. His patience had been rewarded. He caught her first and claimed her as his Valentine, blushing as he offered her a pretty blue paper with her name writ on it in gold. He'd labored over it for hours in secret, knowing his parents would not approve. It was well worth the effort. She stood on the tips of her toes and kissed him, and it warmed him all the way home.

He stopped in the middle of the field, as happy as he'd ever been in all his twelve years. The woods were still. The silence so deep he could hear the excited beating of his own heart. And then a distant shriek. A night owl, he thought, desperately hungry to be searching for food so late. He heard it again.

A panicked scream, coming from the manor house. Caroline!

He raced through the field and skidded across the stone-flagged courtyard, only to be brought short by the sight of five blooded horses wandering loose in front of a smashed and broken door. Heart pounding, his terror for Caroline a sick lump in his throat, he eased into the entrance hall and inched his way along the corridor. The servants must have fled or hidden and there was no sign of his father's men at arms. As he neared the drawing room he heard Caroline sobbing, and the sound of hoarse shouts and the laughter of drunken men.

He leaned against the doorjamb and peered around the corner. The drawing room was littered with broken furniture, shredded hangings and paintings that had been torn from the walls. A lone man at arms with a sword in his back laid sprawled across a table. Caroline huddled in a corner in a tight little ball. Her dress was ripped, her favorite blue ribbons were torn from her hair and her face was bloody, bruised and beaten. For a moment he thought he was going to be sick. This wouldn't be happening if not for him. He should have been there to protect her.

There were five men wearing the brightly colored garb and plumed hats that marked them as His Majesty's cavaliers, but under their elegant trappings they reeked of unwashed clothes and alcohol. He bared his teeth and bit back a feral growl. They were ignoring Caroline for now, tapping at walls with the butts of their swords and digging at the floorboards. He considered darting in, grabbing her and making a run for it, but he didn't even know if she could walk. He wished he could give her some signal to let her know she wasn't alone. But he couldn't risk alerting her captors.

The guilt, the terror, the boiling rage at seeing Caroline so abused, gave way to an icy calm. His breathing slowed, his heart steadied and his attention focused to a razor's edge as he assessed his opponents. A bullet-headed man next to Caroline without his sword. A handsome black-haired man dressed finer than the rest, commanding the center of the room. A rat-faced fellow and a blond man with a split lip knocking on walls, and a bookish-looking fellow with a wickedly curved dagger poking at floorboards in the corner. He observed each in turn before slipping past the doorway and continuing down the hall.

The longsword was mounted on the wall in his father's study. He'd eyed it many a time, fascinated by its lethal beauty and the chilling inscription etched into the blade. Lex Talionis, *the law of revenge.*

The blue steel blade snicked and hissed as he slid it from its mounting. Gripping the wolf's-head pommel with both hands he laid the weapon cross-shoulder and went back for his sister. He ar-

*rived just in time to see the bullet-headed man grab
Caroline by her arm and wrench her to her feet. His
fingers itched and he brought his weapon forward,
silent, shifting his grip so he held it like a spear for
stabbing. Not yet, though. He waited for them to turn
away.*

*"Come, little mistress." The man gave Caroline a
shake. "Tell us where it is, or what you've heard, and
we'll leave you in peace to play with your dollies."*

*"Speak for yourself, Harris," the blond man said.
"She's too old for dolls, that one, and we've other
things she can play with."*

*Bullet Head shook her again, then fisted his hand
in what remained of her dress and lifted her off the
ground, so her feet had to scrabble for purchase. "Is
that right, pretty mistress? You want to play games?"
he cooed.*

*Caroline was sobbing and pleading, fighting
for air as the collar of her dress cut off her breath,
trying to tell them she didn't know. She didn't understand what they wanted.*

*"Get on with it, gentlemen," the black-haired
one snapped, apparently more sober than the rest.
"There's militia in the area. We haven't all day. It's
clear she knows nothing. Finish her, Johnny, and let's
be gone."*

*"Well, that's a bloody waste of an evening,"
Johnny Harris protested. "I've got a use for her if*

*the rest of you don't. Move on if you please, lads. I
shan't be long."*

*"Pah," Golden Hair spat. "Let's all have a go,
then. 'Tis only sporting." He joined the one named
Johnny and yanked at her skirt.*

*Caroline began a desperate struggle, clawing and
kicking.*

*"Enough, you damn fools," the man with the
curved blade shouted. "If I have to, I'll cut her throat
myself." He rose and started in her direction and
there was no more time left.*

*The force that held him frozen loosened its grip. It
was as if time had stopped, trapping him outside it,
only allowing him to observe, then started again, so
that everything came at him in a rush. He raised his
sword high over his head and it was then that Caroline saw him. Their eyes locked for an instant, hers
horrified, imploring, trying to give him some message, but it was lost in the commotion as he charged.
He barreled forward with all his strength, screaming
his fury, his target the man approaching her with the
knife.*

*Slow and sodden and unprepared, his target
wheeled too late, his curved blade just nicking his
young attacker's cheek, and then the longsword
caught him through the belly and impaled him
against the wall.*

*The child who'd never killed before blinked in
shock. It didn't feel real. It felt like the force of sur-*

prise and his own momentum had carried the thing, not him. But now he'd lost both, and try as he might, he couldn't pull out the sword.

A liquor jug hit him full force in the back of his head, knocking him off his feet.

"Bloody hell! Poor Humboldt! Killed by a marauding child! And he was to marry his heiress next month." It was the blond man.

"Aye. A pity. And not how one wants to be remembered," the handsome one said to sniggers all the way round.

He scrambled backward on his elbows and heels, desperately feeling for the dropped sword he'd seen earlier. The moment he found it he jumped to his feet. He pointed it at them, holding it steady. "Let her go!"

"Do you know what I'm going to do with that sword, boy?" the rat man whispered. "I'm going to slit you from throat to belly, and fry your entrails."

Caroline, still struggling in Harris's grip, managed to loosen his chokehold on her throat. "Run, Robbie! Please run! Run!" his sister screamed.

"I'll let her go, lad, if you say so," Harris said with a leer, and then he lifted her high in the air and flung her hard against the wall.

He had always been reserved and she the merry prankster. Sister, boon companion and best friend, she was his strength, her charm and personality both larger than life. But when she hit the wall and slid to the floor in a broken heap, she was so small...so fragile. She looked at him a moment, willing something from him. He whimpered, taking one step back as they advanced toward him, and then his sword clattered to the ground and he ran. He looked back one more time before he reached the doorway, but she was gone.

He ran and ran as they shouted behind him, out of the house and back into the night. He fell on his knees when he could go no further. People were coming, running toward him, their torches bobbing in the dark. A great screaming pain tore through him, rising through his blood and nerves, seizing his throat and ripping his heart. He threw back his head, letting loose a wounded-animal howl.

"JESUS!" HE WOKE WITH A LOUD GASP, doubled over and clutching his midsection, trying to catch his breath. His dreams of Caroline were the worst. They had none of the distance of memory, none of the detached quality of his other nightmares. They hurled him back in time, forcing him to relive that night, a frightened child who failed his sister, over and over again. He groaned and went to the sideboard to pour himself a drink.

"You needn't ride me quite so hard, Caro. I'm doing the best I can," he said to the empty room. But she never stopped. In the light of day he could push such thoughts and images away, but other than the occasional glimpse of a cheeky grin, violet eyes and a muddy face, blood and horror hounded him most every night. He wished he was one of those lucky souls whose dreams did not pursue them when they woke. He wondered what her thoughts would be if she knew he had lost her home.

THE SECOND ROYAL MESSAGE, commanding his presence at Whitehall, came two days later and was almost as great a shock as the first. Robert could imagine no reason for it, other than suspicion regarding his possible involvement with enemies of the crown. Some of those who fought for parliament during the English civil wars were fanatics. The Fifth Monarchists had been a powerful force. Men who saw the war and Charles the First's execution as a prelude to the start of a golden age where Christ and his saints would reign on earth. They had once hailed Cromwell as a second Moses, leading God's chosen people to the promised land. Just three months past they'd launched an uprising in London resulting in a bloody street battle and forty deaths. One couldn't blame the king for dealing with them harshly. Two of them were regicides and one a major general. His first thought upon learning his lands were forfeit was that he was suspected of being one of them.

It couldn't be further from the truth. His war had been a personal one. His brothers weren't Puritans and preachers, but the loose collection of steely eyed soldiers who killed who they needed to, to get the job done. They cared little for religion and had few scruples, and their honor was to their fellows, their craft and their word.

Even as his staff stored three generations of family heirlooms, he contemplated rejoining the fold. Provided, of course, he wasn't arrested for treason. They were after all among the most highly prized mercenaries in Europe, and there were opportunities aplenty in Germany, the Netherlands and further afield. Though he'd thought himself weary of war, he couldn't deny a prick of excitement. There was something about daring death head-on with only skill and luck to save you that could bring even the most jaded spirit sharply back to life.

He'd already claimed his two thousand pounds of goods in weapons, clothing and horseflesh. He would travel to London and satisfy his curiosity, trusting to his wits should things go awry. While there he would look to finding employment for his servants and a well-paid position with a company of mercenary for himself. He'd also check amongst old friends and acquaintances to see if he might pick up a trail grown cold.

CHAPTER FIVE

London

ROBERT STALKED THE LONG stone gallery at Whitehall with a ground-eating stride. His clothing was sober but elegant, and an oversize sword clearly meant for killing hung easily at his side.

He'd been waiting most of the afternoon and his patience was at an end. Now, as the orange glow from the west sank below the horizon and somber shadows lengthened to the east, he decided it was time to find some supper and a bed. He was not a petitioner, after all. It was His Majesty who had asked to see *him*. If his oath-breaking, manor-stealing monarch had need of him, let him come and find him at his lodgings. Tomorrow he'd—

"Captain Nichols!" A sonorous voice echoed through the near empty gallery. "Captain Robert Nichols. His Majesty will see you now."

He stepped into a richly furnished chamber. In the center of the room, parallel to a sculpted marble fireplace flanked by Bacchus and Cupid, a beautiful oak table cast its own lustrous glow. His monarch sat there with his sleeves rolled up and his crimson coat thrown over the back of a chair. He played cards with an auburn-haired beauty perched on his lap. It took a few moments before he looked up.

"Ah, Nichols! Here you are at last, and just in time. Do you play?" The king seemed to be regarding him with great curiosity.

"My lord." Robert removed his wide-brimmed hat with a flourish, and gave him a deep bow. "My Lady Castlemaine." He gave her a deeper one. "Yes, I do. It's a common pastime amongst soldiers."

"Have we met?" the lady purred, her eyes traveling his length with obvious appreciation.

"I should have remembered if we had, madam, but tales of your beauty leave no doubt as to who you are."

"Handsome, well-mannered, with a modicum of charm. If we can…" The king made a frustrated gesture with his fingers as he searched for the right words. "If we can jolly you up a little, you just might do."

"I beg your pardon?"

His Majesty shrugged. "I dare say some women find such a military air dashing, but you don't want to look like a country parson. Particularly not this evening."

"My Lord?" Robert was growing more confused by the minute. Was the man addled or drunk?

"I assure you he doesn't look at all like a parson,

Charles. He looks big and powerful and a little bit frightening, and not the least bit meek or mild." The lady held her hand to her bosom and gave a slight shudder.

"Mmm. And that's quite enough from you, my pet. Leave us now. I will see you later." The king gave his pouting mistress a pat on the rump that she returned with an angry hiss, and sent her on her way. "She has a point, though, Captain," he said returning his attention to Robert. "You *are* very well dressed for a fellow who has just been stripped of his possessions." He gestured toward the sword. "You came ready to do battle?"

"I came because you summoned me."

"Yes?"

"And I was curious."

Charles nodded. "Naturally. That's a wicked weapon, Captain, if not terribly practical. Worth a good deal of money, I expect. Most prefer something lighter, with more flexibility. A rapier or cutlass perhaps."

Robert shrugged. "It is not meant for dueling or to impress the ladies, Your Majesty. You might call it…a personal possession of sentimental value. It was left me by my father."

"Ah!" The king looked at him with a grin. "Call me Charles. May I see it?"

The moment he drew the sword four men at arms stepped from the shadows, along with two gentlemen who'd been playing cards in an alcove across the room. Robert didn't know if it was a display meant to warn him, but as an officer he was impressed. Charles motioned them back with a negligent wave and, after Robert laid his sword on the table, gestured for him to sit.

"Germanic perhaps. They do like their wolves." He examined the blade with interest. "But I'll wager this is a Spanish steel." He turned it over. "*Lex Talionis.* Tell me, Captain—" he leaned forward, and there was hint of playful challenge in his voice "—on whom do you seek revenge?"

Robert leaned forward, too. "If it were some fellow seated in this room, Majesty, he'd already be dead."

"God's blood but you're a bold and impudent fellow!" Charles's laughter rang through the room. "You're not exactly what I expected, but damn me if I don't think you'll do. Here. Take it back." He slid the sword to Robert. "It's bound to be an accursed nuisance when dancing. Have a care not to trip up the ladies tonight."

Is our interview over? Why in God's name did he summon me to court? "Your Majesty. I came here at your summons. I've been waiting all day. Might I enquire as to—"

"All in good time, Captain. Come. Hurry now or we shall be late."

Robert knew the king was notoriously informal.

It was said he attended private parties, taverns, even brothels, and played the country gentleman at New-market every fall. It was unheard of in any other court in Europe, yet he and his brother James could be seen frequently at dinner and supper, dispensing with formality for the sake of entertainment. It took remarkable courage and confidence in the love of his people to allow them to see and interact with him as simply a man. He felt a grudging respect. But it was a shock nonetheless to be bundled into a carriage and told they were off to a party that his other mistress and he were hosting in their town house on Pall Mall.

It was almost May, a beautiful night, and though dusk had already settled it wasn't yet full dark when they rolled to a stop in front of a grand three-story house on the desirable western end of the street. Shaded by elms, with a garden adjoining the king's garden at St. James's Palace, it backed onto the park. Several carriages were arrayed on the street out front, and it looked as if the gathering was already well under way.

There were occasions in battle when despite train-ing, planning and good intelligence, one found one-self cut off and lost in a situation one couldn't foresee or control. When that happened, one trusted to one's instincts and waited, going with the flow of things, watching for that moment when direction and mo-mentum could be wrested back again. Robert Nichols still had no idea why the king who'd stripped him of his lands had summoned him to court and made him his boon companion, so with no answers forthcoming, he prepared to observe.

CHAPTER SIX

HOPE MATHEWS HAD NEVER felt happier. Hosting this
evening with Charles and his friends made up for a
thousand tiny hurts.

For the past year and half, just like Cinderella,
she would appear at Whitehall, set tongues to wag-
ging, then hurry home at midnight with nothing but
the remnants of a dream. But tonight it was she who
was hosting the ball! Well…dinner party. Tomorrow would be May Day, and tonight was an informal
private celebration for only his closest friends. To
hold it at her lodgings was to acknowledge her importance to him in front of those whose opinion he
valued most. She knew she wouldn't have him much
longer, but while she did, she couldn't help but love
him for letting her enjoy the fantasy, and pretend for
one night that *she* was his queen.

He had left her to manage it, telling her to spare no
expense, and she was almost bouncing with excitement, waiting for him to see what she had done. She
had worked day and night for two weeks to prepare,
turning the house into a feast for the senses. A place
to celebrate the summer to come, in luxury, comfort

and ease. She surveyed it all with a wide smile, confident it was a night everyone would remember. A night that would make Charles proud.

The air was fragrant with scented beeswax candles, baskets of fruits and masses of flowers, many of which she had grown in her own beloved gardens under the tutelage of Charles's gardener, her mentor in all things floral, John Rose. Boughs of greenery decked the banisters, mantels and arches, and flower-covered arbors and miniature maypoles marked private grottos both inside and out.

The servant girls wore floral garlands and the footmen were painted as jack-in-the-green and dressed in leaf-green linen. Music drifted through the salon from hidden alcoves, cheerful and unobtrusive, weaving into the happy hum of laughter and conversation as people flirted and gossiped and played at cards. A crystal chandelier blazed overhead and side tables sparkled with decanters of malmsey, Rhenish, sack and canary, and beautifully wrought glasses trimmed in silver and gold.

In the dining room opening off the salon, a long table stood ready, draped in white linen, piled high with platters of chicken, mutton, lobster and tarts from which people could serve themselves. A silver dinner service with the initials *H.M.* shone splendid in the candlelight, and there was a large silver bowl filled with rosewater for guests to dip napkins and wash their hands.

They had invited about fifty guests in all. The king's brother James and his son—the Duke of Monmouth—had already arrived. Buckingham was busy at cards in the corner with Elizabeth de Veres, Lord Rivers's pretty wife. Hope regarded her curiously. She liked the poet. He'd been kind to her, despite her lowly background, treating her as well as any court lady, though it was clear he found her faithfulness to Charles amusing. How curious now to find him in love with his own wife. Charles admired her, too. *What is it such men crave from these virtuous seductresses? Virtue is something no man will look for in me.*

All that was missing was Charles. A cheer made her look to the entrance. A tall and ruddy dark-haired man, wearing an ostrich-plumed hat tilted at a rakish angle and a gold-braided crimson coat, came sweeping through the door, dwarfing most of those around him both in presence and in size. Charles at last! Her face broke into a happy grin and her heart raced a few beats faster. No doubt he had the same effect on every woman in the room. *But tonight he is mine.*

Her gaze sharpened and she looked with interest at the man who walked beside him. She'd never seen him at court before or she would have remembered. Lean-waisted, broad-shouldered, with a powerful frame, he topped Charles by a good two inches. He seemed solid in a way one seldom saw among men living the soft life at court. He moved like a swordsman: lithe, graceful, yet there was something almost wolfish about him. It was easy to imagine him strapped in armor atop a war horse like some vengeful knight of old. He was familiar somehow, as if he might have walked into her home straight from one of her dreams.

She watched him, mesmerized, as she wove though her guests to greet Charles. He wore a rich black suit with a white-plumed slouched hat. A matching officer's sash served as a sword belt, and through slashed sleeves she could see crisp white linen showing at the wrist and neck. In a room of gaily bedecked courtiers he looked elegant and dangerous. It suited him well. Her heart sped up and a guilty flush warmed her cheeks as she imagined him naked.

He turned to speak to Charles and she got a good look at his features, and for one brief moment her heart stood still. He had a harsh beauty set off by a faded scar that creased his cheek. His hair was swept back off his face in a neat queue tied with a length of black ribbon. It gleamed in the candlelight, burnished gold with streaks of dark and light. Flickering shadows from hundreds of tapers accentuated chiseled features: strong cheekbones, a firm jaw and a full, almost sinful-looking mouth. *I wonder what color his eyes are?*

She had almost reached Charles and she rushed the last few steps to greet him. He caught her and hugged her and bussed her cheek. "You've done us proud indeed this evening, Miss Mathews. And you are as pretty as the first day of summer." She beamed with delight, his words making all her hard work worthwhile. He released her and removed his hat, then gave her an elegant bow. "As you can see, I've invited a friend. I pray you have room for one more. My dear, may I present to you a dashing fellow, both brave and bold, Captain Robert Nichols."

He placed an arm around her shoulders and for some reason, the overly familiar public gesture made her feel slightly embarrassed. She fought the urge to shrug him off. The captain stepped forward. His face looked grim, as if he were in the presence of something distasteful. She flushed, surprised at her awkward reaction. What did she care what a disapproving stranger thought? Her life was full of them. Let him think what he pleased.

Unaccustomed modesty overcome, she greeted her new guest with a playful smile. "Welcome, Captain Nichols. It's an honor to have you join us for an evening of celebration. Please treat our home as if it were your own." She held out her hand, forcing him to kiss it.

He tucked the hat he was holding under his arm and took her dainty hand in his large one. Her heart beat violently in her chest. And then he bent to kiss it. His fingers were cool beneath her own and his breath warmed her skin as his lips brushed her knuckles. Two of his fingers lingered a moment, pressing the soft underside of her wrist. She shivered and pulled her hand away, filled with dangerous new sensations. He rose to his full height. A stray lock of hair had escaped its bounds, softening his features.

"It's very kind of you, madam, to welcome a stranger so warmly."

His rich voice was deep and mellow. She raised her eyes to his. He was regarding her intently. Riveted, she returned his searching gaze. There was something sad about him, *and* something frightening. Despite a reassuring air of competence and strength, he struck her as a troubled soul. His eyes were green. A haunting shade of olive-green with flecks of black and silver that captured and mesmerized. She imagined loneliness and sorrow and great pain hidden in their depths. She blinked and looked away. He was a very handsome man.

"Hope, my dear. We have duties to attend. It's time you escort me through the salon to greet our other guests. Then everyone can relax and enjoy the evening."

Released from whatever spell had bound her, she stepped back to the relative safety of Charles's arms, for one wistful moment wishing she might be the virtuous seductress. The kind with whom men fell and stayed in love.

"Can you muddle about on your own for a space, Captain?"

"I expect I can manage it, Your Majesty."

ROBERT WATCHED WITH cold admiration as his new
friend the king took the arm of his beautiful courtesan. She wore a distinctive gown, with deep purple
skirt and sleeves, white, flower-embroidered petticoats and black stomacher. It captured the eye
and drew attention to her trim waist and the sway
of her hips as she walked. Surprisingly, given who
her lover was, the only ornaments she wore were
a floral crown of willow, violets and ivy, with one
errant green sprig trailing down her cheek, and a few
stray flowers woven into her hair.

Hope Mathews. He'd heard of her. The orange girl
who'd leapt from the stage and stormed the palace to
become His Majesty's "country miss." She was finer
than he had expected. Neither coarse nor vulgar,
quite charming in fact, and a breathtaking natural
beauty. With soft creamy skin, a full pouting mouth
and a luxurious mass of rippling waist-length black
hair, she had no need of enhancement, but it was
those eyes that had stopped him dead in his tracks
and held him captive. Arresting eyes full of secrets,
glowing violet then blue, beneath full sweeping
lashes.

He marveled at his own unaccustomed whimsy,
but he'd always been fascinated by violet eyes, and
true ones were exceedingly rare. He reminded himself that despite those delicate wrists and wounded
eyes, she was no pure and innocent waif. She was
a royal concubine, possibly more striking than her

court-bred rival, and definitely fit for a king. Creatures such as she exuded a powerful sexual allure. They were meant to be enticing. Yet she looked like a wild thing sprung from the forest, her smile sparkled and enchanted like a warm summer's night, and she smelled like spring. He hadn't expected to be quite so…entranced.

She looked back at him from over her shoulder, as if she had heard his thoughts. A few sprigs of greenery escaped her crown and tangled in her hair. His breath quickened and he felt an unaccustomed twinge of longing. For a moment everything went still around him, and there was only him and the girl. He tilted his head in a slight bow and she answered with a sunny smile and the merry eyes of a mischievous child. He couldn't help a slight chuckle. Whatever she was, the lass had lightened his spirit like nothing had done in a very long while. Definitely not an innocent waif, but perhaps a wayward elf.

CHAPTER SEVEN

ROBERT COMMANDED A QUIET ALCOVE in a corner of the salon. It was a relief to leave the reception room behind him. He had no idea why any sane person would line a room from floor to ceiling with mirrors. When he first walked in, the whirl of gaudy colors and bewigged heads had left him feeling nauseous and faintly dizzy. He wondered how those who drank too much ever found the door.

The stir around the king had diminished somewhat. The courtiers had made their greetings, the king had accepted them, and now everyone seemed intent on enjoying themselves. Several sat at tables playing hazard and basset, and people streamed in and out of the dining room eating when and what they pleased. The Duke of Buckingham and the charming Mistress Mathews performed a skit in the salon. He thought it somewhat childish, but others seemed to find it uproariously funny. He hid his impatience. He didn't like surprises and had yet to discern why he was here.

It was a pleasant surprise to see Elizabeth across the room, though. He hadn't seen her since she'd left

London close to a year ago. By the looks of it her husband was back in favor. He was deep in conversation with the king. She kept smiling and beckoning for him to join them, but Lord Rivers had a grip on her arm as strong as the one he used to keep on his drink. He looked up from his conversation from time to time, and his eyes held a warning and a possessive gleam. It was enjoyable to watch them. A touch on the arm, a whisper in the ear, private looks that spoke volumes; their intimacy was palpable. It warmed him to see it and it made him jealous. *Is it Elizabeth I crave...or simply to feel something like that?*

Yet on this strange night filled with laughter and music, old friends and old rivals, beautiful seductresses and whimsical kings, the room glowed with color and all that was in it came dancing to life. It almost felt as if *he* were creaking back to life. He grinned as he watched the king's lovely courtesan, no longer impatient, for she was the enchantress who'd first cast the spell.

General Monk, the kingmaker who'd engineered Charles Stuart's return to the throne, stepped forward to greet him.

"Sir Robert Nichols! What a pleasure it is to see you, sir! You've been far too scarce in London as of late." They exchanged a hearty handshake. "Where *have* you been, Captain? I've been trying to find you."

"I have… I *had*…a small estate in Nottingham-shire, sir. I've left the field of battle for fields of grain, and fighting armies for battling floods and heavy rains."

"Ah! Indeed, sir. I know it well. One *thinks* that's what one wants. Away from the smoke and thunder. At last a little peace. But one grows bored. There's a longing. Something's missing and the days take on a sameness that… Do you know what I mean, Robert?"

"Yes, sir. I do."

"As it happens, I may have a cure."

"Sir?" He felt a keen thrill of anticipation. Could this be why the king had brought him here tonight? To take one thing away but give him another?

"You're a superb warrior, Sir Robert, but more importantly for my purpose, you were always a man one could count on to keep a cool head, think for himself and get the job done. How do you like the sound of Colonel Nichols?"

"I like it, General! I—"

"General! I see you know our captain." Charles Stuart came up behind them and embraced them both.

"I do indeed, sire. He's a fine soldier. One that I—"

"And of course you've met Lord Rivers. A dear friend from my exile and a war hero himself. Allow me to introduce his lovely wife, Lady Elizabeth."

The general bowed and kissed Elizabeth's hand.

"Congratulations, madam. All London has been abuzz about the capture. Only an extraordinary woman could manage such a feat."

"Thank you, General. You're very kind. But I assure you it was William who captured me." She turned to Robert with a bright smile. "Oh, Robert, it's so good to see you here! I miss our old visits and I worry about you all alone."

Robert greeted them all with a formal bow, but Elizabeth threw her arms around him and gave him a hug. As he set her back on her feet he took a quick glance at the handsome poet who had stolen her away. Though de Veres had never met him, he'd seen the man in taverns and coffeehouses many times before. There was a brightness to his face. Perhaps Elizabeth had done for her libertine what he had hoped she would do for him.

The man stepped forward and offered his hand and he had no choice but to accept it. "Lizzy has told me many times what a comfort you were to her in the past, Captain Nichols. I offer you my thanks for watching over her when I couldn't do so."

He bit back a scathing reply and managed a polite nod. This was the man who had put her in danger in the first place.

General Monk put a hand on his shoulder as if re-claiming ownership. "If it pleases you, Your Majesty, Sir Robert is a mighty fine soldier. I've a proposition to put to him regarding the Coldstream Guard."

"Ah, reunions. Aren't they grand. I had no idea the captain knew so many of my friends. But I'm afraid it will have to wait, General. In fact I must ask you all to excuse us. As it happens, the captain and I have business to discuss before the dancing begins. Will you forgive us?"

A beaming Elizabeth curtsied while the general and William responded with a bow. His Majesty put a companionable arm around Robert's shoulder, led him into a small dark paneled study and closed and locked the door. He motioned for him to sit and poured them both a drink.

"Well, Captain. You're doubtless wondering why you are here."

"Indeed, Majesty, I am."

"It is that tyrant Elizabeth de Veres's doing. I am fond of her, of course, but she's been very cross with me for taking your lands."

Robert clenched and unclenched his fists. "She had no business discussing it with you. I had not thought of her connection to you, nor did I seek her aid. I thought, as an old friend, she was discreet." His voice was stiff.

The king threw back his head and laughed. "Captain! You are a warrior, sir, and know little of the ways of women. Now you must accustom yourself to softer things. They are weaker than us physically, but any man who things them weaker in other ways doesn't know them at all. I, sir, make a study of them. I know them and love them very well.

"So one hears, sire. Might I ask your point?"

"Some women were born to be generals. Elizabeth is one such, as I'm certain you know, and she has chosen to champion your cause. You mustn't be annoyed with her. She feels loyalty and affection for you. She values you enough to ask me to return your lands, and I value her enough to have thought on it. It is a great inconvenience of course. I shall have to find other lands for Lord Harris, though he was very keen on having yours."

"Jonathon Harris? A bald man?"

"Yes, that's him. Do you know him? I swear you've met every soul in London."

Robert bared his teeth in a cold smile. "I am certain I crossed his path during the wars." A thrill of ice ran through his veins. The hunt was on! The man he chased now circled his home. Did the hunted think to become the hunter? Or was there some divine plan at work? Whatever happened, Harris must not be allowed to walk the halls of Cressly.

"Doubtless you did. He fought for both sides as it swung to his advantage. Royalist, parliament, then royalist once more. I'm not terribly fond of him. Such men can't be trusted. But there is a matter of politics involved. He is a useful man, much needed at the moment. You were an honest soldier, Captain, and a very good one. The general speaks highly of you. A commission for you based on his recommendation is something I've considered, but I've a problem you can help with, and the solution I have in mind should aid us both. If you agree to it, you will keep your lands and I will add the adjacent ones, as well."

"And how can I be of service to Your Majesty?"

"Please, call me Charles."

"What is it you want from me...Charles?"

"I want you to marry my mistress."

Robert covered his shock by downing his drink. Had he heard the man correctly? "You want me to marry your mistress?"

"Yes. Hope Mathews. The one I brought you to meet this evening. She's a charming little thing. I'm very fond of her. But I am to be married soon, Captain. The court already cavils at her presence. Her social status is such that—"

"She is the one they call the orange girl? The one who was a whore at The Merry Strumpet?"

The king stiffened. "They may call her what they like. I assure you she's far more innocent and has a finer character than many of the ladies here at court."

"I don't understand, Your Majesty. Why would you ask such a thing of me?"

"As I said, I am to be married soon. My bride will be on English soil three weeks hence. No doubt you've noticed the preparations. Hope is very dear to me, but she is not of a fit social status to be accepted in the presence of my queen. If my court is to accept my will in this it must be made palatable. A married mistress is far more acceptable than an unmarried one, and a titled lady far more acceptable than a street waif."

"Can you not simply give her a title?"

"For her service to the crown?" The king chuckled heartily and poured them both another drink. "She has been a better friend to me than many who are more amply rewarded, but that I cannot do. Not without turning my court upside down and sending my wife in a fury back to Portugal. England needs this marriage. *I* can't give her a title—" he pointed a long finger at Robert "—but *you* can. Appearances matter here, Captain. The play is the thing, you see? She must marry a title and leave court for a while. Until after the wedding and things are settled between my wife and my *maîtresse-en-titre,* Barbara. Then she may returned as a married lady—"

"Matters between—"

Charles held up his hand. "It is nothing. A bagatelle. Matters that are no concern of yours. What *is* your concern is my proposition. You will marry her. Tonight. You will remove her from London tonight. You will keep your estates and those adjacent, and I will give you a coronet to add to your coat of arms. You will be named Baron Nichols, *and* created Earl of Newport. Henceforth Miss Mathews will be a lady. A countess, no less. And those who felt themselves too grand for her shall look to you and regret it. You will keep her well and safe, and when I summon her to court, you will parade her as a lady before them all."

"So she won't be my wife but your whore?"

"You will treat her as the lady she is." There was a sudden frost in his tone.

"And why have I been chosen for this singular honor?" Robert asked, ignoring it.

"Because Elizabeth assures me you are an honorable man who has shown her only kindness. I trust her judgment and assume you will do the same for Hope. And because no other *suitable* gentleman of my court will have her due to her lowly birth. *Your* great-grandfather had no title. He was a junior officer, barely a gentleman. Your grandfather was given a knighthood and your father made baronet for service to King James. You are a gentleman, but without noble roots so deep that you should fail to see the honor. I will, of course, provide her with a generous dowry, as well. Such things never go amiss." His eyes were calculating now, and slightly cold.

"And if I prefer General Monk's offer?" He didn't really know why he asked. The matter was decided the moment the king mentioned Harris's name. Perhaps it was the casual assumption that his honor was for sale he resented. He wasn't inclined to make the thing easy for them when they both thought so little of him.

"You will not be given that choice, Captain Nichols. General Monk has proven his loyalty to me. His service to myself and England are incalculable. You, on the other hand, could be a dangerous man. A disgruntled landless soldier, prepared to give his allegiance to a military commander before his king. We've had our fill of those. *You* have never served me. You have proven nothing. Do so now, Captain. It is an opportunity that will not come again."

"To be clear…you are asking me to be a knowing cuckold, an accomplice to your own adultery, in order to save my lands?"

"Exactly. Yes. And you shall be amply rewarded for it. It doesn't please me to put an honorable man in this position, Captain, but I can hardly entrust her to anyone less." His Majesty's sudden smile was full of warmth and charm. "But what a poor host I am! Have some dinner. Enjoy the entertainment. Take some time to think. I must see to my lady. We will speak again later, yes? Think carefully, though, Captain. It's always better to make new friends." He gave him a kindly pat on the shoulder. "She really is a lovely girl. What have you got to lose?"

CHAPTER EIGHT

FROM DISPOSSESSED TO NOBLEMAN, suspect to royal favor, and hunter to hunted, the king had set his world to spinning like a master magician, with suggestion, distraction and sleight of hand. Though most of it was smoke and mirrors, two things were perfectly clear. His prey had resurfaced and was within his grasp, and the elfin beauty who had made him laugh had in fact been laughing at him. Tired of overwarm bodies and cloying perfume, Robert went in search of the garden. He passed the king and his hostess on the way. His Majesty, head bent, was listening intently as his lady whispered something in his ear. Those innocent eyes were sparkling, her laughter sweet as music. Wondering if they laughed at him, he stepped outside.

The sounds of murmured conversation and distant laughter followed him. He settled on a bench beside a gently flowing fountain, leaning his back against an arbor wall. He would never have imagined being summoned to court for this…honor. What did one call the paid cuckold to a king? *Baron Nichols, Earl of Newport,* he thought with mordent humor. Titles he was supposed to accept with pride.

Well, accept them he would. There was no other choice. He could never allow one of his sister's murderers to walk Cressly's halls. Not even for the length of time it took to kill him. To do so would be an unconscionable desecration and he knew a part of her, the last part he had, would be lost. He had to accept the girl...this marriage. *Then Harris will be enraged, and will come after me. If he provokes a duel no blame will lay on my door. If he attacks me it will be self-defense. Either way he'll be dead, and Caroline avenged.*

He was well aware of his future bride's background. All of London followed the exploits and intrigues of their amorous king. She was little better than a common prostitute, likely was one before she became the mistress of rich and titled men. He'd seen too much of war and abandoned women and children to judge what a person did to survive. Still, it wasn't the pedigree one sought in a wife, and it angered and offended him to be so casually used.

Cuckold, pimp, pander, blind man. This is the duty my king and his lady look for from me. Better men have refused them. Prouder men have said no. General Monk serves England as soldier and statesman. I will serve her as stage dressing, for my adulterous king and his whore. They had expected it of him. They had assumed him so grasping and venal that he'd sell his honor and his pride for a coronet, some land and a bag of gold. *And I will. Not for riches, but revenge.* He thought back to his last happy moment. That crisp midwinter night he'd kissed Kate Bishop, just moments before he heard his sister's scream. Poor lad. He'd had no idea vengeance was about to swallow his life whole. He let out a long sigh. *Or bring me so low.*

The soft laughter he'd heard earlier had grown closer and wilder, interspersed now with shouts, clapping and cheers. He got up to investigate, walking down the hedgerow and through a small gap into the big garden backing on the park. The moon was new, barely a sliver, but the pitch-black sky glittered diamond bright overhead. It was a beautiful night, the air soft and gentle, and the trees stirred softly in the breeze. The doors from the salon were opened and the celebration had moved outside. Torches and candlelight illuminated the garden, bathing everything in it with a magical glow. There were acrobats and tumblers doing cartwheels and handsprings, and conjurers performing tricks with ropes and fire.

Mistress Mathews's smiling servants skipped through the crowd handing out garlands and May baskets overflowing with tulips, iris and daisies, and stuffed with sweetmeats and nuts. His parents had disapproved of May Day celebrations, but he had often snuck down to the village to join the fun. The king's nymph was enchanting, clapping and dancing, and her merry laugh made him smile. He couldn't stop a rueful chuckle. The wicked Miss Mathews wasn't really at fault. It wasn't she who had chosen him, and for the sake of enjoyment he let his resentment and anger slip away. *Besides, they may think to use me for their own ends, but after tonight she is mine.*

His smile turned into a grin as the sound of drumming, clapping sticks and jingling bells announced the arrival of a troupe of morris dancers, traditional entertainers costumed as beast men. There were wolves and bears and antlered gentlemen, and some half man, half horse. They performed a number of lively folk dances as the servants brought the food outside, the household musicians joined in and the wine freely flowed.

A fiddler and piper broke away, slipping through a slim gated arch in the hedge. Mistress Mathews was close behind them. Wearing a necklace of wildflowers, her midnight hair hanging loose to her waist, skipping barefoot over the moon-silvered grass, leading her flock of gaily bedecked guests into the starlit groves and fields of St. James Park. He followed, completely enthralled. They stopped in the middle of a brightly lit clearing to exclamations of delight. Standing in the center was a tall birch pole, its branches removed except at the top. Garlands, ribbons and wildflowers wrapped around its length. The piper blew a high note, calling for silence, and

Miss Mathews's voice, sounding fine and clear, carried above the crowd.

"Ladies and gentlemen! Dear friends all. His Majesty would like to remind you, 'It is now past midnight and tomorrow is today.' He bids me tell you, 'There's not a budding boy, or girl, this day, but is got up, and gone to bring in May.'"

There were shouts and cheers and laughter. The piper played a sprightly tune and clapping and dancing and singing along, some of the greatest lords and ladies of the land joined in to dance around the maypole. Robert watched her dance with her arms thrown up to the heavens. Not for her the intricate folk steps or careful prancing of her neighbors. She gave herself completely to the music and the moment. He envied her passion. It was something alien to him for far too many years. *I wonder...does she do that with everything? Does she do the same when joined with a lover? What would it be like to take her in the soft grass, under the moon and stars?*

"She is enchanting, isn't she?" The king stood at his shoulder.

"Yes, she is," he replied absently, before realizing who it was.

"As my poet used to say before he was waylaid. 'Such sweet tempting mischiefs women are.'" There seemed an air of regret in his voice.

Robert sighed, his eyes still on her. "Yes...I know. She's very beautiful."

"Will you have her?"

"Yes." What other answer was there?

"Excellent! I am well pleased. It will be the finest entertainment of the evening."

Robert did look at him now, his eyes narrowed. "I'm afraid I don't understand what you mean."

"You will, Lord Newport. I promise you'll know when the time comes. Just play your part and you'll see soon enough."

A gilded carriage had pulled up at the edge of the clearing and His Majesty hurried away to greet it before Robert could respond. Ah, well. What matter how the thing was done? The marriage was pure farce. Why shouldn't it be a part of the evening's entertainment? Resigned, he put it from his mind and lifted a glass of Rhenish from the tray of a passing jack-in-the-green roving the woods.

He wandered closer to the maypole and leaned against a tree, his arms folded, curious but not inclined to join the dance. Several ladies were on the edges of the clearing, rustling in the brushes on hands and knees and crawling in the grass. He cocked his head and watched with bemusement.

"They are collecting the dew," de Veres said from beside him. "Surely you've heard the nursery rhyme.…

"'The fair maid who, the first of May
Goes to the fields at break of day
And washes in dew from the hawthorn tree
Will ever after handsome be.'

"'Tis also said it will help her capture the heart of the man of her choosing. Are you annoyed with Lizzy? She seems to think so."

Robert took his eyes off his fiancée regretfully and glanced coolly at de Veres. "I've yet to decide. When I know I'll be sure to inform you. I take it she's curious as to what comes from her meddling. You can tell her she'll see for herself soon enough."

He returned his attention to the dancers in the glade, stiffening when he felt a hand on his shoulder. Robert didn't look back when he spoke. "For reasons I can't fathom she seems fond of you. But if you don't remove your hand…"

William opened his hand and lifted it, then straightened the back of Robert's coat. He spoke close to his ear, his voice a combination of amusement and warning. "Anything that concerns Lizzy is my affair, Captain. A thing you'd be wise to remember."

Robert shrugged and a moment later the poet was gone. He smiled to himself. Good for Elizabeth. It seemed her courtier poet was more of a man than he'd thought.

A SOUNDING OF HORNS and the ringing of bells marked the arrival of a tall man wearing a sun mask of beaten gold. His left hand held a gilded staff wrapped with flowers and ivy. He bent his knee and held his right hand out to Hope. She took it with a jubilant smile.

He rose and turned to face the crowd and led her out, presenting her. "Lords and ladies, fellow revelers...

"'Hail, bounteous May, that dost inspire
Mirth, and youth, and warm desire!
Woods and groves are of thy dressing;
Hill and dale doth boast thy blessing.
Thus we salute thee with our early song,
And welcome thee, and wish thee long.'

"I present to you our lovely May Queen!"

"Oh, Charles! What a wonderful surprise!" Hope almost had to shout for him to hear above the cheering, so she threw her arms round his neck. "It's a night I will always remember. Thank you!" It was a great honor to be chosen Queen of the May. In villages and towns and cities across Britain all the unmarried women vied for that prize. Yet Charles had chosen her over a bevy of noble beauties.

Her eyes were shining as bright as any star as Charles gently extricated himself from her embrace and placed the leafy staff in her hands. "Your scepter, my lady. And now..." Charles slowly circled the glade, his finger dipping and rising as if he were counting each man that he passed. "The May Queen—" there was a hush of anticipation "—must have...a May King!" His finger tapped Robert's shoulder.

"Why not me?" the Duke of Buckingham shouted to roars of laughter.

Ignoring him, Charles drew Hope and Robert to

stand in front of the Maypole. "It is my decree that Miss Mathews be the Queen of May, and Lord Newport, Baron Nichols, be her consort." The announcement generated excited whispers as well as applause. "I call now for a priest of the wood to step forward, to bestow a blessing on the joining of the Lord and Lady of May."

Hope was a little surprised at this turn of events, but she grinned and tried to straighten the flower wreath that was sliding over her brow, then gave up and turned to give her towering consort a winsome smile. Buckingham would have been a more comfortable choice, but the captain made her heart beat faster, and she supposed it might be fun continuing the game she'd started earlier, trying to make him smile.

Bright red roses were thrown at their feet and Hope was adorned with a necklace of willow and ivy entwined with flowers matching those strewn through her curls. Robert felt himself grow impatient when he was crowned with a wreath of flowers and draped with a rainbow-hued scarf, but Hope was glowing, her smile was contagious and she looked so delightful with her flowered crown that he couldn't play the churl. He felt a pang, keen as a blade, for innocence lost. He was a child once, and it seemed that she still shone with the innocence of joy and youth. *She's aptly named. I wish the past held no sway and*

*we both stood here unspoiled. I wish this night was
real and we were lovers joined in truth.*

The merry din around them rose as the crowd
made way for a corpulent man in the robes of a
priest, except for a green mask, a chaplet of leaves
and a mantle made of flowers. "I will perform the
blessing, great lord," he said with a deep bow. He
went to stand between Hope and Robert. The crowd
hushed, straining to hear him. "Children of the maypole! The woods have echoed with joy and mirth and
now the hour is at hand. The winter is put behind us,
and before us the joys of summer await." He made
a sweeping gesture to the king. "Sweet May has returned, and awaits the dawning of the sun." The sun
bowed graciously to wild cheers as the priest took
Robert and Hope by the hand.

"To honor this gentlest, merriest month, fertile
and sweet and toward lovers inclined, here stand the
Lord and Lady of the May, whom I shall join in marriage. Up with you now and to the dance. Join us in
laughter and song, and wish a toast on the marriage
of the Lord and Lady of the May!"

Suddenly jack-in-the-greens were everywhere,
bearing trays of wine. The guests surged forward to
join the May King and Queen in a toast, and several
barrels of mead were broken open. A fiddler started
up and a piper joined in and a ring of animal men encircled them. As the morris men resumed their bell

ringing and drumming, the heathen priest led them through some surprisingly traditional vows.

The game being over and still an hour before dawn, Hope curtsied to her consort then rose to her toes, looking for Charles, ready to dance. But despite his height she couldn't find him. Ah, wait! There to the left. A flash of gold mask from beside a leafy bower. His head was bent. He was engrossed in conversation with a tall auburn-haired woman masked like the moon to his sun.

A physical pain like a blow to the gut forced the wind from her lungs and almost doubled her over, and though a glacial chill froze her blood, her cheeks burned hot and she blinked back scalding tears. A resplendent Lady Castlemaine was holding court, surrounded by sycophants, her waist encircled by the king.

CHAPTER NINE

TAKING SEVERAL DEEP BREATHS, Hope clenched her
fists, tamping her fury. Even so, as she crossed the
glade with a cool smile pasted on her face and her
head held high, her limbs felt so weak she almost
stumbled, and the aching in her throat made her fear
she couldn't speak. "Lady Castlemaine." She refused
to give her nod or curtsy. "Charles."

Charles looked only vaguely uncomfortable. "Ah!
'Tis the Queen of the May! Are you enjoying yourself, my dear? You've done a splendid job. Everything is going marvelously well."

Few had noticed Lady Castlemaine's presence yet,
but now they all did. Conversation died as people
strained to hear. It had been a wonderful night, and
to have it end with a brawl between two of His Majesty's mistresses would surely make it the best entertainment of the year so far.

Hope's voice rang out, carrying through the glade.
"Surely even as illustrious a whoremonger as you
needs only one of us at a time. Tell her to leave."

Lady Castlemaine gasped in outrage. "Charles!
Will you allow your guttersnipe to address me this

way? If she were one of my servants I'd have her whipped. She needs to be taught respect for her betters!"

Robert sighed, and downed his drink. For a short while he had been glamoured, caught in a dark enchantment of glitter and gaiety and sweet summer's night, but the spell was broken, exposing the cruel deception that lurked beneath. *And I am part of it now.* Should he play his part? Step forward as husband and defender? *She's not really mine. Why should I step between them? Let His Majesty sort it out himself.*

Yet despite his new wife's seething anger, there was an aura about her of a wounded child. She was clearly in distress and there was no one else to come to her aid. He tossed his empty goblet to a passing footman and stepped forward. "Forgive me, Lady Castlemaine. We met earlier this evening. No doubt you speak in jest and mean no insult to the countess. Lady Nichols is neither guttersnipe nor servant, madam. She is my wife."

"Quite so, Barbara. You remember meeting Captain Nichols earlier. He is also Earl of Newport and has married our May Queen. She is a countess now like you, so you must be polite." England's king favored them all with his most charming smile. "Off you go a-maying, then, Lord Newport, and congratulations to you and your lovely bride."

Robert went to take Hope's arm but she tore it

from his grasp. "This game is over! I am not play-ing anymore." She tore off her crown of flowers and flung it at Charles's feet. "How could you do this? After all the work I put into it. To please you! This night was supposed to be ours! Not hers! Yours and mine."

"Don't make a scene, Hope. Lord Nichols, it is time for you to take your wife home. You may borrow my coach." Charles motioned to a footman, who came running over, nodded and then hurried away.

"Come, sweetheart." Robert reached for her elbow.

Hope whirled on him. "*Don't*...put your hands on me. I don't even know who you are! I have *not* given you permission to touch me. Mind your own busi-ness, this is not your affair." He released her im-mediately, stepping well back as if he'd been stung. It was then she saw the jolly priest puffing toward them, one hand holding his cumbersome robes as he walked, the other clutching the green mask he'd been wearing just minutes before. She recognized him in-stantly. She had seen him earlier in the evening and before at court. There was a very sick feeling build-ing inside her.

He approached them, smiling and wheezing, com-pletely oblivious to the tension around them waiting only for a spark to explode. "Your Majesty! I come to pay my respects before taking my leave. I trust all was to your satisfaction?"

"Indeed it was, sir. Lord and Lady Newport, might I introduce the Right Reverend Edward Durham. You have him to thank for your happiness."

"Oh, Charles, you didn't! You couldn't have!" Hope's face drained of all color as the depths of his perfidy sank in. She had thought the marriage ceremony part of an elaborate pageant and nothing more. Charles's surprise contribution to the elaborate entertainment she had arranged. But in one cruel moment her fairy tale came crashing to the ground and her dreams of an independent life, just within her grasp, were cruelly yanked away. *Trust me,* he kept saying. *Trust me.* And then he had tricked her into marrying some hungry fortune hunter, new-come to court. A judgmental Puritan soldier who had looked at her with thinly veiled distaste from the moment they had met.

"All of you! Leave us. Now. That means you, too, Barbara." Charles took Hope by the arm and, too stunned to resist, she followed him to the far side of the glade where curious listeners couldn't hear their words, only her angry voice and his soothing one.

Robert watched it all, his face grim. The king had hurt and humiliated her by bringing his senior mistress. This he understood. But the chit's outraged scorn at his own attempt to help her left him mightily offended and was a very poor sign for what was to come. Clearly the change from monarch to newly minted earl was so far beneath her she felt no need for courtesy. *Imagine what she'll think when she sees my country home. How have I come to marry such a venal creature. How have I fallen so low?* All his sympathy as well as his budding admiration for her were gone.

He stood amongst the spectators, ordered to leave his bride and wait like a servant as the king and his courtesan put on a show. *He rebuffs her in public with his high-born whore, at the same time showing the world that she is his and not mine. And she abets him in it.* He was tempted to leave her and the king and his titles behind. It seemed a travesty to allow this shallow grasping creature to walk Cressly's halls. *She may reside there as a guest but I'll be damned if she'll ever be its mistress.* He stopped a passing jack-in-the-green and reached for another drink. "'Tis my wedding day," he quipped with a sardonic smile. He downed it in one swallow, plucked another from the tray before the man could leave, and settled in to watch the show.

Across the meadow, Hope tried to put her feelings into words. Charles had broken a bond that to her was sacred, and he'd blithely stolen her free will. She would never return to his arms again, but she was determined to speak her piece. "How could you do this, Charles? What in God's name have I ever done to you but be a faithful companion and friend? I would rather return to the stage than let you turn me into that dull slave called wife."

"It is for your own protection, sweetheart. A husband will—"

"A husband will what? Mind me? Rule me? Protect me from rich, entitled, dishonest, faithless, heartless, deceiving, oversexed men?" She hurled each word like a stone.

He had the grace to redden slightly. "Hope, I—"

"How much did you pay him to take me off your hands? Is that what you were doing with him in your study? Discussing me as if I were a fine joint of meat? And neither of you had the decency or courtesy to tell me? Neither of you even asked? What right have either of you to decide my fate without consulting me?" The last was said on a plaintive note. She was perilously close to tears.

The king avoided conflict as assiduously as his courtiers and women seemed to seek it, though Hope had never been a problem before this day. He was becoming uncomfortable and vaguely annoyed. "I am your king, Hope. I am also your lover. And as you yourself keep pointing out, my bride is on her way. Is it not my responsibility to see you cared for?"

"By passing the responsibility on to someone else? Someone a stranger to you as well as to me? Had you even met him before this night?"

"No," he said defensively. "But I had very good reports from those who know him well. And frankly, my dear, I thought you'd prefer a younger handsome man, and it was deuced hard to find one who was both a gentleman and willing."

"Of course it was. I am your whore. I want responsibility for my own life, Charles. I've told you before I have money saved. By giving me to this man you let him take it. You give him control over me and everything I own."

"He would not dare abuse that which I value."

She snorted, anger and disgust drying her tears. "That which you value? By bringing your creature you've shown how much you value me to everyone here this night."

"You know I don't tolerate jealousy, Hope."

"And I don't tolerate being sold as if I were a slave. I will not go with him. Nor shall I burden you. I will return to the stage and—"

"You will not! Neither the King's Theater nor that of my brother will accept you as a player if I tell them no."

"Why do you hurt me this way? You didn't have to do this. You didn't have to bring her. You don't have to take my future away. You betray me in every way imaginable. You may be a king, but what I gave you was worth far more than anything you ever gave me, Charles Stuart. I gave you my friendship. I gave you my loyalty. I gave you my trust!"

"Then trust me now, Hope. Things are not as you paint them. You must believe that I know what is best for you. I have made you a lady. A countess.

The same rank as Barbara. I promise she is no more pleased this night than you. Once I've settled things between her and my wife I will call you back to court as a married lady and—"

"You are banishing me from court?"

"I am sending you to the country for a brief stay. You will be gone by morning. When you return you shall be welcomed at Whitehall as a lady and I shall introduce you to my wi—"

Too angry to hear his words, she did the unthinkable. She turned her back on him and walked away.

Barefoot and bedraggled, she wandered though her guests, shivering with cold, her toes wet with dew. Even though it was dark, streaks of light played on the horizon. Gone by morning? What of her clothing, her jewels, her shoes?

A tall footman approached. She watched him with wary eyes. He stopped by her elbow and nodded to a gravel path that wound into the woods. "My lady… your carriage arrives."

"Yes, of course. Charles has thought of everything."

The man who was her husband, who'd seemed cold and forbidding until he had smiled, now looked impatient and cruel. *You were a part of it, too. You both conspired without a thought to my wishes. Well, you traded for a title by marrying a whore and you'll get just what you deserve. I hate you both.* She gave him a cold smile as she took his arm and let him help her into the plush interior of one of the royal coaches. She sat down, rigid with anger, and looked straight ahead.

Charles stood just outside the window, Lady Castlemaine by his side. "Here now, William," he said with forced joviality. "Have you any words of wit to speed the Lord and Lady of May on their way?"

William looked at the too-familiar tableau. Charles and two mistresses. Tears and humiliation. Courtiers gawking with salacious appetites whetted amidst every form of excess. "Why, yes, Charles. I think I have just the thing.

"'Whence comes this mean submissiveness we find

This ill-bred age has wrought on womankind?

Fall'n from the rights their sex—'"

The king sighed and raised a hand to silence him. "That will be all, Lord Rivers. Thank you. It's good to see some things never change. Drive on, coachman!" The coach lurched forward, its bells jingling merrily, as Hope embarked with a stranger, leaving her beloved house on Pall Mall, all of her friends, and all her dreams behind.

William stood next to the king, watching the coach disappear. "That was unnecessarily cruel, Charlie. You've changed more than I'd allowed."

"Sometimes one must be cruel to be kind, Will."

"Lizzy and I will be leaving tomorrow."

"You will not. You will remember I am your king

and you will stay for my wedding. Do not mistake my patience with you as endless. Besides…haven't I given Elizabeth what she wanted? Her captain keeps his lands. She should be pleased."

ELIZABETH'S CAPTAIN WAS FAR from pleased. The girl sat but two feet away from him and she was clearly upset. Jealous courtesan or haughty jade, she was his responsibility at the moment, and she was folded tight in a corner, her eyes glistening with tears. He didn't know a damned thing about keeping a woman. He'd never had one of his own before. Camp followers and friendly tavern wenches on a cold night, yes. Perhaps a widow now and then. One kissed and cuddled them and left some coin or a gift, and then one was on one's way. They didn't *cry!*

This one was his wife now. The prospect was daunting. It would surely be better for them both if they got along, but it seemed so damned complicated. All he knew for certain was he'd yet to do a single thing right and his efforts had been met with nothing but coldness and disdain. Even the mighty Charles Stuart seemed hard put to keep her happy. Though be she barmaid or great lady, any fool should know better than to favor another woman over the one he was with. *What was he thinking?*

Her quiet tears disturbed him. He preferred it when she was angry. Actually, he had preferred when she was happy. A vision of her dancing barefoot through the grass made the corner of his lips turn up slightly. He knew how to make a woman smile, though not in ways he intended to practice with her. Nevertheless he was an intelligent fellow. Resourceful. Cool under fire. A leader of men. Surely he could find a way to stop a jealous chit's tears.

He decided to try and manage her again. He leaned forward and reached out a hand to pat her shoulder. "There now, lass. There's no need to cry. That redheaded, long-legged shrew is built like a garden rake, and she's nowhere near as pretty as you. I promise you, His Majesty will be regretting it soon."

Her eyes snapped to his, boring into him. "I am not crying! Now...take...your...hand...off...me." She bit out each word. "Don't speak to me. Don't touch me. You haven't the right!"

His good intentions evaporated. He was not at all accustomed to being spoken to in that tone. He was not going to live with hostility, condescension and grand airs, nor be spoken to like an impertinent servant. He sat back in his seat, his eyes blazing and his mouth set in a hard line. "But I do have the right. You would do well to show me some respect." His words were clipped and cold.

"Why?" She sat up. "Why should I? You think yourself better than me? You think me little more than a common whore? I saw how you looked when you first walked into my house. Spare me any pious sermons. What kind of man are you? You take another man's leavings, ready to give her back as soon as she's needed. You sold yourself as surely as I ever did. And your prize is a title and a woman who belongs to somebody else."

"You and your royal lover are both mistaken there."

Though his voice was soft, there was something about it that reminded her she was at the mercy of a stranger.

"We may both be whores. I'll not deny it. But you were paid for with what little is left of my honor. Whether Charles willed it or not, and whether you agree, I bought you, and now I own you. By law you belong to me."

"That's unfortunate for us both. People have been telling me that all my life. I don't like being owned. You'll find I make a very poor slave."

"That's not what I meant! You are an impossible woman. No wonder the... Pah! I should have asked for a dukedom and a palace to put up with you."

She turned her head away to look listlessly out the window. She was barefoot still, and her cheeks were stained with tears. The necklace of flowers rose and fell with her breath and violets and buttercups sprouted here and there in her hair. She looked like a sad little girl, and despite himself he was moved.

Hope closed her eyes, shutting him out, though she'd learned long ago it wouldn't change a thing.

Her heart was near to breaking. Deceived. Betrayed. Sold. Humiliated. Again. Anger warred with hurt and she didn't know one from the other. *How dare he? Hypocrite, liar, beast!* As she fought back bitter tears she wasn't sure if she meant Charles or this arrogant brute of a husband.

CHAPTER TEN

HOPE STUDIED THE LONG-LEGGED gentleman sprawled across the opposite seat. His large frame seemed cramped even in the spacious confines of the royal coach. *He takes up too much space.* They had traveled all through the day yesterday, stopping just before nightfall at an inn a few hours short of their destination. The captain had secured her a room and promptly disappeared. She didn't know where he slept. From the smell of him, probably in the tavern. The sanctimonious prig had been half-shot even as he deceived her with his trickster vows. Perhaps he had needed to drown his delicate scruples to complete the ceremony, or maybe Charles had married her to a drunkard. Either way he was a duplicitous rogue.

She resisted the urge to kick him. If he woke she might have to speak to him. Not a word had passed between them since they left St. James Park. Not even this morning when he'd tossed her a worn pair of shoes to cover her bare feet.

This dissipated Captain Nichols bore little resemblance to the stiff and formal soldier who'd glowered his disapproval in her reception hall. The revels and rigors of the past two nights had left him disheveled. His lids looked bruised and heavy, his rugged jaw bristled with stubble and his hair hung loose about his shoulders. The elegant black coat with its silver trimming hung open, exposing the lines and muscles of his collarbone, and the strong column of his neck. Her eyes were drawn to the hollow where they met and her heart beat a little faster. No knight of old now. He looked tarnished and disreputable, though every bit as dangerous.

She still couldn't believe that Charles had simply handed her over to this stranger, trusting she'd be safe with only his words to protect her, and disconcerted to say the least that despite her anger and resentment, his face and form still held the same fascination for her that they had at Pall Mall. *It is a perfectly normal and entirely manageable reaction to a ruggedly handsome man. The kind one seldom sees at court. A novelty. And novelty fades fast.*

He began to stir, muttering something incoherent under his breath as he shifted position, and she turned away, face flushed, to look out the window.

The road was bounded by a forest of beech, willow and oak. Sunlight dappled the forest floor and a playful breeze lifted fresh spring leaves so they tumbled and swayed, their undersides exposed in a mosaic of light and dark. She climbed up on her knees and poked her head out the window, the better to see. A gleaming band of silver light almost blinded her as the sun reflected off a distant river that appeared and disappeared through a curtain of trees.

As they approached it, the traffic grew thick with carts and people. Cattle and horses forded the river in a noisy churning of water, beasts and men, while a gathering of folk stood gossiping on the bank, waiting their turn to be ferried across. It was wider and swifter than she'd expected, though not as broad as the Thames. Beyond the far bank she could see imposing stone buildings and, eager as ever to see new things, she leaned further out, keen to take it all in.

Robert, who'd been awake the past half hour, watched her, completely bemused. Ladies of his acquaintance didn't perch, elbows on windowsill, with their heads poking out and their bottoms in the air, their unbound hair gleaming in the sun. It was highly indecorous and utterly charming. A smile tugged at the corner of his lips.

He liked her this way. Gone was the haughty courtesan, replaced by the unaffected maid who'd danced barefooted beneath the sky. The night before last she'd appeared a wide-eyed nymph, wild and free, an enchanting visitor from a magical realm. He'd almost thought his imagination had conjured her in a haze of drumming and dancing, spirits and song. Yet here she was back again. *She has a sense of wonder. What fool would let her go if this is who she is?*

She was still barefoot despite his gift, bought for

an exorbitant sum from a saucy flaxen-haired bar-maid who'd offered herself along with her shoes. He wondered if his…pretend wife would care that he'd declined. Somehow he doubted it. Still, she *was* his wife by law. It would hardly be fitting to tumble a maid with his new bride sitting upstairs. Besides, she'd suffered more than enough humiliation in front of her rival for him to risk adding more.

As reward for his chivalrous behavior, he decided to keep silent and enjoy the show. Bad-tempered and haughty she might be, but there was no denying she was a seductive minx. Just not in the way one expected. Mind…the sight of trim ankles and pretty toes peeping from silk petticoats was certainly arousing. She'd discarded her stockings before the dancing the other night, and he had only to stretch his arm a little to claim her skin, sliding his hand beneath her skirts to caress her naked thighs. *She's mine. She sold herself to me so that she might have a place at court.*

Her couldn't help but notice how her arched posture made her dress cling, accentuating every luscious curve. Her breasts thrust forward, straining in her bodice, bobbing as she turned and twisted, trying to see. It must be painful to be so tightly constricted. *I've but to move behind her and loosen her stays.* Then he might reach around to cup those succulent globes, and tweak her nipples, before slipping his hands into her bodice and setting them free.

Christ! I've been too long without a woman. I

should have taken the barmaid's offer whilst I had the chance. An aching erection strained rock hard against his breeches and his fingers itched to touch her. He bit back a groan, suffering in silence with no immediate way to relieve himself. *I could slide her skirt up the smooth skin of her haunches, exposing that pretty rounded behind.* His hands could almost feel her pert buttocks: soft, smooth, firm, demanding to be squeezed and fondled, positioned and— *Stop!*

He took a deep breath, fighting to master his body and his senses. His imaginings fueled a hunger that alarmed him. One that mustn't be allowed. The situation was far too complicated. She wasn't simply another man's mistress. She was mistress to his king, to be called at His Majesty's pleasure. It was clear she had no liking for him as a husband. She didn't wish to hear his voice, let alone feel his touch. And he was not a man to share his woman. As long as he made no claim on her as such, their marriage was in name only. There was no true adultery, no true cuckolding, no pandering of wife or honor, where there was no true wife. She was a pretend wife. A royal charge. He was honor bound to see her safe and well cared for and to strive to be civil and that was all.

Pleased at having reasoned an accommodation that left his honor intact, he returned his attention to the window.

She stretched, arching her neck and back like a contented cat before settling back on her elbows and shifting her knees to get comfortable again. Her bottom wiggled and bounced as she managed her contortions.

"God's blood, that's quite enough! Would you please sit down?"

Hope jumped, startled from her reverie, smacking the back of her head on the top of the window as she pulled herself back inside.

He winced in sympathy but made no move to help her, remembering her angry reaction the last two times he'd tried.

"Does this suit you better?" she snapped. She sat primly, her hands folded in her lap, and gave him an angry accusatory stare.

"Yes!" He sat up straight, as well, his hat resting on his lap. "Thank you."

As they waited their turn to be ferried across the river she stared straight ahead, all trace of the curious young lady gone. Robert felt a pang of guilt. Her excitement had been innocent, and his interruption of it anything but. He'd passed this way so many times he didn't pay attention anymore, but it was clearly a new experience for her. One she had seemed prepared to enjoy.

They crossed the river in an awkward silence. He hadn't meant to ruin her pleasure but damned if he knew how to talk to the chit. He was skilled at war and killing, competent at managing his affairs and more than adept at satisfying a woman's physical needs, but he was learning—to his chagrin—he had little idea of what it took to keep one happy. Each time he tried he felt more inept, a feeling he didn't like at all.

Still, a man didn't shirk his duty no matter how difficult. He cleared his throat.... "As I'm sure you know, this is the town of Nottingham, and the river we've just crossed is the Trent. You might not be aware that Nottingham is famous for its cheese and fine pale ales, which are considered the strongest, clearest and best tasting in England. It is also renowned for the Goose Fair, which is several hundred years old and held here every fall. My... Cressly Manor is but eight miles away. You may wish to come here for shopping on occasion. It has the largest marketplace in England and my housekeeper says it has the best shopping before London. They make fine lace and stockings, which of course you'll be needing as you left yours..." His voice trailed off.

Hope stared at him as if he were a two-headed calf, astonished at the lengthy speech after more than a day of frosty silence. Her eyes glanced to his lap and back to his face.

"There is a castle, as well," he ventured.

He was clearly making an effort to be civil and she felt obliged to do the same. Besides, he had piqued her interest and despite her anger and mistrust, she had never been one to cut off her nose to spite her face. Her voice was flat, but she made an effort to respond. "Nottingham Castle?"

"Yes," he replied, encouraged. "One can climb the castle rock and see for twenty miles around." He felt a stab of pain, remembering how he'd climbed the stairs to look from the turrets with Caroline and his parents as a child.

"Robin Hood's Nottingham Castle?" Her voice was a little more animated.

"The one from the stories, yes. Unfortunately, the castle's commander dismantled it rather than let it be used by the enemy during the war. I believe your friend Buckingham owns it now and is making some repairs."

"Can you see Sherwood Forest from there?" There was excitement in her voice now.

"Certainly some of it, though it is only a shadow of what it used to be. A good deal has been cut down for lumber for building and timber for the navy, and much has been cleared for new estates. Cressly has some trees that would have once been part of it, and the king has deeded me a property that encompasses much more. I intend to preserve it as best I can."

"Ah! So you married me to protect a forest."

"In part. What better dowry for a pretty elf?"

Her face brightened and she answered with a slight smile.

Perhaps he was getting better at managing a wife. He'd set out to improve her mood and so far it seemed to be working. She had to be taken care of, just like his servants, his tenants, his soldiers or his horse. A horse needed hay, water, oats and exercise. What did a wife need? If he applied himself to the problem he was sure he could puzzle it out. He realized he'd been at loose ends for some time now. A soldier with no war was an aimless thing. His first thought had been that Hope Mathews would be a burden. *Perhaps she's just the project I need.*

"Are you hungry? Would you like to see the town? Perhaps we can find you stockings and better shoes."

Despite her best efforts at cool nonchalance a wide grin split her face. "I would love to climb the castle rock and see the forest, and then have a taste of your famous cheese and ale."

Animosity behind them and the light of excitement back in Hope's eyes, they set out first for the mercers. She did need stockings, and brushes and petticoats, shoes and combs, and at least a couple of comfortable gowns. Everything she owned had been left behind her in the town house on Pall Mall.

Nottingham was a well-planned, bustling town with broad streets lined with substantial homes and buildings made from red brick and stone. The market was just as Robert had claimed, commanding two very large streets with a pillared mile-long piazza for strolling along one side. She trotted along beside him, trying to keep up with his easy, loping stride. They stopped to watch a man spinning glass, and to her delight he let her try it, heating a piece and flattening it out, then applying a second glass rod to the first one to pull and shape a delicate strand.

She looked with longing at an array of exquisitely crafted fanciful glass birds and beasts, and then her gaze caught a mirror, its oak frame carved and painted with green leaves and acorns. She picked it up to take a look and Robert spoke over her shoulder. "You look like a woodland fairy seeing her reflection in a forest pool. We'll buy it. The poor man needs some recompense for his tutoring." She pursed her lips and frowned but was pleased with it nonetheless.

She found everything she needed with little effort, and though she hoped to retrieve her belongings from London, to be safe, she bought a little more. Within a couple of hours her purchases were safe in the coach and they were ensconced in the cellar of the Crown Inn drinking ale and eating cheese. The cheese *was* very good and the ale exceedingly clear and, more importantly, fortifying and full-flavored.

Since their undeclared truce their conversation had been careful. The fine weather, local points of interest, the history of the town. Hope found she was actually enjoying herself. It was thoughtful of him to take her shopping and she was thrilled with the mirror. He'd been very generous. He had already achieved what he wanted, yet he seemed much nicer today than yesterday, even though he didn't need to be.

As if he could read her thoughts, he pulled a lovely glass swan from his pocket and set it on the table before her.

She blinked, a little flustered, wondering what had come over him. She had needed a mirror, though not one so fine, but this was clearly a present. *Be careful, woman. He's far more dangerous bearing gifts than glowering and cursing.* She must do her best to remain wary, but he was so handsome and she'd drank three pints of ale and it seemed so very hard.

"I...don't know what to say. Thank you, Captain Nichols. But that really wasn't necessary."

He shrugged. "I know. You needn't look so worried. I'm a man of my word and well aware of how things stand. You'll have your own room again tonight. But though we got off to a difficult start we *are* in fact married. Every woman should have a gift to mark her wedding, and if that sits ill with you, you can think of it as a peace offering."

I love the sound of his voice. It's warm and reassuring, yet seductive at the same time. She tossed back her ale and reached across the table, turning the swan so it caught the light. It was beautiful, fluid. With its long neck arched and its wings unfurled it looked like a living thing about to take flight. She was intensely aware of his fingertips, just inches away from hers. She felt them as surely as if he touched her. They sent a shiver up her arm and down her back, leaving an exquisite aching in her chest and a delicious hollow twinge in the pit of her stomach.

She lifted her eyes and her gaze locked with his, drawn deep into shadowed green pools, glinting with intricate patterns of dark and light. There were fine lines etched on his face around his eyes. Laugh lines, some might call them, but she didn't think he laughed much. She imagined she saw loneliness and grief there, She wondered what terrible things he'd witnessed, and what wonders he had seen. She imagined they held promise...wanting...need. She wanted desperately to kiss him.

She cleared her throat, remembering how to breathe, and pushed back to sit upright. "Thank you, Captain. It's very lovely. Shouldn't you show me the castle soon? Before it gets too dark?"

"Yes, of course." He drew back, as well, whatever unspoken communication that had crackled between them cut as cleanly as if by a knife. "Don't you think it strange, given the circumstances, to keep calling me Captain Nichols? You might try Robert, or husband."

"Or sir?" She said it with a cheeky smile and he chuckled.

"I am sorry I annoyed you, in the carriage."

"I'm not comfortable with husband—" *nor with being a wife* "—but perhaps Robert will do."

"Good!" He stood, being careful not to hit his

head on an overhead beam, and extended a hand to help her up.

It was a steep climb to what was left of the castle, perched on a promontory with cliffs over one hundred and thirty feet high, known as the castle rock. The castle itself was a ruin, with only the gatehouse and part of an old bailey remaining, along with the outer walls. The view was magnificent. Hope surveyed it all with a gardener's eye and the curiosity and wonder of a tourist. The land was rich and fruitful, painted with great swathes of forest to the north and west, and lush meadows and rich farmland in the valley, following the sinuous course of the silvery Trent.

While she enjoyed the view, Robert watched her with a pang of hunger. The wind whipped her hair and clothes tight against her body, molding to her curves, tugging at her skirts and lifting her petticoats like an eager lover trying to coax them off. The idea made him grin, something he was getting accustomed to since he'd met her only two days ago. He stepped close beside her, ready to steady her, a little anxious she stood so close to the edge. "There is your Sherwood Forest, and about seven miles to the northeast on that twisting bend lies Cressly. One can almost see her chimneys and turrets through the trees."

Hope nodded, as if she could. It almost seemed so. She stood on her toes and shaded her eyes and imagined she saw a curl of smoke escaping from a distant chimney. Much to her surprise, she felt a thrill of anticipation, curious to see this new country home.

Dusk was fast approaching. The sun hung low on the horizon. The sky had taken on a smoky orange cast, topped with streaks of brilliant gold and shot through with wisps of magenta and purplish-blue. They watched together, side by side, and Hope stopped herself a moment before she leaned against him. How had they become so familiar so quickly? Only two days ago she'd had her heart broken, and yet she hadn't spared a thought for it all day. Was she really so shallow? There were many men who'd tried to pursue her, but she'd never been attracted to a man the way she was to this one. She knew that couldn't be trusted, but might they be friends? It would make life easier. *He says he understands. He said he keeps his word.* Maybe to a man…but to a woman?

She shivered and he gave her his coat. It smelled like him. Musk and smoke, spice and leather. It was still warm from his body and she hugged it close. *How has he slipped under my guard like this?*

"We'd best move on, elf. There's something I'd like to show you, and these ledges grow tricky as it nears dark."

She looked at him, pleased and surprised by the casual endearment. *Elf.* She liked the sound of it. Elves were wild, beautiful and mysterious. No one had ever called her that before. He offered her his hand and she took it without thinking. As they neared the castle walls she caught the scent of a powerful perfume resembling meadowsweet and blackthorn, coming from luminescent white flowers that climbed the walls and blanketed the ruins. "Robert, they're lovely! How is it I failed to notice them before?"

"I've noted your penchant for flowers and thought you might enjoy them," he said smugly. "'Tis why I didn't bring you before late afternoon. They are called white catchfly, and grow here at the castle. Their petals only open from dusk to dawn. It's only then one smells their perfume. Come now. We must hasten before it grows full dark." He took her arm to steady her as they continued down the path.

"Thank you, Robert. It's turned out to be a wonderful day. I've quite enjoyed it."

"As have I, Lady Nichols. You've helped me see it all again with fresh eyes."

Her eyes sparkled in the twilight and she warmed him with her smile. "Do you think Robin Hood and Little John might have trod this very path?"

"Perhaps. But not as most like to think them. Doubtless they were highwaymen and villains more than gentlemen thieves."

"But they only robbed from the rich!"

"Yes, I know the story. But all thieves rob from the rich. There's really no point in taking from the poor, is there? They'd not be worth the risk in time or loss of life." It was too dark for him to see her warning glare.

"Well, they also gave to the poor."

"I rather doubt that," he said reasonably. "Paid them for their silence, more like, and paid them for drink and food…. It would only be good policy to do so. They were not in a position to do him harm, but they could do him some good. Scouting, intelligence, warnings and such. No doubt a coin dropped here and there was a good investment at the time."

She was almost sputtering now. "The stories say he suffered no woman to be oppressed or otherwise molested. He was a prince among thieves. A gentleman thief, the spirit of liberty for common folk against cruel taxes and forest laws made by the church and tyrants and…and people like you!"

"People like me?"

"Yes! Nobles and barons and earls who live in luxury feeding off the spoils of other men's labor."

Live in luxury off the back of other men's labor? Was she was comparing him to those soft-handed useless courtiers and sycophants that suckled at the royal teat? It stung. And two days of being *her* bought husband didn't make it true. "Might I remind you, *Lady Nichols,* that you are people like me now, too? And what have you been living off in your palace and town house in Pall Mall?"

"Oh! I will never be people like you. After all I'm

not good enough, am I? Nor would I want to be. You are all hypocrites and liars!"

"The man was a cutthroat, a robber and thief," he snapped. "No wonder he's admired by people like you."

She stopped and jerked her arm from his grasp. "No doubt you would have seen him hang, Captain Nichols. Or maybe drawn and quartered. And you know nothing about people like me! Maybe I *have* lived off other men's labors, but believe me, I've worked and paid for every bit of it. Who are you to judge? I have done what I must to survive and prosper. Have you not done the same on the battlefield? Do you not do the same in holding your nose to marry me? At least *I* have never killed anyone!" She shoved past him, continuing down the path on her own.

"Hope, wait! The trail is dangerous in the dark." He hurried to catch up with her, grasping her by her upper arm when she wouldn't stop. "All I meant was that you grew up amongst the poor, who tend to take their heroes from rebels and those who flout the law."

"And to remind me I am a glorified whore."

"No! To remind you that now you live the life of those nobles you insult, which makes you just as much a hypocrite as me."

"Let go of me! I've told you before not to touch me," she snarled.

"And I'm telling you that you're not walking home

alone in the dark." She made to pull away from him and he hoisted her in his arms as easily as if she were a child.

"Put me down, Captain. I'm well able to walk on my own two feet." She struggled in his grasp but it only made him hold her tighter. She could feel the strength of him in his easy stride, the muscles of his stomach, arms and chest—every inch of him was hard. There was no escaping. She ceased her struggles but refused to relax against him, her body as tense and rigid as that of an angry cat. He dropped her to her feet at the entrance to the inn.

"*Now* I put you down."

He needed a drink. He couldn't remember ever drinking as much as he had over the past few days. She was exactly what he'd thought her. An impossible woman. He was almost grateful for their argument. At least things had righted themselves and were back the way they should be. He walked away, leaving her to find her own way to her room.

"And who are your heroes, Captain?" she called after him, her voice mocking.

"I have none," he replied without looking back.

"I will tell you how many men I have fucked if you tell me how many you have killed."

He slowed and stopped, then turned to face her, leaning against a pillar, his arms crossed and his head cocked as he looked her up and down. "I don't care how many men you've fucked, Mistress Mathews, and I don't keep count of how many I have killed."

CHAPTER ELEVEN

HOPE WAS BACK TO STARING out of windows. Anything rather than acknowledge his presence. She must have imagined the brief warmth between them, for all traces of it were gone. After a day of pleasantries and simple pleasures, the thin veneer of civility between them had shredded as easily as flimsy tissue, leaving them encased in frigid hostility once more. One moment they were enjoying the sunset and the next they were on the attack. She wasn't quite sure how it had happened so quickly, nor why she'd deliberately provoked him when he'd dropped her at the door. *Did I want him to go? Or did I want him to stay?*

That there was an attraction was undeniable. She'd felt it from the first moment she'd seen him. But he wasn't the amiable companion he'd pretended to be yesterday. It embarrassed her to remember how she'd warmed to a few kind words like an abandoned puppy, but perhaps that was to be expected after being humiliated and betrayed. Well, it wouldn't happen again. She was a courtesan, not some soft and brokenhearted dewy-eyed miss, and it hadn't taken him long to show *his* true colors.

It was better this way. Truly. Without masquerade or pretense. He was arrogant, high-handed, superior and judgmental. When he came to collect her this morning, his cold gaze had flicked over her as if she were a bale of linen or a sack of sugar, just one more purchase to be carted home.

She snuck a sideways peek at him from beneath her lashes. He seemed cramped and uncomfortable in confined spaces. The inn, the coach, even in her town house. He'd neglected to shave again, and dark shadows accentuated firm lips and strong chin and jaw. She didn't know why she found this rugged look so appealing, particularly when it appeared he had spent the night drinking again. She should feel nothing but contempt, yet her body betrayed her. Despite her anger and his disdain, she felt the same intense awareness of him as she had when he sat across from her at the inn. It was the sensation of touching without being touched. She could almost feel the rasp of his stubble against her tender cheeks. Her lips burned as if his sullen mouth hovered just a heartbeat from hers.

She took a deep breath, acknowledging a tender aching that weakened her limbs and squeezed her heart. *This man is a danger to me like none other if I let my senses rule my head.* A woman like herself, feeling alone and unwanted and prone to childish fantasies, must always take care that her head ruled her heart. Yesterday had been an aberration. It was well

they didn't like each other. It was far too easy to con-
fuse lust with something else when friendship mixed
freely with desire. Desire unchecked was a treach-
erous weakness, but desire acknowledged could be
harnessed and used.

She turned her gaze back out the window. *He feels
it, too. The evidence in the coach yesterday was…
unmistakable.* Her lips curled in a satisfied smile. *He
is not the only one with power here.*

They passed a prosperous-looking village of
thatch-roofed brick and half-timbered houses, clus-
tered in a shady dell nestled in the woods. Its cool
green depths, pierced by thick white shafts of sunlight, were bordered by large pasturages to the west
and boasted a handsome forge and substantial ale-
house. Yesterday she would have asked him about it
and its people, but today she was rendered mute.

Not long after the village, they turned up a winding drive. The approach to Cressly was through a
magnificent alley of towering oaks in the midst of
an oak-and-silver-birch forest. The ancient trees,
as magnificent in size and shape as any she'd ever
seen, created a cathedral-like sense of awe. Ignoring her surly keeper, she perched halfway out the
window when she spotted a small herd of deer. Their
ears pricked forward but they made no move to bolt,
watching the passing coach with mild interest as it
circled round the bend and moved deeper into the
valley.

Her eagerness to see Cressly had been growing since yesterday, when she'd seen the vista from
castle rock. The pretty village and regal forest were
something she might imagine from a fairy tale and
she was excited to see the rest. At first she caught
only flashes; teasing glimpses of red brick, soaring turrets and towering chimney stacks, but as the
drive straightened it revealed a beautiful three-story,
rust-tinted house with banks of white-trimmed
windows. Set amongst a copse of trees with ample
boughs to shelter and protect from eastern blasts, it
was draped by many years' growth of dark green ivy
and widespread Virginia creeper.

Edged by a moss-and-lichen-covered terrace, it
sat on a gentle rise on a protected bend of the river.
The Trent, girded by stately trees, some of whose
boughs dipped gently, almost trailing in the water,
flowed right in front of its windows, and a backwater made from its overflow seemed to be home to a
pair of swans and various other waterfowl. She had
never seen a home that looked more like it belonged
just where it was. It seemed as if it had grown there,
amidst the forest and fields and hills, a part of them
rather than something that had been built.

They came to a halt in an empty stone-flagged
courtyard. A sweet scent wafted from overgrown
beds of tangled flowers on either side of a broad
gravel walk. There was no bustle of servants, no
clutch of chickens, no curious children or barking

dogs. As she stepped from the coach it was eerily silent. Just the rush of the river and the sibilant whisper of wind stirring the leaves. She accepted the captain's proffered hand, though he offered her no greeting or welcome to his home. *My home, too, now, Captain Nichols. Whether it pleases you or not.*

A peregrine cried overhead and the breeze made a cold shiver crawl up her spine. For a moment it seemed as if the house was watching her, taking her measure, judging. She swallowed her anxiety, lifted her chin and stiffened her spine. *He* was judging. This lovely home had been forsaken and neglected. It was almost ghostly with its unkempt gardens, smothered walls and silent courtyard. But it was the home she'd always dreamt of. It called to her, begging to be loved and cared for, and her heart ached to embrace it. *I need it and it needs me and I won't let him drive me away.*

But in her dream her house belonged to her. In her dream she was happy and free. Charles and this stranger had stolen her dream. This house could never be hers. It belonged to someone else. If Charles called her back she would have to leave it for whatever pretty cage he chose to put her in. If he forgot her here, as she knew he might, it would become her prison and the captain her jailor; a place where she would live unwanted and unloved. At least in Drury Lane she'd been useful and she'd belonged.

Her emotions threatened to overwhelm her. It had

taken such effort not to let this cold, harsh stranger see her pain. One kind gesture and she'd been drawn to him immediately, taking his arm, leaning on his strength. But the truth was she was alone and she always had been, and that is where she must find her strength. *Oh, Charles! How could you do this to me? Why?* It hurt so bad she had to bite her knuckle to keep from crying.

"Good evening, Sergeant Oakes. I have brought a guest. The Countess of Newport. I would appreciate if you would have the staff see to her comfort, and then I will see you in the library straightaway. There are important matters to discuss."

I have brought a guest? So that was how it was going to be. She took a deep breath, regaining her composure, and turned to greet the newcomer. He seemed almost taken aback by his master's appearance, tilting his head with what looked like puzzlement before shifting his attention to her. As he approached she noticed he walked with his left hand curled by his side. He seemed to be missing a couple of fingers, and a scar across his cheek and brow passed perilously close to one eye.

"It's a great pleasure to meet you, my lady." The grizzled old veteran gave her a beaming smile. He had the rough-edged growl of someone who'd spent years barking orders, but his tone was friendly enough. He wore a military uniform rather than livery, and it was hard to tell his position in the household, but she didn't care. Like recognized like. The sergeant was a survivor and so was she.

She stepped forward and threaded her arm through his. "It's such a great joy to meet one of Robert's colleagues, Sergeant Oakes. He can be rather taciturn and I feared he had no friends. It pleases me greatly to see him play the jester, but he really shouldn't tease you. I am Lady Nichols, our gallant captain's new wife."

The sergeant's eyes rounded and he blinked several times. His mouth opened and closed twice before he recovered the capacity to speak. "You're married, sir? When? How? Why didn't you inform us, Captain?"

"The whole thing was rather sudden. I ought to have sent a messenger from London or Nottingham, I suppose." The captain signaled his indifference with a yawn.

"Indeed, sir. Then we might have greeted your lady properly. You are most welcome here at Cressly, madam. We have missed a lady's touch. Er…" The sergeant reddened and cleared his throat. "That is to say *Cressly* has missed a lady's touch. Pray forgive the miserly welcome, my lady. I'll have the staff assembled to greet you at once."

"There's no need to apologize, Sergeant." Hope patted his arm. The sergeant's surprise was almost comical, but her husband's look was one of cold indifference. Returning it with a sweet smile and eyes full of scorn, she let go of the sergeant and took her husband's arm instead. She smiled when she felt it stiffen. Leaning her head against his shoulder she looked up at him with melting eyes. "We were both overtaken by a grand passion, weren't we, darling?"

He grunted in reply. A wiry dark-haired young man with an eye patch had come to help with the horses, and a footman with a scar across the bridge of his nose and down his cheek was assisting with the bags. People with scars and missing limbs were a common sight on the streets of London since the war, but not in gentlemen's homes. She almost asked a question of the sergeant, but the doors to Cressly opened and she was swept inside.

CHAPTER TWELVE

HER FIRST THOUGHT was that it was dark, the second that it was cold and unwelcoming, much like its owner, and the third that it was empty inside. A superb wood staircase rose in front of her, massive and elaborately carved with wide landings, leading from the basement to the upper floors. A billiard room was close by the entrance, the doors to a library were to her left, and what looked to be a drawing room and a long hallway were to her right, but other than heavy, dark-colored drapes, the walls were bare and the furnishings, many of which were covered by sheets and rugs, were sparse.

It must be easy for the maids to clean, but it felt funereal and much too quiet. A clock ticked in a distant room and she felt a tightening dread. *How can I live in this house?* She was used to music and color, laughter and gaiety, company…friends.

Once Sergeant Oakes had assembled the staff, the captain introduced her as the Countess of Newport, then waited with a look of bored impatience as the sergeant told her their names and explained their duties. Clearly her fortune-hunting husband was eager to be shed of her and off about his business. *He is ashamed to call me wife.* She felt a quick stab of hurt and anger. Refusing to acknowledge it, she straightened her spine and raised her chin, doing her best to look gracious and regal.

He seemed curt with his servants. They showed no fear, no sign he was a difficult master, but they were efficient. There was no evidence of the excitement and bustle one might expect when a new mistress came home. They stood in order of precedence. Maggie Overton, the housekeeper, a small, severe-looking woman with nut-brown hair, watched her with eyes as cold as her master's. Mrs. Fullerton, the cook, gave her a businesslike nod, as if she had other places to be. The scarred footman was introduced as Corporal Ryan, along with another handsome fellow called Mr. Yates, who was missing two fingers on his left hand. Last, two maids named Lucy and Patience bobbed their heads, their eyes sharp with speculation.

It was a small coterie of servants, particularly given the size of the manor. There was no butler, valet or lady's maid, though she would correct the last as soon as she could. She wasn't sure what to make of them. The sergeant seemed friendly, the footmen correct, but the housekeeper looked her up and down contemptuously, almost bristling with disapproval, and the maids, though not outwardly insubordinate, stared with a curiosity that bordered on rudeness.

I might as well have whore *stamped on my forehead. They think they know what I am even if the men don't.* His introduction would have confirmed their suspicions. Even Sergeant Oakes hadn't known they were married and respectable unmarried ladies didn't come to stay with men alone. Well, she was not about to stand here and try to defend and explain herself to a collection of surly strangers. Who were they to judge? If she had faced down dukes and duchesses, she could certainly manage this lot. She held her head proudly and returned the housekeeper's withering look with a haughty stare.

The captain cleared his throat and stepped forward. "Well. There you have it. Now you've met the household staff. I'm sure Maggie will be pleased to show you the house while a room is prepared for you. Oakes and I have business to attend to. I shall see you at dinner." With that, he abandoned her, leaving her to cope as best she might on her own.

"This way if you please, mistress. Quickly now. I'll show you the drawing room. Your unexpected arrival has left us with much work to do."

Hope's eyes narrowed. The housekeeper's annoyance was obvious and disrespectful. After cleaning and serving in her mother's establishment, she usually felt a kinship with servants and staff. She tried to respect their dignity, be sensitive to their needs, and she made every attempt not to be burdensome, but she never tolerated rudeness. She hadn't asked to be countess, lady, or wife, but she was. And it had cost her dearly. She had earned respect and she would have it. The housekeeper would have to be put in her place.

Unlike parts of the house she'd glimpsed so far, the drawing room was well-appointed, luxurious and clearly lived in. Dutch tiles ornamented a fireplace of gigantic proportions and plush settees, chairs and couches sat upon a brightly colored Turkish carpet with a beautiful star-burst design. The broad casement commanded a beautiful view of gently rising hills, grand old trees and the gleam of water edging the deer park, and a portrait of a handsome if stern-looking man and an elegant woman graced the walls. The family resemblance was unmistakable. *He is more handsome than his father,* she mused. *His face is hard—not harsh—and I doubt the man before me ever smiled.*

The housekeeper cleared her throat impatiently. They all seemed impatient around here, though from what little she'd seen of this cavernous house there could not be that much to do. She studied the painting a few moments longer before turning to respond. "Yes, Maggie?" she inquired mildly.

"It's Mrs. Overton to you, miss," the housekeeper snapped. "I've work to do. You can settle yourself here until one of the lads has got your luggage and the girls have fixed your room."

"I should like someone to show me around, *Maggie*. That is the housekeeper's duty, is it not?"

"That's the housekeeper's prerogative, when she has spare time for amusing guests...*miss*." She almost hissed it.

"Not when her mistress requires it, Mrs. Overton. And it's Lady Newport, or my lady, or ma'am to you. I am married to your master, and the lady of this house now, and like it or not, I am your new mistress. You will show me the appropriate respect if you wish to remain employed here."

"You be mistress all right, *ma'am*. And we all know whose. Notts is not so far from London as you might think. They talk of the king's country miss there, with her enchantress eyes and witch-black hair. None else has eyes that color, nor would come to the country dressed so fine. I've seen you with the king at Newcastle when I visited me granny. Lord knows what you've done to the master. He's never brought a woman here before, but he's been through enough and deserves better than the likes of you. We be hard-working folk here, *ma'am*. There's no palace full of servants at your beck and call. If you want to pretend to be his wife, go ahead. But don't expect the rest of us to pretend it with you!"

Shaken by the housekeeper's vituperative attack, Hope's heart raced and a red haze of anger threatened to engulf her. She had suffered worse at court, but this was completely unexpected and one thing too many after three days of betrayal, upheaval and uncertainty. Not five years past she would have taken a fist and knocked her flat!

"Mrs. Overton—" she managed to keep her voice even "—I advise you never to take that tone with me again. If you know who I am, then I'm sure you've heard stories. The one about Orange Moll is true. I have been polite with you, and given you no reason to be so rude with me. You leave me no choice but to talk to your master."

"Go ahead then, my lady." Her tone was still pugnacious but she took a good step back. "I've been with him seventeen years, and you…? What? A week? A few days?"

"Get out of my sight, Mrs. Overton. Now!"

"Aye, with pleasure, ma'am. Enjoy yourself finding your way around."

Still seething, Hope stalked down the oak-paneled hall, opening door after door as she went. This was *his* fault. The servants would treat her with the same courtesy and respect that he did.

The hallway was furnished with several green carpets, a long trestle table covered in leather and a cupboard and several chairs. One of the carpets slid out from beneath her and she fell to the floor, smacking her elbow on the table on the way down. She struggled to her feet cursing, no easy feat in her cumber-

some skirts. Sitting on a chair she cradled her elbow,
fighting back tears of pain.

*He hates me. The staff hate me. Now the house
hates me, too!* "Well, I hate you!" Speaking it out
loud made it seem rather silly, which made her feel
better, until she saw a tiny open-mouthed redheaded
girl with a bucket in hand and her cap askew, staring
at her with round startled eyes. Petite herself, it was
seldom someone made her feel tall. It wasn't Lucy or
Patience. Doubtless a lowly house or scullery maid,
not meant to be seen above stairs.

"Can I… Are you… Do you need some help?" The
girl's voice was barely a whisper. But it was the first
offer of help she'd received all day.

"You needn't look so frightened. I'm not mad. Just
angry, and I'm no intruder or ghost."

"Oh, thank goodness, my lady. For a moment I
thought you was her." She bobbed two quick curt-
sies, as if making up for one she'd forgot.

"Her?"

"The ghost girl. The one some in the servants'
quarters say walks the halls both day and night."

"Ah, I see. No. I am Captain Nichols's new wife,
and at the moment I'm a little lost. What's your name,
my dear?"

"My name is Rose, my lady. It's most kind of you
to ask. I best get back below stairs now, though. If
Mrs. Overton sees me she'll have my hide." The
girl was clearly nervous, looking up and down the

hall and anxiously wringing her apron in her hands. "I was supposed to scrub the front hall for Lettice, who's taking on Patience's duties, who's cleaning the parlor for—"

"That's quite all right, Rose. There's no need to explain." An idea was forming. "Do you know your way around Cressly, Rose?"

"Yes, my lady, I do. Every nook and cranny, though I lay the hearths and such when most are still asleep."

"Do you think you could help me take off this dress?" The girl's scandalized look was so comical that Hope smiled for the first time that day. "Like a lady's maid must do. She helps the mistress with her clothing when she's needed and such."

"Oh, yes! I'm certain I could do that, ma'am. Mrs. Overton's needed my help before, and I'm often called on to assist Patience and Lucy. I can stitch and sew, too," she added proudly. "I used to make all the clothes for my family back home. I can also help with hair."

"Why, that's excellent, Rose! My marriage was very sudden and I am much in need of a lady's maid." Which was nothing less than the truth. She might have relied on the help of Patience or Lucy, at least until she could find a girl from the village, but their attitude had not endeared them to her. Taking on Rose would shake the household up. They'd be sullen and angry at first, something she knew from her own service days. But they'd understand quickly that advancement and position relied upon pleasing her. "How is it such a talented girl works in the scullery?"

"There's been no lady here so long as I can recollect, ma'am, though I am expected to help the other maids with whatever they need. And then, of course, I'm Irish. You won't see an Irish lass rise beyond the scullery, ma'am. Not in an English home."

"Is that the captain's will?"

"Why, no, ma'am. I shouldn't think so. The master doesn't concern himself with such things. It's just the way things are. I do believe it's much the same in other homes."

"Well, not in this one. A lady chooses her own maid and I choose you."

The girl squealed in delight, clapped her hands and accidently knocked over the bucket. "Oh, ma'am! I'm so sorry. I'm so clumsy! I'll clean it up straight away!"

"Oh, dear! I fear we're much alike. I just tripped and fell on my head. We can't be constantly apologizing for it, though. We shall traipse this place together, and take pride in leaving mayhem in our wake. And don't clean that up, Rose. You are a lady's maid now. Such duties are beneath you. You take your orders only from me."

Rose's grin was contagious and Hope felt optimistic for the first time that day. An ally gained. One whose loyalty would be only to her. Sergeant Oakes was at least friendly, and she would win the rest of them one at a time. Rather than fight Mrs. Overton for control of her home, she might simply walk around her.

After Rose pointed her to the door of her husband's study, Hope sent her to find her room. "Come back when you know where it is. If anyone questions you, direct them to me."

The girl was practically skipping. "I will, my lady. Right away. When I got up this morning I had no idea, ma'am. You coming here has been the best thing to happen in my life!"

Well, at least someone is glad to see me.

She looked down the hall to the captain's study with some degree of trepidation. Though she fought when she needed to, she really didn't like it. She avoided unpleasantness whenever she could. Yet except for a few brief hours in Nottingham, every conversation with this man ended in strife. He didn't like her, he saw her as a burden, he would resent the intrusion and it would end in a fight. Nevertheless, if she wished to take charge she must beard the lion in his den. She did her best to armor herself with calm indifference, took a fortifying breath, knocked on the door and, without waiting for an answer, she opened it and slipped inside.

IT WAS A DARK, SPARTAN ROOM, with a fireplace, desk, two chairs and and a collection of shields and instruments of war mounted on the wall. The sword he wore in London hung above the mantel, lethal in its beauty, but beyond carved wood and weaponry, the room boasted no color, no decoration, no warmth at all.

If a man's private study reflected his interior life, her husband was dark and dangerous, and his life was war.

CHAPTER THIRTEEN

"WHAT IS IT, HOPE? Do people not knock at the palace? Surely you can see that we are busy here."

"But I did knock!" She blinked in surprise when Sergeant Oakes gave her a wink and a commiserating smile. "I need to talk to you about the servants. It should be settled now, before things get out of hand. It really can't wait."

The sergeant rose and bowed, gallantly offering her his seat. "I pray you excuse me, my lady. And you, Captain. I should pass the happy news to the staff without delay." He stopped at the doorway. "You bring us good fortune, Lady Newport. I pray in return much happiness comes your way."

Hope looked back at Robert, somewhat bewildered. Of what concern were forest lands to his staff?

"Well? You interrupted a meeting in my private study. Pray tell me your complaint."

"Your housekeeper is insolent and terribly rude."

"Is she really? All these years and I hadn't noticed."

She strove to keep her voice as indifferent as his.

"I asked her for a tour of the house, so I might find my way around and she refused me."

He shrugged. "What do you expect me to do about it? I haven't the time to take you by the hand. We work here."

"How droll! That's almost exactly what she said. I expect you to do your duty. You must introduce me properly, as your wife. The servants will not respect me until you do."

"But you're not my proper wife, are you? Yet you feel empowered to invade my privacy, tell me my duty and order me about."

"Your pretend wife, then, devil take you! And I shouldn't *have* to tell you your duty. I would never abandon a guest, allow my servants to be rude to them, or treat them as you are treating me." Her voice was heated now. Despite her best intentions, no man had ever made her as angry, or made her lose control time after time as this one did.

"What shall we do, then? Stand in the great hall, hand in hand, and lie to them? Fueling speculation about dynasties and heirs and generations of Nicholses yet to come?"

"Let us speak plainly here. You mean generations of Stuarts, don't you? If it irks you so much why did you agree?"

"I mean you are not to play with my servants or retainers, my lady. And that includes the sergeant. They are not your toys or here for your amusement.

Mrs. Overton is useful to me, and she has been with me for many years."

His cool voice and calm demeanor infuriated her. "I see. She is useful…and I am not. Except, of course, as a means to acquire land and a title. Now that you have what you wanted…it is too much to honor and respect your side of the bargain. I am a peaceful creature, Captain. I mean harm to no one. But I swear, if I'd known you were going to be my husband I would have been sorely tempted to put poison in your May Day wine!"

"Madam, if I knew you were to be my wife I would have been sorely tempted to drink it."

"Oh, but you did know, Captain. And you were very well rewarded for it, too."

Her grand disdainful exit was marred by a brief collision with the door. She had always been a bit clumsy but this man, this house, this situation had her so off balance she was covered in bruises, and so frustrated she was on the verge of tears. They almost came when she stood in the hall and realized she had no idea where to go.

"I've found your room, my lady. It's ready for you now." Rose was such a welcome sight she could have hugged her. She must do something nice for the girl. She and the sergeant were the only bright spots in an otherwise dismal day. Until she saw her room.

It was a sumptuous and cozy corner suite with a polished oak floor inlaid with a sunflower pattern made of ebony and honey-colored wood. A recessed window seat looked out over the river, and a heavy oaken desk sat next to a bank of windows with doors that opened onto a terrace to the south. Pale blue satin and colorful Aubusson tapestry covered the walls, while the furniture was upholstered in darker hues. Rich hangings of gold damask and sky-blue velvet graced a comfortable bed, a mantelpiece of snow-white marble conferred a classical elegance, and a jungle of ferns and flowers grew in potted profusion in every corner of the room.

"Oh, my, Rose! It looks like a beautiful and airy summer's day."

"Doesn't it just, ma'am! I'm afraid to touch anything lest I get it dirty."

Hope chuckled, her mood greatly improved. "We shall have to see to that. You'll need a good bath and some better clothes. I believe I may have a dress that will do you for now. I'll dine in my room this evening, Rose. Please inform…whomever. Then fetch me a jug of wine and a loaf of bread while I see what I can find."

The little maid scurried happily away, only to be stopped at the door by Mrs. Overton, who seemed every bit as surprised to see the room as Hope was. "I… But this isn't… Your room is… Rose O'Donnell! What is the meaning of this? No one has been able to find you all day. Get back to the scullery at once!"

"Rose will not be returning to the scullery, Mrs.

Overton. She's been a very great help to me today. I'm in need of a lady's maid, as I'm sure you'll understand, and I've decided that Rose will do nicely."

"Well, you can't have her. It's entirely inappropriate and it will leave me short of help."

"Then hire someone. The matter is closed. She has already begun her new duties, haven't you, Rose?"

"Yes, my lady!"

"Off you go, then."

Rose ducked past Mrs. Overton and out the door.

"The master—"

"The master can go hang himself, and you may tell him that I said so. It's been a long day and a difficult week and my patience is worn thin. Take your complaints to him. Leave me now. And if you see Sergeant Oakes, please thank him for the lovely room."

The housekeeper sputtered in outrage.

"Good night, Mrs. Overton. Please close the door on the way out."

Rose returned with a plate of cheese, ham and fruit, and a jug brim-full of cold, sweet sack. She was turning out to be a little gem. Her reward was a simple dark blue taffeta dress and a dark green woolen, both of which would complement her complexion and hair. "Oh, my lady, these are mine? I've never seen the like. In all my life I never thought to wear such beautiful things!" She twirled around the room, the blue taffeta clutched to her chest. "How can I ever thank you?"

Hope smiled to remember the days when her first real dress transported her. "I'm glad you're pleased, Rose. And I think with a little adjusting they shall suit you very well. A lady's maid must be well-dressed or it reflects poorly on her employer. Proper clothes are part of your wages. Now, if you would help me out of my dress, that is all I'll be needing tonight. Then you should go and find Sergeant Oakes. Tell him you're now my maid, and I would be grateful if he can find you a suitable room. And tell him I say 'Bless you' for finding this one for me." She knew it had to be the sergeant who'd assigned her this room. It was fit for the mistress of the house and it explained his wink and smile.

After Rose left, she settled with the wine jug in the window seat, watching as a yellow moon rose slowly from the mist and trees. For the first time in days she had a place to ponder and be alone. No one came to disturb her and she wasn't surprised. It should have been restful and God knew she was exhausted in body, mind and spirit, but the events of the past week had happened so quickly and been so chaotic, it was as though she'd been shipwrecked and washed up on some distant shore. While she was moving, walking, fighting, planning, talking, she had no time to dwell on it. But now, when she rested, it crowded in.

Charles's betrayal had been devastating, for both the substance and the manner in which it was done. What did she do to make him hurt her this way? To make him abandon her in this half-empty place amongst strangers. To give her to this coldhearted man? *Nothing! I didn't do a goddamned thing!* She felt a white-hot bolt of anger and washed it down with a glass of wine. She'd given him more of herself than anyone else ever had. Her body and her friendship, and she'd never asked him for a bloody thing. Not jewels nor favors. Only the freedom to leave in peace. And that he'd cruelly denied her, through trickery and deceit.

I hate him. She had made him no promises. She owed him nothing anymore. She was not some toy to put away while he played with a new one. *He thinks to treat me like a whore and rule me like a husband.* And her proxy husband? He married her for what he wanted while scorning her for who she was. He blamed her for a bargain she'd had no part in making, whilst he'd entered it freely and claimed his prize.

One was a liar, the other a hypocrite, and both had treated her as an object of little value, to be used and moved to suit their own ends. *The captain gets his title. Charles gets to hide me without letting go, at least until he's sure he wants to, and what is there in this for me?* Humiliation, exile, the loss of freedom, and from menials to master, nothing but scorn. If anyone had a right to anger, she did. It was she who suffered, and she who'd done nothing wrong. All that she owned, everything she'd worked for, had ceased to exist or belonged to her husband now. Charles had even denied her the stage.

I will take what I may from both of them, and both of them will pay. She would make the honor-bound captain desire her, despite his disdain. She would seduce him, thereby gaining revenge on both captain and king. She would show Charles he didn't control her, and the captain he was no better than she was. *I will force him to admit his honor is no better than mine.*

She tossed back another glass of wine, trying to soothe the sharp edges of anger and loss. Her childhood fantasies had featured a place like this, with towering trees, clear flowing water and vibrant gardens alive with flowers of every hue. Cressly was neglected, but its beauty shone through and its charms ran deep. It almost felt as though it needed her. Yet somewhere at its core, the house felt cold and empty. Surrounded by silent, staring servants and tied to this distant, icy man, she felt lonely, weary and trapped, and she was so tired of being strong. A hollow ache took her breath away and tears threatened at the corners of her eyes, but she ruthlessly beat them back.

She reached for the wine jug again, then let her arm drop. Wine did soothe ragged edges, but its powerful alchemy had turned her anger to self-pity. The moon had risen now, a heavy globe of sallow light, hovering above a blue-black horizon. Though the sky was clear, a creeping bank of fog was winding up the river, and somewhere in the distance, thunder groaned. She shivered and hugged her knees tight to her chest. She should have asked for a fire. It was time for bed.

She felt her way carefully in the dark, but still caught her toe on the edge of the massive oak bed. The pain welled through her, rising the length of her body and making her cry out as she collapsed in a heap on the mattress. It was a small thing, but it was a small thing too much. As the pain subsided to a throbbing ache, tears spilled down her cheeks. She bit her knuckle to hold it in but the pain and hurt she'd been holding for days finally overwhelmed her. The tears came in gut-wrenching sobs and she cried and cried like a lost little girl.

ROBERT NICHOLS SETTLED into his bed, exhausted. He'd spent twenty minutes listening to the frantic complaints of Mrs. Overton. It seemed that despite his warning, the Mathews chit would insist on upsetting his household. She was as thoughtless and selfish, spoiled and shallow, as he had first feared. She had not even deigned to join them at dinner. One would think she'd have come, if only to gloat after making off with one of Mrs. Overton's scullery maids. Still, one had to admire her courage and cunning. Mrs. Overton was a formidable opponent who had, to all intents and purposes, been mistress of Cressly for the past fifteen years.

According to Oakes, whose unseemly amusement had not been helpful, it had been a veritable coup d'état. One the redoubtable housekeeper never saw coming. Now the staff were confused, wondering who was in charge. Mrs. Overton, or the unexplained countess. Say what you will, she was a brilliant tactician. He was going to have to deal with the ensuing uproar, though, and petty disputes were the last thing he needed to be bothered with right now.

Harris was his main concern. He must have known that he was hunted as his cronies died, one by one. *I hope it kept him looking over his shoulder all these years. I hope it keeps him up at night as Caroline does me.* It was no accident the man had asked the king for Cressly. He'd still be seeking the treasure he thought was buried here. Did he also seek a confrontation? *I doubt it. I'm no twelve-year-old girl.* The man was a coward who'd hidden his tracks until now. He saw an opportunity and greed had overcome caution. But he was exposed and dangerous now. *Will he seek to destroy me? Or will he run?* If he did attack it would be by a coward's way.

I should be in London. He needed information. He needed to find and follow the man. But the king had wasted no time in sending him and his inconvenient mistress on their way. There had been no opportunity to discover more about Harris. Where he lived, what he was up to, what were his weaknesses, his habits, his plans. He'd alerted the sergeant to take the necessary precautions, but after all these years a reckoning was coming, and he'd prefer it be in London or further afield.

This…wife. Hope. She was a complication and distraction he certainly didn't need. He still couldn't believe that within hours of learning of Harris, a man he'd hunted for years and who might be hunting him, all he could think of was her barefoot dance under the stars. He'd taken her shopping, *sightseeing,* for God's sake, while the man who'd killed his sister might be slipping from his grasp.

Unable to sleep, he shifted onto his back and clasped his hands behind his head. She was right, though, and none of this was her fault. It was because of her his servants still had jobs. He had made a bargain for his own reasons, and he had a responsibility to see that she be treated well. An uncomfortable stab of guilt precipitated a drawn-out sigh. *Today can't have been easy for her.* He should have shielded her from Overton and made her feel at home. He should have made arrangements for a maid, and shown her the house himself. He was an experienced and capable commander, after all. Surely he could manage two things at once.

He hoped he'd got the room right at least. It was one of the lightest and brightest, and arguably had the best views in the house. He'd told Oakes she liked her plants and flowers and the footmen had scoured the house for everything living and green. It was not as grand as what she'd have been accustomed to in London, but he was fairly certain that she'd be pleased. *I will try and be more attentive to her needs, if only to keep her from trouble. But I must attend to Cressly first.*

He closed his eyes and let himself drift as his dark dreams overtook him. Far away, as always, he heard a woman weep.

CHAPTER FOURTEEN

ROSE CAME THE NEXT MORNING to bring Hope her tea and help her dress, proudly wearing her new green frock and bubbling with excitement. The girl's enthusiasm was contagious and it wasn't in Hope's nature to sit and wait for things to happen. By midmorning they were well embarked on a household tour.

Her first impression the day before had been correct. Most of the house was empty and closed. *I suppose I shouldn't take his abandonment personally. He seems to have little interest even in his own home.* Certain key rooms were well maintained, though. The handsome dining room, boasting carved walnut panels and a sideboard graced with a colorful Turkish rug, was situated in the north wing across from the drawing room she'd been left in yesterday. The captain's study was further down the hall, and a cozy room with a ceiling painted with wispy clouds and a blue summer sky was hidden off an eastern corridor at the far end. The sofas, chairs and desk were draped in sheets, but the walls were covered with tiny oil paintings, and several cabinets and small tables held displays of wondrous curiosities.

Brightly colored corals and polished stones stood on low bookcases. Small sculptures were housed in cabinets alongside clockwork automata of people, animals, the solar system and even a coach-and-four complete with footmen running alongside. There was a unicorn horn and glass figurines and a spyglass set on a stand. She was particularly taken by a lovely three-story dollhouse furnished in exquisite miniature detail. She ran her hand along a cabinet top and flicked dust from her fingertips. "What a marvelous room! It's a curiosity cabinet and study. Does no one come here, Rose?"

"No, ma'am," Rose said with a shudder. "Folk stay away from this part of the house. Some say 'tis here that's most haunted. I've never seen this room before. I didn't even know it was here."

"Excellent! We shall keep it that way. I love this room and I intend to claim it for myself. That will be much easier if no one else wants anything to do with it."

"But who will have to come here to clean it, ma'am. Or lay a fire?" The little maid was clearly nervous the task might fall to her.

"Help me today, Rose, and I shall see to it myself thereafter. I'm not afraid of a little work." She began removing sheets and coverings, and with Rose's reluctant help, spent the rest of the morning dusting, polishing and cleaning windows, so the floors sparkled and the cabinets, furniture and collection of curiosities shone with a luminous glow. She stopped to examine a couple of exquisite miniatures of a beautiful golden-haired girl with lovely rounded features and a sweet sunny smile. They were carefully placed in one of the cabinets along with other little treasures. She stood transfixed. It seemed almost as if the girl was trying to send her a message from some distant place or time. Something about the eyes reminded her of the captain. *Will he ever tell me of his family? Would I ever tell him of mine?*

She shook off a sudden chill. There was still more of this fascinating hideaway to explore. There was a window seat that looked to the water, much like her room upstairs, and with the casement opened she could hear the busy twitter of nesting birds, the soft rustle of wind through the leaves and the soothing murmur of the river. She was further delighted to find a partially concealed door to the right of the fireplace that led to a flagged terrace flanked by a high wall covered in sweet-smelling climbers.

She followed the fragrant path to an unkempt garden complete with a sundial and an overgrown fairy fountain. The garden needed pruning and weeding, the fountain had to be cleaned and cleared, but it felt like her own little piece of heaven.

They finished the tour in the late afternoon. Other than a richly appointed billiard room attached to a lofty, well-lit library, the south wing was unused. Their footsteps echoed behind them as they wandered down the hall. At the far end Hope discovered an empty stone conservatory two stories tall, with an upper gallery that overlooked the woods and fields below. Who would leave such a lovely room empty? She imagined it fitted with mirrors, its white marble fountain burbling merrily amidst exotic plants and trees from around the world. A conservatory was a luxury she'd not had in London and she resolved to write the king's gardener, her friend Mr. Rose.

Rose tugged at her sleeve and directed a worried look outside. The sky had darkened quickly, with towering pillars of leaden cloud. "We've no candles to light our way, my lady, and it's growing late. Shouldn't we hurry back now? I'd not like to be caught in these halls once it's grown full dark."

Hiding her own uneasiness and exhausted from her explorations, Hope readily agreed. They hurried back to the comfort of lighted rooms and the smell of slow-roasting beef. Too tired to endure forced conversation and stiff politeness, she ate her supper in her room and promptly sought her bed.

Across the hall and three doors down her husband sought a bottle. He didn't want company either. He wanted brandy, and he wanted to be alone. Today would have been Caroline's birthday.

HOPE TWISTED AND MOANED, restless in her sleep. Somewhere a loose shutter banged on a wall and she shifted and whimpered as half-heard sounds invaded her dreams. Her heart beat faster and her breath came in shallow gasps as she clutched her blanket, gripping it tight. She twitched and started violently, fighting to wake, trapped by whatever chased her through her nightmare. She woke suddenly, as if dragged from her sleep, with the eerie feeling that someone had been calling her name. She often woke at night. As a child in a brothel on Drury Lane one always needed to be on guard. But she liked it, too. Walking alone, enveloped in the soft mystery of the dark. It never used to frighten her, but it did tonight.

The wind had picked up since early evening, and was blowing from the east. Unfamiliar houses made unfamiliar noises. But did they sound like whispers? Footsteps? Or the sound of something lost, calling in the dark? Something clattered in the hall and she stifled a startled scream. Creaking floorboards, slamming windows and eerie whispers were nothing more than what was to be expected. The normal grumblings of an elderly house as its joints complained. It was nothing but an overactive imagination that made it seem like anything more.

Fighting a panicked urge to hide beneath her blankets, she lifted her chin and stiffened her spine, deliberately challenging her fears. Reminding herself that she loved storms. They filled her with anticipation and a sense of power, which was something she needed desperately right now. She drew a loose, floor-length silk robe tight around her and set off for the library, with its magnificent view.

She walked back and forth between the library and billiards room as the rain drove across the river in great angry gusts, slamming against the windows and rattling doors. Rather than excited, she felt distinctly on edge. In the city one watched a storm from a bulwark of buildings, but here in the country, one stood directly in its path. It felt wilder, rawer and far more dangerous, like a wild beast approaching, roaring its hunger and snapping off limbs as it moved through the forest. There were the same familiar rumblings as thunder loomed closer, but other sounds, too, were born on the wind. Shrieks and wailing and mournful cries. *It's nothing but the wind tearing through the woods.* Yet she couldn't help thinking of Rose's fearful tales.

Something shifted and stirred in the air around her and a bright crack of lightning illuminated the sky. A face flickered in the window and she turned to run with a startled cry. She slammed into something warm and hard.

"I see the storm woke you, too. I'm sorry if I startled you."

He held her tight, to keep her from falling, and she clutched at his shoulders with a gasp of relief. She could feel his strength, coiled beneath her fingers. It made her feel safe in an oddly familiar way. He held her a little longer than necessary, before letting her slide down his body until her feet touched the ground. He seemed different somehow. His movements were relaxed, his voice was husky, and she could smell brandy on his breath. His arms were still wrapped around her, and his arousal pressed firm against her belly, weakening her limbs and making her melt inside. It was the chance she had been waiting for. To teach him he was no better than she was. To make him hers.

"I heard noises in my room. They frightened me," she whispered, smoothing and straightening the front of his robe before sliding beneath it to place a dainty hand on his hard, muscled chest. His naked skin was hot to her touch and his heart beat strong beneath her palm.

"So you came down here all by yourself in the dark?"

"I came down here to better watch the storm." She took a step closer, so the soft curves of her body molded against him. He was naked beneath his banyan and her fingers trailed across his taut belly, then curled around his arousal with a firm squeeze. He swelled in her hand, smooth as velvet and hard as iron and she stood on tiptoe to whisper against his throat. "They make me feel alive and restless. They make me ache with longing and feed some nameless need. Do you feel their power, Captain Nichols? When is the last time you had a woman?"

He took her hand in a hard grip and forced her to

take a step back. "Madam, I am drunk, but in the morning I shall be sober, and you will still be the king's whore."

"And your wife. I'll still be that, too," she said, stung.

"Good God, madam! You act like a bitch in heat. You are his. Would you have it otherwise?"

"And you a hound with the scent, sir." It wasn't going at all as she'd planned. She was angry, and despite herself her feelings were hurt. "You want me. Your prick can't lie. You're just not man enough to act on it. I may be his bitch, but you are his cur and the master is far from the kennel. Why shouldn't we please ourselves?"

"Have you no love for him, then? Are you truly so venal? He has treated you well enough. At least show some honor to the man who has fed and clothed you. You owe him that much." His voice was laced with disgust.

"No!" Her angry shout startled them both. "Love for him? Honor? I owe him nothing. I'll not love a man who doesn't love me. He's no better than you! You are hypocrites both. And I am a courtesan, not a whore. I am educated. I can dance and sing and play cards. I can use a napkin and speak some French and write and read. I have even learned to do my sums. I have known only three men. Yes. They bought and paid for my company, but I've been faithful to each one. I daresay that's more than you or he can say."

"I pray you forgive my doubts regarding your faithfulness when I have just removed your dainty hand from about my cock. I'm a man, Hope. And yes…I have your scent. I spring to attention whenever you walk by. It's in your voice, your look, your walk. Women like you were born to entice, but like it or not, you're not some strumpet I can walk away from. Your name, and thus your honor, is now bound to mine. As long as you're his, I'll treat you as guest, not lover or wife."

"Hah!" Her laughter was harsh. "Listen to yourself. You think that refusing to acknowledge we're married makes you any less a cuckold? You have no honor left to lose, Captain. You sold it for a title, *my lord.*"

Robert sighed. He didn't really want this constant animosity. There didn't have to be a contest. She was what she was and he was what he was. A whore and a killer who'd failed in his duty. Far better if they could just let each other be. He carefully modulated his tone. "The title means naught, Hope. All I cared about was keeping Cressly, so I might honor a promise made years ago. There must have been other men to suit your purpose. If you find me so distasteful, why in God's name did you choose me?"

"Choose you? What choice did I make? I was not even forewarned. As you and he decided how I was to be disposed of, I was seeing to his guests and readying the maypole and doing my best to make him proud. He thanked me by denying me the thing I want most. I know what you think. Jewels. Money. Position. But what are they when dependent on the good graces of another? I wanted my freedom, Captain. I had no wish to be there when his queen arrived. I begged him to let me leave court and retire to a place of my own before he married. And what did he do? He sold me to a man who hates me. Married me to someone I'd never met and forever denied me my freedom. He does not love or honor me, so why should I him?"

"He is your monarch."

"As someone who has slept in his bed I can tell you that all that he is, is a man."

Her hair was disheveled, her lovely face stained with tears, and Robert felt a gut-wrenching ache that spread to his chest and squeezed his throat. The thought that she might not have known, might not have been complicit, had never occurred to him. If what she said were true, Charles had treated her badly indeed, and she was no more at fault for their current predicament than he. She was as much a pawn if not more. At least he had been given a choice. "I didn't know, Hope. I thought it was something arranged between the two of you."

She looked taken aback but quickly recovered. "And I thought it was something between you and him. He used us both, Captain. When I saw you in London my pulse quickened. I had never been so interested or attracted to a man. It's not something I would have acted upon, but we are far from London now and so much has changed. Why not seek comfort from one another? There is sorrow in your eyes and I am lonely this night."

His body tightened and he took a harsh breath. She was such a lovely creature he ached to possess her, from her tumble of night-dark hair to her pretty toes. He looked into violet eyes that shone with their own inner light. "And when he calls for you?" His voice grated.

"You know as well as I do that I will have to go."

He took a step back. "I will not take advantage of a guest, madam."

Rippling like water, her gown slid from her shoulders to lie in a silken pool on the floor. Her body shone like alabaster as lightning lit the sky. Her breasts were firm and high and sweetly rounded, with tight dark nipples that begged to be teased and kissed. A slim waist curved into luscious hips and he could feel the heat from the soft dark thatch between her sleek and shapely legs. His nostrils flared as he smelled her musk. Her fingers brushed his penis, trailing up and down the underside, and he groaned and leapt in her palm.

Her other hand found his, and guided it unresisting to the juncture between her legs. She was wet and silky and he cursed beneath his breath, taking her by her hips and bottom and lifting her tight against him.

She wrapped her legs around his waist as his straining erection pressed hard between her naked thighs. Rubbing up and down against it, she purred like a stroked cat. This man set her body aflame.

Succumbing to imaginings that had plagued him for days, he let go of his good intentions. His hands worked with her, rocking her against him. He captured her mouth in a scorching brandy-soaked kiss, his tongue plunging deep into the hot inner recesses of her mouth, thrusting to the same rhythm as her hips. There was nothing tender about his kiss. It was hungry, demanding, greedy with need. Her breasts were mashed against his chest. He could feel her hardened nipples rub against him as her moist and eager heat teased and embraced his swollen cock. A violent gust of wind blew open a French door but neither of them noticed.

He had been too long without a woman and his hunger overtook him. He leaned over the heavy oak billiards table and lowered her onto its green worsted surface, one handing knocking ivory balls aside as his body followed hers down. His mouth devoured hers as his hands traveled her length, pinching and teasing her nipples, brushing her belly and squeezing her waist. He blazed a trail of hot kisses down her throat, across her breasts and over her stomach as he stroked her quivering flesh.

Hope had imagined his kisses in London. At the inn in Nottingham his nearness had been a touch.

She didn't know what wild magic this was but she reveled in the feel of him as he boldly claimed her body. She arched against his hands, and turned into his kisses as his bristled jaw abraded aching skin and left her lips burning and swollen. Every part of her was exquisitely alive.

She whimpered an incoherent protest when he withdrew his heat from hers. Her eyes opened to find him standing, watching her from the edge of the table. His body was all that she'd imagined. Lithe, hard and lean-waisted, his torso was taut and sleek, his stomach ridged with muscle, and he had the corded shoulders, sculpted chest and rippling arms of a swordsman. She moaned in frustration and lust, and gasped in shock and excitement when he grasped the back of her thighs in his large hands, roughly hauling her toward him so her buttocks rested against the felt rail cushions and she lay completely open to his gaze. Her face blazed as he stood naked between her legs, a proud erection jutting, brushing against her soaking curls.

"Good Christ, I could devour you." It was the first words either of them had spoken since she'd slipped out of her gown. He knelt between her legs, hooking them over his shoulders, and gripped her hips, holding her firmly in place. Despite the chill wind and rain spattering through the open door, her body burned crimson. When he kissed her lightly, just brushing her with his warm breath, she almost leapt from the table, twisting and squirming, but her gy-rations didn't free her, they only forced her tighter against his seeking mouth. As he pleasured her, kiss-ing and tonguing, her moan was one of wild surren-der, but her hands gripped his head, and her hold was as fierce and possessive as his was of her.

"Robert, please," she gasped. He rose and entered her, slamming into her, and she grasped his shoulders and arched to meet each thrust. Thunder reverberated in the distance, rumbling as it echoed off buildings, trees and hills. As wind slammed the shutters hard against the outer wall and white sheets of lightning lit the sky, he filled her body, he filled her senses and he rode her through the storm.

He lay atop her for several moments. She could hear the rain sweeping across the flagstones. She could hear his heart and his ragged breathing, but he didn't say a word. He pushed himself up on his arms and she shivered, watching in silence as he adjusted his robe. Retrieving hers, he handed it to her, and of-fered his hand to help her to her feet.

"I think it's time for me to retire. Do you need me to escort you back to your room? Or can you find your way alone?"

His cold politeness mortified her after abandoning herself as she had. "Now that you've taken what you wanted, you will simply walk away?" She couldn't keep the hurt from her voice.

"It was what you wanted, Hope." His manner was

distant, his voice weary. "It's been a difficult day. It's better I'm alone."

"And now I suppose you feel dishonored. You ooze judgment like a weeping sore."

"It's not judgment. You have no idea what I…" He sighed and raked his fingers through his hair. "Was that your purpose? Was it what you wanted?"

She had the grace to flush. Why *had* she pursued this man? She didn't know herself anymore. She was so lonely, so far away from all that was familiar, and she had never felt so lost. She blinked back her tears. They served no purpose and he would not appreciate them. No doubt he hated her now.

She rounded on him with a fortifying surge of anger. "If you feel you've sullied your precious honor, you have no one to blame but yourself. Yes, I teased and provoked you. Yes, I offered myself. Blatantly! But no one forced you to accept. Don't act like I ravaged you. Like you are some sort of victim. That is laughable. You are a man. The world and all the things in it belong to you. You are bigger than me. Stronger than me. You took what I offered. You took what you wanted. 'Tis you who has the power here."

"Is it?" he said mildly. "It's you who has the king."

She called after him as he turned and walked away. "Whilst you try and sleep in your lonely bed you will think of me willing and warm."

"Leave it be, Hope." His voice was flat, rasping, barely more than a whisper. "It's not you who haunts my dreams."

CHAPTER FIFTEEN

HOPE WOKE WITH A blinding headache. Doubtless it came from crying herself to sleep. It was a wretched habit, one she seemed to be growing used to. Perhaps she should turn to the bottle when upset. It would be far better, and certainly much less humiliating, to wake sick and hurting from too much drink. She should be feeling powerful and victorious. She'd decisively turned her back on Charles and shown the captain he was no better than she was, yet all she felt was guilty and confused. Not that she had any reason to. Perhaps the captain had not knowingly tricked her into marriage. But he was still a hypocrite, who'd married someone he held in disdain in a situation he disapproved.

And how must he feel today? *All I've done is proven to him I'm nothing but a whore.* With a moan she buried her head against her knees and wrapped her arms around her legs. *I'll never be able to look him in the eyes again.*

That was how Rose found her almost twenty minutes later. Unable to deal with the girl's relentless good cheer, Hope flopped onto her stomach and pulled a coverlet over her head. A determined Rose prepared her tea with a loud clatter of silver on porcelain. The delicious hot drink was the latest rage among sophisticated folk, but she'd been surprised to find it here in the country. It seemed Nottingham really did have shopping to rival that of London.

"Here we go, my lady. Open your eyes and see what I've got. I've brought you a special treat!"

"Go away, Rose," she mumbled into her pillow.

"My lady, I know what it is to be far from home, and I know sometimes you're sad and lonely. If you'd just open your eyes I have something I promise will cheer you up."

Giving a very unladylike grunt, Hope stretched out her arm and pointed. "It's not the magic potion people say it is. Just put in on the side table, Rose, and leave me be." Something warm and silky soft rubbed against her hand, and she opened her eyes to see an amber-eyed, snub-nosed, fluff-ball of a kitten. It stared at her with a mix of curiosity and mischief, and she stared right back and grinned.

"You've been awfully nice to me, my lady, what with the dresses and all. Before you came here nobody even bothered to ask me my name. I wanted to do something nice for you."

"Well, God bless you, Rose O'Donnell. I daresay this is one of the nicest things anyone's ever done for me." Giggling and cooing, they played with the kitten as it reared and pounced and wriggled in ambush, attacking a feather they tied to a string.

"I should warn you though, my lady. We best try to keep her a secret. The master is very strict about animals in the house."

As the week wore on, Hope managed to avoid the captain, who had returned to Nottingham on business with Sergeant Oakes. She expected he was busy avoiding her, too. She ate in her rooms rather than alone in the dining room, and procured a matronly apron with wide pockets that could discreetly carry her kitten inside. Mrs. Overton saw its tiny head peeking from her pocket and screamed as if she were carrying a rat.

"You'll not be keeping that in the house once the master sees it! Far as he's concerned the place for animals is outside."

Hope shrugged her shoulders and ignored her. The palace had been full of dogs and they often made a filthy mess, but cats were cleanly. Rose wouldn't stay long in the curiosity cabinet she'd claimed as study, and one little kitten to keep her company was surely not too much to ask. She continued her exploration of Cressly, hiking through pasture and woodland and riverside with her kitten at her side. And if the night was filled with mournful calls and eerie creaking, she was too tired from her travels to pay it much mind.

Midweek a coach from London arrived bearing

her jewels, her cosmetics and clothes. She had little use for them here at Cressly, and much to Rose's horror, after giving her another dress, a coat and a very smart feathered hat, she packed them away, contented with a few simple dresses, some India gowns and the men's clothes she'd worn in London when that fashion had been the rage. She wondered what her soldier husband would think of those.

There was little she could do to improve the house without cooperation or resources, so she contented herself with adding her own touches to her study, and weeding and tending its hidden garden as best she might.

ROBERT NICHOLS WAS IN a quandary. He had slept with his own wife. That she was another man's lover hadn't mattered until now. So long as he hadn't touched her, so long as he was convinced she'd deliberately used him, knowing his desperate situation with Charles, all he owed her was the minimal civility one had to offer an unwanted guest. Her perspicacity had taken him completely by surprise. *You think that refusing to acknowledge we're married makes you any less a cuckold?* It was exactly what he'd thought. But refusing to think of her as his woman was going to be far more difficult now.

In spite of his words the other night, he'd been lying to himself and her. His nights were still filled with flashing steel and cannon fire, the battlefield,

fear and blood. He still heard the shouting and cursing and the screams of trapped innocents, and her
crying still followed him through his dreams. But
ever since London, as he drifted off to sleep, his
thoughts were filled with a sad-eyed elf with violet
eyes.

It was bad enough before, when he was constantly
thinking of her dancing like some wild pagan queen,
or the movement of her shapely bottom as she leaned
out the carriage window. But now, the image of her
spread in open invitation on his billiard table, the
scent and taste and sound of her, invaded his every
thought. She was making his life complicated in
ways he'd not imagined. She was certainly not a wife
he'd have chosen for himself. But a fever was upon
him and he'd have to find a way to resolve the thing
because he was not a man who shared.

He dealt with easier complications first, sending
Oakes to hire five more men, ex-soldiers all, to act as
footmen, grooms and extra coachmen. It wouldn't be
hard. The country was full of displaced soldiers ill-fit
for other jobs. The sergeant would see to it they were
armed and ready if their other skills were required.
He'd also swallowed his pride and sent a message to
de Veres. He needed eyes and ears in London. The
man knew things, and Elizabeth trusted him.

And then there was Hope. It was clear she was
unhappy, and true he'd been neglectful. He could
only imagine how she'd felt at the way she'd been

betrayed. She had not come of her own accord and given that, and what had passed between them, he felt a greater responsibility than he had before.

He knew she'd been avoiding him. He hadn't meant to insult or offend her after their…encounter, but she'd been in no mood to listen, and he in no mood to speak. Not about Caroline. Not to anyone. A little time and distance should make it easier to talk. Too much might make it impossible. Fortified with a shot of brandy, he set out to track her down. She was not in the drawing room or library, and there was no answer when he knocked on her door. He was about to take the search outside when he saw the housekeeper.

"She'll be in the same place she goes every day," Mrs. Overton told him. "Down the old east hall off the north wing."

"She'll be where?"

"In the room you told us all to stay out of. It seems she's got it in her head to make it her own."

Bloody hell! The woman was a damned nuisance. What gave her the right? She went where she pleased. Took what she pleased. Did as she pleased, and now she'd launched an invasion of his privacy and his home. He stalked down the hall.

The door to the little room was half-open. She was perched on the window seat, gazing outside. She was simply dressed and wearing an apron, and there was a streak of soot smudging her cheek. A snow-white kitten sat in her lap, pawing at a bit of lace trailing from her sleeve. She patted it absently as she watched out the window, looking for all the world like a lost little waif. He was arrested by the scene. Moved in a way he hadn't expected, as forcefully as if he'd been punched in the gut. In the past he had wondered what she was, but for the first time he wondered who she was.

The kitten saw him first. It arched its back and hissed. Hope looked up, startled, her face white with surprise. He collected himself quickly. "What is that thing doing in here? Cats are for vermin, not for pets. It should be in the kitchen or outside. There are… there are many valuables in this room."

"She's only a kitten, Captain. And she's very well-behaved." There was a note of pleading in her voice.

"We are not at the palace now, where every idiot has a dog or monkey or other small pet stuck in a muff or sleeve. Send it to the barn where it can make itself useful. You may have had your way with your lover, but… Oh, bloody hell! Stop that!"

She tried to, but she'd been under a strain for days. Her eyes welled with tears though she fought to keep them back. She'd poured all her affection into the kitten and it tore at her heart that she was helpless to stop him taking it away.

"Stop it at once, Hope. You'll find I don't respond well to such tricks." The kitten jumped from the seat and ambled across the floor to rub against his boots, then pounced on the toes, its tiny little claws digging into the leather.

Hope stiffened in fear. "Please, Captain, I beg you. She meant no harm."

Robert reached down and pinched its nape, plucking it off his boot. It squirmed in his hand and scratched him, and his face twisted in displeasure. "Really? Your bloody little savage meant no harm? And you call this well-behaved? One can only wonder what havoc she'll wreak when grown." He plunked it back down on the window seat beside her.

"Here. Take your Fluffy or Princess or whatever you've decided to name it, and keep her out from underfoot. See that it doesn't cause a bother. No climbing curtains or scratching furniture, or out to the barns she goes."

"I can keep her?"

He sighed as he settled into an armchair, taking note of what she'd done with the room as he stretched out his booted feet. It shone with a luster he didn't remember and he was more comfortable than he'd expected. "This is your home, too. Teach it some manners."

"Her name is Daisy."

He nodded. "White hair, those colored eyes. Naturally she's named for a flower."

Hope wasn't sure if he was making an effort at conversation or was simply being sarcastic. She decided to give him the benefit of the doubt. "I had a kitten very much like her when I was a child."

"Was it ill-behaved, too?"

She was about to make a defensive retort when she caught the slight smile playing about his lips. "Yes," she said with a grin. "I'm afraid she was. I will find a way to replace your boots."

"There's no need. My boots have withstood far worse than the fangs and claws of a rampaging kitten. Hope, has no one told you that I prefer this part of the house to remain unused?"

"You haven't told me. And the servants don't speak to me except for Rose."

"Ah, yes. As you told me your first day here. I have to remedy that."

"Why don't you use this room? It's a wonderful space filled with marvelous things and has a beautiful garden out back."

"It was my curiosity cabinet when I was a boy." He gave her a grim smile. "I suppose you might say I've lost my curiosity since then, and I generally prefer not to revisit my youth."

"May I use it, though? I'll take good care of it and be very careful."

He chuckled. The chit could read his thoughts. "I can see how you value it. It looks better than I remember. But you'll need the fireplace working, a servant's bell, and a supply of liquor to really do it justice."

"I tried to poke around the fireplace and clean it out, but it's a bit too complicated for me."

That explained the soot-stained face. "You should leave that work to the servants. Oakes can tell you who's best for the job."

There was an awkward silence between them, but it was the first civil conversation they'd had since the afternoon in Nottingham. Hope didn't want it to end, and she didn't want him to leave. When he exerted himself to be pleasant she found him likable indeed. She struggled for a topic of conversation. "In the drawing room…"

"Yes?"

"There are two portraits. Are they your mother and father?"

"Yes."

"And where are they now?"

"I have no idea. In heaven one hopes, should there be such a place. They died several years ago while visiting London, during an outbreak of the plague."

"I'm sorry, I didn't—"

"As I said, it was many years ago."

"And in this room. There are two miniatures."

"My sister, Caroline, yes. She is dead, too. If it pleases you, I have no wish to discuss it. There are other matters, though, that—"

He stopped in surprise as the housekeeper barged into the room. "Ah! I see you have found her, my lord. I tried to tell her about keeping that creature but she would not listen, and—"

"Mrs. Overton, you have forgotten to knock. My wife and I are speaking. In future please remember that you are the servant here and she is the mistress. It is not her place to listen to you, it is yours to listen to her. When it comes to the household, you shall take Lady Newport's word as mine. You will see this is understood by all members of the staff. Have I made myself clear?"

"Yes. Yes, my lord, my lady." Red-faced and stammering, Mrs. Overton curtsied to them both and hurried from the room.

"Well! There's that taken care of. "

Hope found herself wincing in unexpected sympathy. "Oh, dear. Perhaps that was just a little bit harsh."

"Was it, damn it? I have no clue when it comes to these matters. One never has to worry about such things with soldiers. I swear I never saw a one of them run away in tears. Now…in fairness to Mrs. Overton, I have to ask, did ever you threaten to punch her?"

Hope gave him her best wide-eyed innocent look. "I most certainly did not!"

"How curious. Why would she say such a thing?"

"Perhaps she can't hold her drink. My mother was much the same."

"Perhaps. Are you certain you said nothing to her?"

She shrugged, and then kissed her kitten's pretty head. "She did accuse me of being Hope Mathews. All I did was agree, and promise her that some of the stories she'd heard, like the one about Orange Moll, were true."

"She accused you of being Hope Mathews?"

"Yes. An evil courtesan bent on no good and the like. I told her I was your wife, but she refused to believe it. I daresay she meant to protect you from my wicked influence and—" She turned crimson as she realized what she was saying.

"Ahem…" He cleared his throat. "Yes, well…I am sorry. That was my fault. I should have made it clear you were to be respected and obeyed from the beginning. I should have listened when you said there was a problem. I hope that it is rectified now. What *did* you do to Orange Moll?"

"I knocked her flat," she said with a wicked grin.

His rich laughter echoed through the halls of Cressly for the first time in years.

"You're an evil wench, Hope Nichols," he said when he had caught his breath. The picture of his tiny guest flooring the fearsome Mrs. Overton with one punch left him with a rueful grin. He didn't doubt she could do it. It was another thing to add to the growing list of images that crowded his brain whenever she came to mind. "As punishment, I leave the entire mess in your hands. If you insist on upsetting my household, the responsibility to deal with it shall be yours. I expect this will mean that these foolish dramas will no longer wash up at my door."

"And what of outdoors? Who do I speak to about the gardens and such?"

"Oakes, I suppose, but that shouldn't concern you." He shifted uncomfortably, and put thoughts of the billiards room firmly away.

"Perhaps he can tell me who might repair the fountain in the hidden garden. And there's so much work that needs to be done outside."

"No! I don't want you tearing up the gardens."

"I don't want to tear them up. Just weeding and trimming and tidying and such."

"There are gardeners for that."

"It hardly seems so. It should be a cheerful place yet it's sad and neglected."

"And what do you know about gardens?"

"I had many a talk with John, Mr. Rose. He is the king's gardener, and a botanist of great renown. He is trying to grow pineapples, you know. Have you ever tasted—"

"Leave the gardens alone. If you grow bored there are other things you can do. The library is there anytime you want it, and you can use the stables, as well. If you wish you can take a carriage to Nottingham for shopping."

"What? I can shop?"

"Yes. It's hardly what you're used to and the roads are rutted, but if you wish to shop then by all means do so. You will wait until Oakes has returned and take a complement of armed men with you, though."

"You'll not accompany me?"

Was that a hint of wistfulness in her voice? "I'm sorry, no. There are important matters I must take care of in London. I will leave by week's end, and expect to be gone a fortnight or so."

She felt a keen sense of disappointment. Just when she was warming to him he was leaving. She remembered their brief truce in Nottingham, and how his smiles and charm had heated her blood. *I want to know this man. I want to know him as a lover, and I want to know him as a friend.*

"I… What should I shop for?"

"I'd never thought to hear a woman ask that!" He pulled a velvet pouch from under his shirt. "When your carriage came from London it came with this. Here are twenty gold sovereigns. They belong to you. Along with another two thousand pounds in a locked box in my study. When I leave I will entrust you with a key."

"It's—"

"Your savings. Yes. Do what you will with it, but don't spend it on the house. That's money that rightfully belongs to you. His Majesty gave us ten thousand pounds when we married. If you want to decorate and claim the place, or if you see a need, use that. Simply put it on my account."

"You would trust me with it?" *So that is what Charles saw as my worth. More than any whore, but less than Castlemaine's necklace.* She felt a twinge of annoyance, but it didn't sting as it might have before.

"You supervised a large town house and staff in Pall Mall. Overall it seemed well-managed and tasteful. I'm sure you know more about such things than me. You don't *have* to, Hope."

"No! I do! I will. You may rely on it."

It pleases me to see her smile. "Good. I have but two conditions. Leave the gardens be, and no mirrors, unless they be for your own room."

"No mirrors?"

"Having seen your home, it's clear you can't be trusted in that regard."

"But mirrors add light and warmth to a house, Captain Nichols, which is something your home badly needs. They bring—"

"Call me Robert. Mirror upon mirror encircling a man simply makes him dizzy and ill. When first I met you I was certain I was going to spew."

"That was why you looked so annoyed? I thought you were glaring at me!"

"No, elf. Despite what you might think of me, I am not in the habit of grimacing at beautiful women. At least not on purpose." He stood up and offered her his hand. "The hour grows late and I've still much to do. Will you join me later for supper?"

"I look forward to it," she said with a brilliant smile. "Robert?"

"Yes?"

His body was almost touching her. She could feel it like a warm caress.

"I…" What to say? That she was sorry for seducing him? She wasn't. All she could think of was doing it again. "I've blamed you for things that weren't your fault and I regret it. I said some things the other night, but despite our differences, I know they aren't true. You are an honorable man, or at least you have been so with me."

He gave her a deep bow. "I have done the same, madam, to you. I thought you part of Charles's scheme and resented you for it, as much as I resented myself for saying yes. I shall do my best to make your stay comfortable here, as I should have from the start."

"Thank you, my lord. Perhaps, on your return from London, we might start anew. I should like us to be friends."

His smile was warm as he bent to kiss her hand. The touch of his lips sent a shiver up her spine. What would it be like to make sweet love with this man? With no anger or hurt or reason beyond wanting. What would it be like to love someone who cared?

"I promise you I should like that, too, though I think it best we are careful, given the circumstances, to avoid a repetition of what happened the other night."

CHAPTER SIXTEEN

London

ROBERT NICHOLS'S RETURN TO LONDON was a good deal more circumspect then his last visit had been. He wore nondescript clothing and kept the brim of his hat pulled low over his eyes. It wasn't easy hiding his height, but seated men all looked the same when hunched over a table. He had arrived in the city just in time to watch the new queen's procession from Hampton Court to Whitehall. Gliding down the Thames on a gilded barge surrounded by a grand flotilla, she and her train of black-clad monks and stern-faced ladies looked like a flock of starlings let loose amidst the peacocks.

He had felt a stab of pity. Confessors and duennas and somber dress would only bring her ridicule here. Even as he had watched, a smiling Lady Castlemaine stood among the king's friends and retainers, draped in more jewels than the queen and the Duchess of York together. He wondered what Hope would have thought to see it all. She wouldn't gloat like Castlemaine. *She'd be more inclined to sympathy.*

His musings reminded him that she, too, belonged to the king. *They say he feels no jealousy, but I do. I should never have allowed the other night to happen. Any man would want her, but I didn't expect to like her so much.*

In truth their talk had gone much better than he'd anticipated. She really didn't seem that hard to please. Common courtesy, a little respect, her Irish maid and a kitten. It was a small enough price to see her smile. When she smiled everything lit up, even her surroundings. Her face glowed, her eyes shone with excitement and she awakened things inside him he'd long thought dead. *I wish I could have stayed to take her back to Nottingham.*

He'd certainly enjoyed their first visit…for the most part. Watching her spinning glass, her thrill at the tales surrounding the city and Sherwood Forest… He'd never really understood how their argument had begun. Somehow he'd offended her, and she'd offended him.

"I will tell you how many men I have fucked if you tell me how many you have killed."

Ah, yes. There was that. Three, she'd said. It was shocking only for its moderation. But she'd be shocked if she knew his answer, or what he did in London now, sitting in a secluded alcove in this Russell Street coffee house with its stink of tobacco and frantic bustle of overstimulated fools, waiting for William de Veres.

Robert disliked asking help from any man, particularly regarding a matter of personal honor, but it was a necessary evil. This wasn't only about vengeance or redemption. For the first time in a long time there was something to protect. Harris was dangerous, and he had disappeared. So…highwayman, spy, whatever de Veres's previous hobbies, hopefully he had something of note to impart, because after two fruitless weeks, all Robert wanted was to be done with his business and go home.

A buzz of excited conversation drew his attention. He laid down his drink and looked to the entrance as a tall, elegant-looking gentleman strode through the door. De Veres doffed a rakish feathered hat and bowed to the room, exchanging a few sallies and nodding politely to a beefy mutton-chopped gentleman who stood near the door. Robert recognized him as Joshua Greathead, a country squire who had fought in the civil war under Cromwell and had also led a company of his own. He wondered what acquaintance he might have with de Veres, as the king's favorite poet sauntered over to join him in the corner.

"Good evening, Lord Newport." The poet rested his booted feet upon the table and folded his hands across his lap. "My, what a great big sword you've got. It's hard to believe the lovely Drury Lane angel could have tired of you so soon after seeing that. Or won't you let her touch it?"

"Call me Captain Nichols…or Robert if you must.

One hopes you're not as foppish as you look. My enemies fight with swords, de Veres, not words."

William grinned in appreciation.

"'On men disarmed how can one gallant prove? And I was long ago disarmed by love.'"

"For God's sake, man. Must you speak in rhyme? It grows damned annoying."

"My apologies, Captain, if my flights of fancy tax your brain." He spoke the words slowly, enunciating clearly.

"You sent me a message to meet you here, Lord Rivers. Why?"

"You made enquiries about Lord Harris. Why?"

Robert leaned back in his chair, drawing lazy circles on the battered tabletop, and didn't answer.

"Perhaps Lizzy is right and I may grow to like you. You could certainly use some friends. You have many enemies, Captain. It's very hard to fathom given your gentle nature. Fortunately for you, I am adept with both pen *and* sword. I know you dislike me, but I do love Lizzy, and I did so long before you ever knew her. If I endangered her it was by accident, and I cannot regret it, for it brought us together again. But you had a part to play. You kept her safe and cared for her. I know you did it for her and not for me, but I am indebted to you nonetheless. I sent you a message because I thought you should know that Lord Harris has been making enquiries about *you.*"

Robert's hand stilled, and he lifted his head to look William straight in the eyes. "That's interesting."

"I thought so."

"What do you know of him?" Robert's tone was mild.

"He is sadistic, vicious, a murderer, but a dab hand at racing and cards. He calls himself Colonel, though he was cashiered from the army a decade ago. He's been twice charged with rape, and once with assault, though he's scampered away unscathed from each charge."

I should have killed him years ago. Who else has he harmed because of my failure? "Is there some reason Charles would want to reward him?"

"Perhaps. I'm not as close to His Majesty as I once was. Charles is rather indolent when it comes to paperwork. The devil is in the details. Literally in this case. I doubt he knows anything about the man's crimes or he'd never be welcomed at court. Harris is wealthy, owns several brothels and has vast properties in Lancashire and Scotland. He's well connected and well protected as he's owed significant sums of money by significant men. He has made several generous contributions to His Majesty's cause. What's really curious is why he should have any interest in you."

Robert nodded. His fingers unconsciously stroked the hilt of his sword. "You've been very helpful, Lord

Rivers. You have my thanks. Do you know where I might find him?"

"Again, I ask why?"

"I have business of a private nature with him, and it would seem he also has business with me."

"There can be no good business with him, Nichols." William eyed Robert's sword pointedly. "And the king is dead set against dueling. You have your lands and you have the king's gratitude and goodwill. And the girl…she is charming, is she not?"

Robert gave him a sharp look.

"Mmm. Yes, I thought so. I refer, of course, to her winning nature. She was far too selective and overchaste to make a convincing courtesan. You have stumbled upon a prize there, Captain. If there is something personal between you and Harris I suggest you let it go and enjoy the bounty fate has sent you, lest you anger our dear Charles and lose it all."

Elizabeth trusts this man. "There is something *very* personal between us, Rivers. A debt that must be paid. Even if I wished to let it go I cannot. I spent years tracking him only to lose him in Europe. Now he is back and a danger to me and mine. It was he who was meant to have Cressly. He asked the king for it specifically. He can't be sure I know it was him. He can't be sure I know he's back. I need to put him dow— I need to deal with him before he does."

William smiled and leaned back in his chair. "Lizzy made me promise to act with discretion and maturity, and to try and dissuade you from impulsive acts. You are my witness that I did. But intrigue, espionage, danger… I am married, Captain, not dead."

"You discussed my message to you with Elizabeth?"

"Of course I did. I tell her everything. There is nothing you can do at the moment. Your quarry is in Scotland. Surrounded by armed men. He left right after you did, supposedly to raise monies for His Majesty's ambitions abroad. By the time you reach his holdings he'll likely be on his way back to London. Go home. Be patient. I will be your eyes and ears. Rest assured I'll keep you informed of all you need to know and help in any way I can."

"I thank you for the offer, de Veres…." Pride, one of his staunchest allies over the years, made a half-hearted effort to refuse, but it was no match for a sudden vision of a sooty-faced enchantress. It was his duty to take care of her, after all. A thing he could hardly do from miles away. "Your help is much appreciated. And please, give Elizabeth my best regards."

"*De rien,* Captain. I always pay my debts. Besides, it should prove entertaining."

Robert set out for home with a sense of anticipation he hadn't felt in years. In the short time he'd known her, Hope had become so much a part of his life it seemed she'd always been there. For the first time in a long time it felt like there was something to go home to.

CHAPTER SEVENTEEN

Cressly Manor

"'ONE FOR SORROW,
  Two for mirth,
  Three for a wedding,
  Four for a birth.'

"Me ma taught me that one," Lucy said proudly. "Magpies know things."

"Everyone's mother told them that," Patience said with a disdainful sniff.

"Well, I've never heard it before." Hope stood, her head crooked to one side, as two of Sergeant Oakes's rather burly footmen repositioned a painting yet again. "I wish I'd known that before *my* wedding."

Everyone laughed, even Mrs. Overton, who couldn't help but add, "The master is a good man. Magpies three was good luck for you, my lady."

As they worked, they all vied to impress their new city mistress with hard-won country wisdom, which in turn led to stories of dastardly deeds and neighborhood ghosts and hauntings. Fortunately

Sergeant Oakes stepped in before stories got started about Cressly. Hope still heard noises that made her jump, and the cry of hunting birds at night sometimes alarmed her.

There was a thirst among the staff to bring the neglected house back to life. Underneath the humming and singing, laughter and joking, there was pride. For the past few weeks, since she'd returned from her shopping, all the staff had lent a hand working together, and it showed. Day by day, in remarkably short order, the house had taken on a new life and brilliance. Plaster walls were whitewashed, panels and floors polished, and light streamed through windows and danced along the halls.

Now they embarked on decorating: hanging paintings and tapestries, removing dusty sheets and laying down rugs. She hadn't needed to purchase as much as she'd expected after raiding the treasure trove of furniture, paintings and hangings packed in storage. She asked Mrs. Overton, over tea, why so much had been put away.

"It was first put there for safekeeping, during the war, my lady. The master was hardly ever home. It was just me and the servants. He was gone for seven years with just one visit. When he finally came home he didn't seem to have much interest. Then Mr. Oakes said the house was going to someone else and we'd all be moving to town so we packed up more.

It does my heart good, ma'am, to see it shining like it is. I never thought I'd see it this way again."

Hope had been careful to mend relations with the housekeeper. The woman's experience and expertise were invaluable, and she had no interest in taking over her duties. "My goodness, Mrs. Overton! You managed this place by yourself for seven years? That must have been an enormous task. What would the captain have done without you?"

"I don't know, my lady, and that's the truth. The sergeant wasn't here neither. I suspect it would have gone to ruin, and himself not even notice."

"Well, thank the lord you were able to preserve it. Between us we'll return her to her former glory and see if he notices that."

The housekeeper grinned. "Aye, ma'am. I daresay he might. At least once he gets the bills."

Hope's heart leapt when a coach arrived from London two days later, but it was just her plate and silverware, not the captain returning home. She flung a note from Charles in the fire without opening it. It was a private note, not a royal missive, and she felt no obligation to treat it differently than one from any other man. She hadn't expected to miss the captain quite so much, but the wild night he'd taken her during the storm had changed things between them, even if he'd left for London before she could understand how.

She couldn't call what happened between them

making love. It was far too rough, too urgent, too angry, on both their parts. But there had been passion, attraction, lust and delirious pleasure. Even though he'd said it mustn't happen again, she felt as if he'd branded her, claiming every part of her, even her thoughts.

She hadn't known he had been so close to losing his home. Had he been in debt? It didn't seem so. Was it because he fought for parliament? Perhaps. In any case, it helped explain what he meant when he said he'd not married her for a title. He'd said other things, too.

It's not you who haunts my dreams.

That meant someone else did. He refused to talk of his family or past, and he rarely laughed or smiled, but even when he did there was a haunted look in his eyes. A man who looked like he did could not have spent his life alone. She wasn't the only woman who'd watched him hungrily in London. Was there a lost love? A broken heart? A tragedy in his past? Who *did* he dream of? Even if it wasn't her, she wanted him to come home.

Despite his prohibition, she turned her attention to the garden. Not the large overgrown jungles that surrounded the house. They had been scavenged for blooms to brighten the dining room and landings, but otherwise left alone. But the hidden garden behind the magical little room seemed to call out to her so loud she couldn't refuse. It was beautiful in its own wild glory and she didn't seek to tame it. She pruned a bit and weeded, loosened packed earth and cleared away dead leaves. Sergeant Oakes came to help her with the fountain and she took the time to thank him for finding her such a lovely room.

"That wasn't me, lass," he replied. "The captain was very clear he wanted you to have it. He said you'd like the brightness and the view."

"He did?" *He thought of my comfort even as we were quarrelling?* The fountain was hot work, and she poured the sergeant a healthy mug of wine from the jug she'd brought to the garden.

"Oh, aye, ma'am. 'She's a fey little thing, Oakes,' says he. 'She's bound to find it gloomy here. Give her the sunny one over the river, and fill it with all the plants you can find.'"

"Well, that was very thoughtful of him. He never said a thing."

"He wouldn't, ma'am." The wine was making the sergeant loquacious and she made sure to keep his cup full. "He's good at taking care of people, but not much of a one for talking. Maggie claims his old nurse said he was more sociable so to speak, as a child, but ever since I've known him, and that'd be nigh on twenty years, he's had a tendency to keep his thoughts mostly to himself."

"Really?"

"Aye. Shut tight as a clam, he is. He was made lieutenant at sixteen. I didn't much like the thought of having a green boy as an officer, and neither did the other men. But even then he weren't no boy. I swear we all thought he was born old. There was something dark about him. He never laughed or smiled and he was always business. Not one to sit and have a beer with the boys. Myself, I thought the lad had demons, but if he did he kept them to himself."

"Demons?" She had noticed something dark about him, but that was not how she'd describe it.

"Aye. Eyes like a shark he had sometimes, before battle. You could see right through 'em like they was made of ice. I swear he could scare a man to death. He didn't need that monster sword for that." He gave a short laugh and spit on the ground as if warding off evil. "But don't you worry none, lass. He's ferocious on the battlefield, but I never seen him abuse his men or a prisoner, and certainly never a woman or child. That's a rare thing to say about men who've been long to war. A gentleman he is, and a damned fine commander. Some thought it were their duty to use up men like ammunition, but the captain, he did a job and did his best to get us out alive."

She nodded solemnly. *That's much as I imagined him the first time I saw him.*

The sergeant wiped his brow and settled on a stone bench in the shade. It was hot for early June. He reached for the jug and helped himself. "Do you know, my lady? You're the first person I can recall ever making him laugh or smile. A real smile anyway. Not one of those cold lifeless ones that freeze you to your bones."

She was pleased to hear it. His smiles and laughter were quick and fleeting, except for the belly laugh when she told him of Orange Moll. She'd learned more about the captain in an hour with Mr. Oakes than she had over the past month, and she pressed ahead, taking advantage of his talkative mood.

"You say he's good at taking care of people..."

"Oh, aye," Oakes offered before she could finish. "Scarred footmen, one-eyed stable boys and short-fingered...well, whatever I am. Most of the men you see here served under him, ma'am. After the war ended there was little employment and too many men looking for work. Many of us never got paid our back wages, and many turned to crime or ended in debtor's prison...or starved. Finding work is hard enough if you're able-bodied and handsome, almost impossible for fellows like Jemmy and me. The captain finds work for any of his men that need it. He always takes care of his own."

"Ah! That explains a great deal. I wondered about that, Sergeant. I was beginning to think you were all a great clumsy lot."

They both broke into laughter.

"You're good for him, lass. You've sparked his interest and that's a rare thing indeed. He's not easy to get to know, but I warrant it's well worth the effort."

"I'll keep that in mind, Sergeant, but surely he's had other…interests…before me."

"Ah! Well, there was the Walters woman. Very protective of her, he was. He served her father a space during the war. He admired her, I think, and felt it his duty to care of her, but she never made him laugh, and he never looked at her the way he does at you."

Hope blushed and looked at her toes. "He's a very handsome man, though, Sergeant. Surely there have been others."

"Ach!" He shrugged his broad shoulders. "Soldiers have needs just like other men, and some of them even have more than one wife." He gave her a cheeky grin. "The captain, well, there's been a widow or three, and more than a few barmaids eager to warm him at night. But he's never been one to play at romance. Many a fine lady has tried and failed. I've never seen him in love, though he liked Lady Rivers. For my money, he's been married to that cold dark bitch called war. You're the first he's ever brought to Cressly. It was a great surprise to all of us to see you married."

"Believe me, Sergeant, it was as great a surprise to me as it was to you."

ROBERT WALKED THROUGH THE HOUSE in stunned amazement. The walls were hung with botanical watercolors, beautiful landscapes and exotic paintings of

Eastern cities. Vibrant colored rugs adorned walls and tables, and some were laid on the burnished floors. A chaotic mix of Flemish and Brussels tapestries told stories from history, legend and myth. He stopped in front of one that covered a wall in the library, depicting a group of colorfully clad astrologers standing on a balcony as they trained a telescope on a black-and-silver sky. He recognized many of the scenes from his childhood. He'd forgotten he had them packed away. Her decoration had no coherence as to style or subject. She had clearly chosen for cheerfulness, warmth and what was pleasing to the eye.

It was Cressly as he had never imagined it. Relaxing, inviting, comfortable and bright. He was astonished by what she'd accomplished in just a few short weeks. *She's taken my empty house and made it her own.* The thought didn't bother him. Indeed it made him smile, until he saw the masses of flowers in the dining room. *Caroline's flowers. I asked her but one thing!* His eye was caught by the gleam of silverware set on a sideboard. There were beautifully wrought candles, an engraved plate and bowl and a stack of linen napkins, all of them marked with the initials *H.M.*

AFTER SERGEANT OAKES LEFT HER, Hope stretched out with the half-emptied jug on a velvet carpet of lush green grass. The sun kissed her face and the delight-

ful chatter from the laughing fountain added the final
enchantment to a lovely day. As white puffs of cloud
drifted overhead she dared think it. *Maybe, by some
strange May Day magic, I have finally found my
home. Maybe I have found my—*

"What in God's name are you doing out here?"

She jolted upright in surprise, smacking her head
on the edge of the fountain, biting her tongue and
seeing stars. *Curse the man!* "I am enjoying the sunshine, you bloody fool! You shouldn't sneak up on
people like that. When did you get back?" Any pleasure at seeing him home was waylaid by his angry
tone and the throbbing pain to the back of her head.

"Just now. And just in time to stop you from
laying claim to the gardens. Must you meddle with
everything, madam?"

"You said to do as I pleased. You said this was
my home, too. While I am here I shall live like it is."
Her voice was defiant, but she was bewildered. She
thought he would appreciate all the work they had
done. She had thought that he'd be pleased. She'd
fixed a fountain and picked a few flowers. What on
earth was wrong with him?

"I gave you the house, woman. All that I asked
was you leave the gardens alone. You and your lover
cannot just walk in and lay claim to all that you
please!"

"My lover? You mean the king?"

"Yes, I mean the king." He took note of her bared

feet and tousled hair. Despite his annoyance his mind was flooded with images of pebbled nipples and snowy thighs and his body tightened. He flung a napkin at her feet. "Sell them, store them, or give them away, but do not use His Majesty as initials to adorn my house."

She snatched the napkin and stuffed it in her pocket. "The initials are for Hope Mathews!" Her lips were parted in anger and her eyes flashed a challenge.

"Well...you are Hope Nichols now, are you not?" he responded after a moment's awkward silence.

She detected a faint red stain on his cheeks. Could it be jealousy? Embarrassment? When some men were angry their lips paled and thinned, but his looked hard and full. "Your point is taken, Captain. You needn't belabor it. I will remove the offending napkins so they trouble you no more."

He cleared his throat. "You can always go to Nottingham and order up some new ones."

"The king is no longer my lover," she said, ignoring his words and offering her hand so he might pull her to her feet.

"Eh? What?"

"You called him my lover. He is not. If he were, I would never have..." She took a deep breath and looked him in the eye. "Whatever you may think of me, I don't entertain two men at once, Captain. He betrayed me. As far as I am concerned our arrangement is at an end. It ended the first day of May. Whatever comes of this, I will never trust him or be with him again."

"But you said the other evening when I asked you…that if he sent for you you'd go." He pulled her easily to her feet. The feel of her dainty hands in his sent an aching to his groin. Her hand, her foot, her every look inflamed him.

"I said I would *have* to go. He is the king. I can't refuse his summons. Neither could you when he called you. But I will never be with him again." She removed her hands from his and brushed off her skirts, deciding she was still angry. "If you'll excuse me now, I'll be on my way before I sully your precious gardens. They are meant to bring a place to life, to be a joy and celebration. You are letting them die through your neglect. It almost seems you want to keep this lovely place a tomb. Be sure to thank the servants for all their hard work. They did miracles here to please you and the least you can do is notice. Oh. And welcome home."

CHAPTER EIGHTEEN

WELCOME HOME? It was a sad welcome when the chit avoided him and had returned to eating dinner in her room. It was all because of the blasted gardens. Was a man a monster for expecting a promise to be kept? If it meant so bloody much to her she should state her case rather than sulk in her room. The gardens had always been Caroline's domain. She'd loved them since she'd first learned how to walk. She'd toddled about on stubbly legs, laughing and chasing butterflies, and they had been her passion as she'd grown. All who lived at Cressly had recognized them as hers. *Hope* would change them and claim them and make them her own and a last part of Caroline might slip away. He couldn't bring his sister back, but he owed her justice, and until she had that, the gardens would remain as they were.

Hope loved her flowers, too, though. Perhaps there was something he could do to assuage her. She wouldn't be happy unless she had something to grow. Doubtless a gift of bushes and a wheelbarrow would please her more than jewels. He grinned at the thought.

On his third day back he spied her sitting by the backwater feeding the swans. He was on the north lawn about to start sword practice. She was wearing boys' breeches and her hair was unbound. She took turns, flicking crumbs out to the stately birds, and then tossing some to a daring collection of song-thrushes and wrens that tiptoed in with sideways glances, then swooped off, flittering away like winged bandits, proudly bearing their prize.

"How is she fitting in, Oakes?" he asked of his companion. "She didn't cause too much trouble while I was away?"

"No indeed, Captain. The household is quite taken with her in truth. Even Maggie has warmed to her considerably. It's a happier house with her in it. She's made it bright and warm and the staff are cheered."

"Do they know who she is?"

"Them that do don't cares, my lord. A pretty woman might catch a king, but only a kind one can tame wild birds to her hand. She makes them feel important and valued. She makes the house feel like a home."

"Mmm. They'd be wise not to get too attached."

"And you, Captain?"

"Oh, the same goes for me, Sergeant. Only more so."

He whirled about and the sergeant barely had time to block his blade.

"Is that why you don't sup with her, Captain? And

why she stays in her room since you've been back? You don't want to grow too attached?"

"Damn!" Robert hissed as the sergeant's sword reached under his guard, slicing his shirt and nicking his skin. He hadn't anticipated that question. He drove the sergeant back with a series of thrusts and feints, careful to keep his focus. "No, Oakes. She sulks in her rooms because she's annoyed that I've forbid her the gardens."

The contest had grown interesting, no longer routine, and each circled the other with a predatory gleam in his eye. "Why on God's green earth would you do such a thing, my lord? Surely you don't wish to drive her away."

"No, Sergeant. I just want to keep a small part of Cressly sacrosanct…for reasons that are no concern of yours." His voice was calm, unruffled, and his eyes never left the sergeant's.

"You're not very good with people, are you, sir?" The sergeant slid forward, attempting to seize an opening, but his sword was caught by Robert's *main-gauche,* a left-hand weapon used to disarm and parry, and flung away. "But you're a hell of a warrior," he added with a rueful grin.

Robert smiled and bowed. "As are you, sir. Shall we try it again?"

THE DISTANT CLANG AND CLASH of metal battering metal invaded Hope's peaceful morning and chased all of her winged friends away. Wasn't it enough he'd chased her from her sanctuary without explanation or reason? It was not the homecoming she'd anticipated. He had seemed nice, friendly, even likeable before he left. She had missed him. Looked forward to his return. But once again it seemed she had imagined things that weren't there. He was as gruff on his return as he'd ever been. It was as if the thaw between them had never occurred. At least she'd won over the servants and made the house livable in his absence. Some things had improved.

Despite her annoyance, she stopped on the terrace to watch them train. She'd be a liar to say she had no appreciation for a fine male form, and her husband had a fascinating one. She'd always found a tall, rugged, masculine body appealing, and it wasn't something one saw every day at court. And the way he moved! It was hard for her to take her eyes off him. Years of fighting and practice had hardened and honed him, but he moved with the same fluid ease that had so captured her in London. He reminded her of one of the great cats she'd seen at the tower.

Some of the ladies at court practiced at swordplay for amusement and exercise, and because it seemed to excite a certain species of man. It was something she'd always wanted to learn. *I wonder if he'd teach me?* She imagined it was her standing toe-to-toe with him, eyes intent, joined with his in a thrilling challenge, her movements matching his as they danced back and forth, anticipating, responding, thrusting, parrying, beaded with perspiration, aching…. As his supple body powered each twist and thrust she felt herself grow warmer. His half-opened shirt clung to his body and an errant strand of hair had escaped its queue. She watched in fascination, her breath quickening and her lips parted as if preparing to receive a kiss—

Damn the man! Even as he banished her from his precious garden she'd been dreaming about his mouth, for God's sake! It was her own fault for seducing him during the storm. In setting out to entrance and capture she had been caught herself. With a snort of annoyance she turned her back on him and went inside.

She was coming up the stairs from the kitchen an hour later, with her nose in Hannah Woolley's book *The Ladies Directory*. It was full of wonderful recipes, medical remedies, instructions for making perfumes, as well as information on running a household and dealing with awkward social situations. Unfortunately there was no entry for managing surly pretend husbands or—

She gave a shriek of alarm as she almost smacked into her hulking husband, who was bounding down the stairs two at a time with a brace of hares. Though they both did their best to avoid the collision, Robert's elbow caught her cheek just below the eye. She lost her footing and began to tumble backward, but he managed to catch her wrist and right her. Her face began to swell immediately. Amidst curses and hastily murmured apologies, he swept her off her feet and carried her upstairs, calling for Mrs. Overton as he went.

"There's no need to make such a fuss, Captain. It's just a bump on the head. Have someone fetch me a cold cloth and in a day or two I'll be as good as new." In truth it didn't feel that bad. She felt more stunned and surprised than hurt, more shock than actual pain, though her eye watered and her face felt tight and heavy.

"Hush, elf. I'm a very large fellow and it's a very big bump. I should have been more careful. I shouldn't have been going so fast and I should have watched where I was going. Damn! Your cheek is black and blue and your eye is swollen shut. You're going to have a very ugly bruise."

"How ugly?" Her voice was a little anxious.

"Ugly enough to scare small children and weak-kneed adults."

Her involuntary grin caused a jolt of pain that radiated through her teeth, temple and jaw and she stifled a moan.

"I'm so sorry, love. I'll make it better. I promise."

He carried her with ease, and despite the pain she let her head fall back against his chest. She was not a trusting soul by nature, but she knew instinctively she could trust him to take care of her. *I think I've always known it*. It was an unaccustomed relief to let go and let someone else take charge for a change, and the comforting feel of his arms tight around her enveloped her in a delicious warmth that far exceeded any pain.

At least for the first twenty minutes. As Rose and her suddenly solicitous husband settled her into her bed with her head and shoulders raised on pillows, the pain and swelling steadily grew. The aching in her temple became so jagged it hurt to move and her jaw throbbed with a grinding pain that threatened to banish any other thought. Her skin felt as if it were burning and stretched so tight that it might burst. She bit back a whimper as her husband, Rose, and Mrs. Overton huddled over her, consulting on how best to proceed.

"Please close the curtains," she rasped, perilously close to tears. Rose rushed to comply and then hurried away on a mission. The captain sat on the bed beside her. She gasped in pain as careful fingers brushed her tender skin.

"Hush now, love. This won't take but a minute. Yours is not the first black eye I've dealt with. My men were always breaking their heads or running into a fist." His voice was gentle and soothing. Expert fingers explored her eye, ears, jaw, teeth and cheek, checking for broken bones and assessing the damage. She flinched and his free hand gave her shoulder a slight squeeze. "Not many of them were as brave as you."

She wanted to tell him she wasn't brave. Her head ached and her eye hurt and she couldn't open it even so much as to blink, but it hurt too much to speak. She started as something cold and wet was laid across her eye and cheek. It surprised her for a moment, then it cooled her face and numbed her pain and she sighed, leaning into it, feeling a blessed wave of relief.

"Better, yes?" He smoothed back her hair and kissed her forehead.

"Better. Yes. Is it really so ugly?"

"Not so much as it will be tomorrow, I'm afraid." He replied without thinking and she gave a sad little groan.

"You'll feel much better soon. Here comes your Rose with something to ease the pain and help you sleep." He settled on the bed beside her, slipping a hand under her shoulders and easing her up, supporting her so she could drink the infusion of opium, saffron and nutmeg mixed in hot wine. Even that slight movement made her wince.

"I've brought ice, my lord, and more cloths. Mrs. Overton says the laudanum should keep her comfortable the rest of the night. I can stay with her now, if it pleases you."

"Thank you, Rose, but it's my fault she's hurt and I'll stay and see her to sleep."

"Of course, my lord." The little maid gave him an odd look as she left the room.

"She thinks you hit me," Hope said dreamily, the potion already doing its work. She would never have dreamt yesterday that today her husband would be lying in her bed. She gave a little sigh and snuggled against him. Her head fit in the hollow between his neck and chin. Her movements were slow and languid, as if she were swimming in treacle. Despite all those hard muscles he felt comfortable and warm.

"I did hit you," he said ruefully, applying the ice-cold cloth to her cheek with a gentle pressure. His cock stirred as she wiggled and the soft curve of her hip settled tight against his groin.

"Mmm," she agreed happily. "Not on purpose, though. I shouldn't read on the stairs. Now I can't read at all." If a voice could pout, her last statement did just that.

"I really am sorry, love." In truth he was mortified. She looked as fragile as a child and he felt like a great bloody oaf. "I've never bruised a woman before."

"Hmm. I know, Robert. Don't feel bad. It was a foolish accident on both our parts." She yawned and wiggled again and he grunted. His breath quickened and his thighs and buttocks tightened. A surge of warmth stirred in his balls, spreading through his body, awakening all his senses and swelling his cock. That unruly organ surged forward, tingling from base to tip, and the constraints of his clothing acted as added stimulation, encouraging it more.

He shifted position but she shifted with him, and the warmth of her bottom only made things worse. He had never been so hungry for a woman. Despite her injury and obvious intoxication he wanted to claim her. To slip his hand under her gown and slide the length of her body, up her soft creamy thighs to brush her heated center, caress her sleek stomach, plump her breasts and tweak her nipples, making them ready for—

"I will forgive you completely if you tell me a story." Her voice was barely a murmur.

"A story?" It took him a moment to regain his bearings.

"Mmm. To help me sleep," she whispered.

He sighed in frustration. She was in this condition because of him but the damned woman might as well walk around naked. It wouldn't make him any less on edge. She'd fired his blood and now even the sound of her voice left him aroused. He skimmed her cheek with his knuckles, pleased that it was cold to the touch. One long finger slowly traced her hairline from her temple, stopping to tuck an errant silk lock behind her ear.

"What story would you like, wife?" He nuzzled her neck, breathing in her scent. She smelled of rose and nutmeg and he longed to taste her.

Hope shivered and it wasn't from the cold. She felt

a delicious lassitude as his warm breath stirred her hair. The butterflies in her stomach fluttered lazily and she could feel a tender swelling in her loins. Her skin felt ripe and tender, pricking from her nipples to her toes, but it was all as if it came from a thousand miles away. Maybe she was dreaming. "Robin Hood," she said on a sigh. "*My* Robin Hood, not yours."

"I am to do penance, then," he said with a chuckle. "Very well. I will be sure to remember that you do not forget. But stop wiggling, love, and pressing your pretty bum close against me. You know full well what you're doing."

She smiled, on the brink of sleep.

"Has anyone told you about the Major Oak?"

His voice was a caress. He spoke in a rich soothing tone that made her think of chocolate. She shook her head. A dull shard of pain shot down her jawbone but it was too far distant to trouble her.

"Ah, well…" He stoked her hair with the tips of his fingers. "It is a venerable ancient oak tree near the village of Edwinstowe in the heart of Sherwood Forest. Some say it might be one thousand years old. Thirty-three feet across its base it is, with a warm dry hollow at its center, and thick broad branches that stretch out like welcoming arms. People say 'twas there Robin and his men slept. My— Someone from my childhood, who loved tales of Robin much as you do, used to delight in reciting me this poem. It's very old. I'm not sure who wrote it."

A fierce ache seized him. It was sudden, more bitter than sweet. It burned the back of his eyes and seized hold of his throat. For a moment he feared he would be swallowed by the past.

"Robert?" She turned toward him and laid a dainty hand on his chest.

He took several deep breaths, beating back something dark and terrible. "I'm sorry. You should be sleeping. Perhaps another time would be—"

"Noooo. Please. I want to hear it now."

He took her hand in his without thinking, and gathered her close. The heat of her body warmed him, melting some of the chill that had seized him so abruptly. "Then I shall tell it to you as it was told to me. Close your eyes and imagine yourself in Sherwood Forest, with Robin and his Merry Men, beneath a starlit sky sheltered by a mighty oak." After a moment's hesitation, he began to recite in a melodious voice a tale he'd not recalled since his last day as a child.

"'Then taking them to rest, his merry men and he
Slept many a summer's night under the greenwood tree.
From wealthy abbots' chests, and churls' abundant store,
What oftentimes he took, he shar'd amongst the poor:
No lordly bishop came in lusty Robin's way.

To him before he went, but for his pass must pay:
The widow in distress he graciously reliev'd,
And remedied the wrongs of many a virgin
griev'd:
He from the husband's bed no married woman
wan,
But to his mistress dear, his loved Marian,
Was ever constant known, which wheresoe'er she
came,
Was sovereign of the woods; chief lady of the
game:
Her clothes tuck'd to the knee, and dainty braided
hair.
With bow and quiver arm'd, she wander'd here
and there,
Amongst the forests wild; Diana never knew
Such pleasures, nor such harts as Mariana
slew…'"

As his voice trailed off he felt her go limp against him. His knuckles brushed her cheek. "Good night, Lady Nichols," he whispered in her hair.

Hope drifted to sleep under a leafy bower, her bow over her shoulder, her husband's hand in hers. Her last thought before she slipped away was that Robin looked a great deal like her Robert.

CHAPTER NINETEEN

FOR THREE LONG DAYS Hope lay abed. Her swollen face was iced for twenty minutes every hour. She felt sorry for creating so much work for the new maid, whose job it was to trek back and forth from the straw-and-sawdust-lined icehouse deep in the cellar. The ice and possets seemed to be doing the trick, though. The pain was down to a manageable roar and she could open her eye again, though the effort hurt and burned. It was still hard to read, or eat or drink, and she had little to do but listen to Rose's chatter and play on her bed with Daisy. The kitten's antics kept her amused for a while, but she was getting restless.

Her husband was a tyrant. He'd given orders she was not to leave her bed until he said so, but he'd hardly visited her over the past three days other than to poke his head in her room and leave. She had a vague recollection of him staying by her side the day she was injured, and even telling her a poem late in the night, but she was beginning to think she had imagined it. It had been about Robin Hood after all, and everyone knew laudanum could make people imagine some very strange things.

It surprised her how easily she had come to think of him as husband, and she supposed she was lucky as far as those things went. He was a taciturn man, not easy to know, but he was young and handsome and honorable, it seemed. It was a trait much mocked at court, yet an important one to her. But it was not going to keep her in bed. No husband was going to rule her. It was her face that was injured, not her legs. She could surely walk.

Her determination withered as soon as Rose brought her a mirror. Her face was no longer black and blue. It was black and purple and a sickly green and yellow, and though her eye could open it was still swollen and misshapen. She let out a low moan. "Sweet Jesus, Rose! Why didn't you tell me? What did he do to me? I look like a monster. I can't leave the room looking like this."

"A little face powder, my lady, would make a world of difference and—"

They both looked up to see the captain standing in the door. Rose glared at him, her eyes flashing, while Hope unconsciously put her hand up to hide her face.

"Ladies." Red-faced and stiff, he bowed and then left.

"Robert, wait! I didn't mean to…" Her voice trailed off. He was already gone.

"Rose, I look awful. No wonder he can't bear to see me this way."

"More like he can't bear to see his own handiwork," the maid replied with a disdainful sniff.

"Oh, dear. You might be right. But it's not what you think. I've told you several times that—"

"That you run into his fist, ma'am. That's what my ma used to say, too."

"Well, I'm sorry for your mother, Rose, if that was the case. But I assure you the captain is *not* that way. He is a gentleman. And it wasn't his fist. I ran into his elbow. I don't want to have to explain it again."

"Yes, ma'am." Rose left the room with a handful of sewing and a mutinous tilt to her chin.

TWO DAYS LATER HOPE LEFT her room. The swelling was down considerably, it hardly hurt at all, and she could see. She did stoop to using face powder, which almost made her more uncomfortable and self-conscious than the bruising did, but she was determined to get outside. It was a beautiful midsummer day. Roses, heavy with bees and perfume, spilled over the garden gates and wended their way, lush and colorful, over long abandoned pergola and broken trellises, and up red brick walls.

She walked across the park to the river path, and rambled along its edge. It was a study in contrasts. Lofty branches made a shady canopy overhead, while the sun reflected diamond bright from off the river in a lovely dance of shadow and light. Moving past flowing eddies and around a narrow bend, she came to a place where the water widened and calmed to a slow and lazy flow. She settled on a small hillock, with her back resting against a stately yew.

It was early still and she could hear the gentle plop and see the tiny ripples as here and there a fish would rise. She flung her line into the glistening waters. Oakes had told her the river teemed with bream and pike and gudgeon, but fishing was just an excuse to enjoy a day by the river, and she flipped her line from the water before a long dark shadow could make its strike.

I love it here. I like the people. This man fascinates me and I think of little else. But Charles is married and might summon me soon. What in God's name am I supposed to do?

Relax and enjoy yourself, a voice seemed to answer, and she determined that as long as she might that was exactly what she'd do.

She had just dozed off to the quiet shushing of the river when a panicked Irish brogue woke her from her sleep.

"My lady! My lady! You are wanted at the house! You must come at once. The king's messenger is here."

Her heart seized in her chest. No! She wasn't ready. She didn't want to see him. She had no wish to go.

The visitor, dressed very smartly in Stuart livery, waited in the drawing room with Robert. His eyes looked startled when he saw her and he perused her up and down. "My Lady Newport?"

"Yes, sir. And you are?" She was acutely aware of her black eye, bruised face and disheveled appearance. What in God's name was the man to think?

"John Carpenter, at your service, madam." He removed his brightly plumed hat to perform a deep bow. "I come with gifts, for your kitchen, and a message from His Majesty. Might we speak in private?"

Hope glanced at her glowering husband, sitting in the corner with his arms folded and his long legs stretched in front of him, his booted feet crossed. "Whatever you have to say, you can say in front of my husband, Mr. Carpenter." Robert gave her a quick look, but she couldn't read his expression.

"Very well! His Majesty has sent you ten barrels of Rhenish and a fine haunch of venison to celebrate your wedding and his own marital bliss. He wishes you to know that he thinks of you often and hopes that you are well." He turned to stare at Robert as if he were some species of insect. Robert straightened suddenly as if he were about to get up and she hurried over to stand beside him, placing a hand on his shoulder. His glower worsened but he grunted and settled back down.

Not to be intimidated, the messenger continued, though his voice was pitched a little higher and his eye seemed to have developed a nervous twitch. "His Majesty is most concerned that he hasn't heard from you. He has sent you several letters but received no reply."

He stared at Robert as he spoke, as if accusing him, and now Robert was staring at her with a look of surprise. "I—I have received His Majesty's letters, of course. I had not thought they required an answer. I…" *I threw them away without even looking. Has he ordered me back to court before now?*

"His Majesty simply wishes to know that you are well. He has asked me to report back on it, madam."

"Oh. Oh! Oh, this. The bruises. You need not concern yourself with that, Mr. Carpenter. His Majesty is well aware of what a fumble-heels I am. I came around a corner mounting a staircase, not paying attention with a book in hand. My husband was coming down in too great a hurry at exactly the same time. I was almost upon him when we noticed each other. I gave a spring to the side to avoid him and he did the very same. Unfortunately we both jumped to the same side. It will be an amusing story once the bruises fade," she added ruefully.

"Indeed, madam. And where are your husband's bruises?"

"My husband's? Why would he have any? He was coming down as I was going up and he is already much taller than me. I assure you, sir, I am not some cowed and meek—"

"Enough!" The captain stood. He towered over the messenger by several inches. "The man is simply doing his job, Hope. See he gets a meal and a bed if he wants it. And you, Carpenter. Your message is delivered. You have asked your questions and my wife has answered. As you can see she is still recovering from her ordeal. The questions are done now. Once you've rested you'll be on your way. I know you're here to see my wife, but please be sure to thank His Majesty from me for *all* his gifts."

Robert didn't know why the messenger's visit had made him so angry but there was no doubt it had struck a nerve. The king had invaded his home, his privacy. To check on her. To remind them both to whom she belonged. And what if the messenger had come to summon her back to the palace? It was just the kind of thing he had feared when he'd first agreed to this scheme. But he'd grown to care for her more than he'd expected. He'd come to think of her as his since then. How much worse now? Was this to be his future? To see his wife at the beck and call of another man? She said not. She said she was done with him. And she hadn't answered his letters. But she knew as well as he did that one day the summons would come. *What then?*

HOPE HAD FELT HIS WITHDRAWAL at dinner. He had barely spoken to her except to say goodnight. She'd been so afraid the messenger had come to call her back to London, but Robert had offered no comfort, no reassurance. Now, alone in her room, she couldn't help but wonder at how quick she was to look to him expecting such things.

A gust of wind scattered her bed curtains and she crossed to the window to look outside. The moon was high and distant tonight, the clouds formless black shadows scudding by. There was no hint of thunder, and no taste of rain. Just a harrying wind whipping moon-washed trees that shimmered silver-grey in the pallid light. She heard what sounded like a sigh behind her, and whirled, heart pounding, but there was nothing there. She picked up Daisy from her nest among the pillows, comforted by her silky warmth and lusty purr. *Why does the wind always blow when we argue?* And why did the house sometimes seem to breathe?

There was a rustling sound from the corner. She scrambled for a candlestick and backed from the room, waving it all around her, Daisy clutched to her chest. *I love this house, but I'm not at all sure that it loves me.* Braving shadowed hallways and echoing floors, she headed for the room where she always felt comfortable. The quaint little cabinet off the north wing. It was too warm for a fire, so she lit several candles for light. Even this little room, her haven, seemed off somehow tonight. Above or below the mournful howl of the wind, she thought she heard someone scream.

"It's all right, Daisy. There's naught to be afraid of." A floorboard squeaked behind her and she gave a small scream.

Robert grinned as he took in the scene. The kitten was hidden behind her back, he assumed for its own protection, and she wielded her candlestick like a weapon, held over her head, ready to throw or strike.

"I'm sorry. I didn't mean to startle you. What are you doing down here at this hour, Hope?"

"I couldn't sleep. I told you before I'm often up at night."

He walked over to her and gently pried the candlestick from her hands, replacing it with a glass of brandy. "So am I," he said with a weary sigh. "There are few who brave this part of the house in daylight, let alone at night."

She gave him a sharp glance. "Really?"

"Indeed." He guided her to an armchair, released Daisy from her grip and sat her down. "Why not read a book, nice and safe in your room?" He settled himself in the chair beside hers and rested his feet on an expensive-looking marquetry table.

"Sometimes, I hear things in my room. Like…a woman crying, or somebody screaming, or footsteps and such. It…it is such an old house. There are many odd noises."

"Yes. Have you been speaking with the servants while I was away?"

"Why?"

"Because they will fill your head with nonsense. Banshees and faeries and ghosts and such."

The brandy warmed her somewhat, and his presence warmed her more. "They say…"

"The house is haunted. Yes. It's not. What you hear are only night birds, calling to their mates. There are many that live in these parts. Tawny owls can sound like mournful calling, and a barn owl's cry sounds very much like a scream. Mockingbirds can mimic many sounds, such as squeaky gates, barking dogs and even people whistling. There's nothing to be afraid of."

"Just because you are not afraid, it doesn't mean there's nothing to fear. Mrs. Overton herself told me about the Fair Maid of Clifton who married a richer man when her betrothed was gone. 'Tis said he was driven wild with grief and drowned himself in the river. This river. Near here."

"Yes, I've heard the story…. 'Then all was still, the wave was rough no more, the river swept as sweetly as before.' Except it happened a good ten miles from here."

"Did it really?" Her eyes shone with excitement.

"Yes. But that's not all. When Margaret Clifton heard of the fate of her lover, seized by guilt she joined her moldering paramour in his watery grave." The last was spoke in a eerie whisper.

"You don't believe in ghosts, do you, Robert?"

The kitten had climbed up his legs and settled on

his chest and he scratched its head absently. "No. No, I don't."

There was a sadness to his voice and she wanted to ask him more.

"If anything haunts you here, elf, it's of your own making."

"And what is it that haunts you, Captain?"

He groaned and poured another drink. "Something worse than ghosts or demons."

"What can be worse than that?" Her apprehension showed in her voice.

"Memories," he answered after a long pause. "Memories haunt me, Hope."

"Ah, yes." She nodded. "I have those, too." She wished she could reach out to touch him without it being misconstrued.

His eyes were far away, somewhere else, but he gifted her with a tired smile. "The gardens were my sister's favorite place," he offered after several minutes of silence.

She looked at him, startled. She'd come to accept that certain topics were closed to her. She knew he was an intensely private man. "The girl in the miniature?" she asked carefully.

"Yes. Caroline. She died several years ago. I apologize. You have worked so hard, all of you have, to restore the house. I really was very pleased with the results. I didn't mean to shout, it's just…"

"You didn't want me intruding."

"Yes… No… It's not you. No one has touched it in years. She had special places there. The secret garden and such. We…" He gave a painful sigh. "I just prefer to leave them untouched. It's like holding on to the last piece of her. There are the orchards, though, and the old conservatory, though it is much run-down. I've been thinking you might occupy yourself with those." He made a fluid motion with his hands and fingers. "Perhaps you can conjure pineapples."

She grinned. "Perhaps I can."

"If you don't go back to London. You didn't answer his letters?"

"No. I didn't even read them. I'm not even angry with him anymore. I just…have no interest. I was afraid today…"

He looked at her carefully. "Afraid that he'd summoned you home?"

"I've never had a real home, Robert. Not one that was mine. The closest thing I have to home is here. I was afraid you'd let me go without a backward glance."

He laughed at that and took her hand in his. "Look at me, Hope." His eyes were warm and his voice compelling. "How would that be possible? Cressly has come to life since you've been here. She was alone and empty and you've infused her with your soul. You *do* have a home. You're sitting in it. Whatever might happen, she'll always await you, and you'll always be welcome here."

She was furiously blinking back tears, but one escaped and rolled down her cheek. He brushed it gently with his thumb. "If he summons me to London, would you come with me? To stand as my husband and bring me back home?"

"Yes. If that's what you want. Now…do you think that we might start over again?"

"How do you mean?" Her eyes were luminous. She wasn't certain that he really meant it. It might all change the next time they had a fight. She'd been given a house to use before, but it was the first time she'd ever been offered a home.

"As if I'd just come home. Before I snarled at you and chased you from the gardens or sent you tumbling down the stairs."

She gave him a bright smile. "Of course we can. I'm so pleased to see you back safe, Captain. How was your business in London?"

He hadn't really been expecting that question, but he answered as best as he could. "I have a powerful enemy I have to deal with, Lady Nichols, who attacks from hiding after many years away. The trip proved unfruitful. The matter remains unsettled. That's all I can tell you at this time."

"I see." She blinked several times, somewhat taken aback, but she had never lacked for persistence. "Are you or Cressly in any immediate danger?"

"No. I've an unlikely ally in London who watches

my back. Now if you please, let's talk of something else."

"Very well. Did you really tell me a tale of Robin Hood?"

"I did. I felt obliged after bashing you in the face."

"I told you then, I tell you now, you make too much of it, but I am pleased to know you've come round to a more sympathetic point of view."

"I haven't," he said with a rueful chuckle. "One should never argue with someone whose head might be addled. I was simply humoring you. Speaking of which, you should really be warm in your bed."

"Would you escort me back and see me settled? My room makes me rather nervous this night." She looked at him from beneath lowered lashes, a mischievous smile on her face, but the tension in her voice was real.

He helped her up and handed her Daisy, then wrapped an arm around her waist and drew her close. She was trembling and he gave her a quick hug before starting down the hall. "I assure you, wife, these days there is nothing that walks Cressly more dangerous than me."

Hope was surprised when they reached her room. The atmosphere felt peaceful, brighter. The tension and heaviness were gone. It was very late and when he bundled her into her bed, he flopped down beside her.

"Captain Robert Nichols at your service, madam.

Household patrol and, ah…spectral night watch. I guarantee you a peaceful sleep." He reached for a coverlet and tucked it around her shoulders, noting as he did the glass swan on her bedside table. His lips quirked in a smile.

"Did I thank you, Robert, for the lovely room? I meant to."

"You mean the one that is crowded with ghosts?" He wrapped her in a warm embrace and she settled close against him. "Sleep now. After a knock on the head you need it. You're safe here with me."

She was too tired to argue. Feeling safe and protected she drifted toward sleep.

"My but you're a naughty wench, Hope Nichols," he whispered a moment later. His voice sounded positively sinful and highly amused.

"Mmm?" Try as she might, fatigue had claimed her and she could rouse herself no further.

"I've only just noticed the mirror above your bed. Where else have you hidden them? Must I look in the salon, the library…above the billiard table?"

With a wicked smile, she fell asleep.

CHAPTER TWENTY

ROBERT NICHOLS WOULD ONCE HAVE sworn he had no strong emotions left. But Hope stirred something in him. Of that there was no doubt. Whatever her past, there was something sweet and genuine about her. Her passion for life lit a spark in everything surrounding her, including him. Caroline would have liked her. He couldn't pretend that he didn't anymore. He liked her far too much, and he was so very tired of being alone. Last night he had talked with her of Caroline, for God's sake, if only a little. It was something he had never done with anyone before. Yet she mustn't know the truth about him, what he had and had not done. She would surely leave in horror if she did. *How many have you killed?*

When he was a fighting man he used to dream of going home. He thought Cressly was what he wanted. But it was nothing but an empty pile of brick and stone, filled with painful memories. Hope made it a home. Last night he had told her so. Last night she had asked him to stand with her should she be called away. Now he had something worth keeping, something that mattered, and something to lose.

Even as he searched the grounds looking for her it pleased and terrified him. A soldier knew how thin the line between life and death. It was a knife edge, a moment, a breath. Only a fool would deny himself warmth and comfort when it came his way like a gift. Her past didn't matter, as long as she didn't insist on knowing too much of his. And though he knew it could only lead to heartache, he couldn't help but seek her out.

He found her on the riverbank just before sunset, as the countryside burned green and gold. A fishing rod lay abandoned on the ground beside her, next to a small basket of fishing corks and clever feather flies. Unaware of his presence, she slowly twirled a daisy in her hand, carefully plucking petals one by one and muttering to herself in French, *"Il m'aime un peu, il m'aime beaucoup, il m'aime pas du tout."*

She'd tied her hair back off her face with a ribbon that threatened to become undone. A lustrous curl had escaped its bonds to brush her cheek and throat. If he hadn't known anything of her background he might have thought her a disheveled angel. Perhaps she was.

Riveted he approached her, hunger sparking in his eyes.

"Il m'aime—"

"Good evening, Hope."

"Merde!" In her surprise she kicked the pole and had to scramble down the bank to stop it from sliding

into the river. He reached for the back of her dress just as she lunged for the rod, and hauled her back upright with her prize clutched in her hand. "Good lord, Captain. You nearly stopped my heart!"

"I also just saved you from a soaking. Who were you dreaming of as you tore apart that poor defenseless flower?"

She was certain he could see her blush, for she could feel it burning her face. "It's just a silly children's game." But there was nothing childish about the thrill of pleasure she felt when he offered her his arm. There was nothing childish about the thrill that ran through her whenever he smiled, or the way her skin pricked and her heart hammered whenever she felt his touch.

"Will you walk with me? Your rod and basket will be safe stowed under the tree."

She answered by sliding her arm through his, and they ambled along the bank together. It was nearing midsummer and the nights were warm. Dusk descended in layers of lavender, streaked with brilliant dabs of orange. A low-lying mist blanketed the river and valley, and the treetops floated above it, resembling islands in a lake.

It was clear overhead, and as they turned back after walking a mile or two, the first stars made their appearance, blinking on one after the other, as if lit by some unseen hand.

"It's so beautiful here, Robert."

"Do you ever miss London?"

"No. At first I was too angry. Then I was too busy. And then…"

"And then?"

"I found I was enjoying myself. With Rose and Daisy and Oakes. Sometimes even you." She gave him a quick sideways glance.

He pulled her to a stop under the yew. "And now?" His voice was rough, warm, and it sent chills up her spine.

"Now I find myself longing for something. But I'm not sure what it is." The sky was glowing now, a vast pulsing mystery. Behind them was the dull rumble of the river, between them, their own heat and the steady rhythm of heart and lung.

"I am sorry, Robert, that you were forced into this. You have been quite kind under the circumstances. When I first saw you, you reminded me of some knight of old. You still do. I can only guess what you thought of me."

He took a step closer, leaning in to her. When he spoke his voice was low and seductive; his lips almost brushed her cheek. "Can you? I remember it clearly. I always will. Those mischievous eyes, that tumbling hair tangled through with vines and flowers." He brushed her cheek with his knuckles, his touch feather-light as he caught the errant lock of hair between his fingers.

"I thought you were some magical creature full of

grace and light and tremendous power." He felt her tremble as he drew her wayward tendril along her collarbone and up the underside of her jaw. "For a moment I was paralyzed and forgot how to breathe. A sharp pain pierced my heart and I grew dizzy. Everything receded. Nothing existed but you." He drew the unruly curl to his lips and kissed it, before tucking it gently behind her ear. "Elf-shot I was. I knew right away what you were."

Her smile was brilliant, her eyes outshone the stars. "You said that was because of my mirrors."

His full-throated laughter was carried downstream on the river.

"What are you doing here, Robert?"

"Chasing you. Following you. Wooing you, I think."

"You think? Oh, look! Look all around us. It's beautiful!" Her voice was hushed and filled with awe.

Her lips were beautiful. Her eyes were beautiful. But he tore his gaze away. Though the moon was but a sliver, the woods were alive with flickering patterns of glowing light. Some danced through the air emitting multiple flashes, some answered with a stately response from the bushes, and others seemed to line the path, glowing on the ground. "Your relatives and fairy friends?"

She grinned and ducked her head.

"It's been so long since I've sat out on a summer's night just to enjoy it. Will you join me?" he asked.

He sat on the ground, his back against a tree, and reached for her hand to help her down. She lost her balance and giggled as she landed in his lap.

"Ooof! You are remarkably solid for a being of grace and light." Despite his teasing, he was quick to grab hold of her when she tried to get off him, encircling her waist with one strong arm while wrapping the other around her shoulders and pulling her down into his warmth. She settled back against his chest. This beautiful night there was no other place in the world she would rather be.

"It almost seems as if they are talking to each other," she said, breathless.

"They are. I used to sit out all night to watch them as a boy. This is the time of year they go looking for a mate."

"It's fantastical. Magical. A creature that makes its own light!"

"Yes, elf. Much like you do. A rare and wondrous creature indeed." He nuzzled her throat, trailing sweet hot kisses along the curve of her neck and jaw. She moaned when he nibbled the sensitive skin behind her ear, and her mouth parted when he caught her bottom lip, caressing it with his thumb. He lowered his mouth, stopping a breath away from hers. She snuggled tight against him, reaching her arms around his neck as he pulled her closer still. Sweet sensations curled around her. She felt as if something deep inside her was melting. Not just in her body, but in her soul. It made her feel tender and wild and vulnerable.

His knuckles grazed her cheekbone and he cupped her jaw. His mouth brushed hers in a feather-light kiss and he growled low in his throat as he tasted her lips. She smelled like sunshine and summer, and her lips were sweet as strawberries. He hugged her, enjoying the feel of her in his arms as she squirmed against him. *Christ!* His cock was stiff and swollen, wedged between her buttocks with nothing but a few thin layers of linen and silk between them. Every time she shifted, every time she squirmed or wriggled, every move she made was an exquisite agony that set his teeth on edge.

He tugged at her ribbon, freeing her hair so it tumbled about her shoulders in a wild cascade. Spreading his fingers through it he claimed her in a devouring kiss. She could feel him, hard and insistent beneath her, pressing against her bottom, teasing the warm juncture between her thighs. Alive with sensation she arched against him, unable to stop a moan of excitement as his tongue found hers, exploring her mouth in an unhurried teasing dance. She sighed against him as an exquisite fire began to burn.

Insistent hands roamed the contours of her dress, stroking and squeezing, exploring every curve. A gasp escaped her when his fingers brushed the pebbled peaks that thrust against the thin material of her bodice. She turned into his arms with an incoherent cry, reaching under his shirt and tugging it open to slide her hand along his heated skin, reveling in the play of skin and muscle beneath her open palm. Never had a man stirred her like this, with nothing more than a touch and a kiss. Never had a man taken such care.

Groaning, he eased her from his aching lap before she made him spend like an untried youth. She whimpered as he laid her down in the bed of moss and violets carpeting the earth beneath the tree. Silencing her murmured protest with a lush kiss, he covered her body with his own. "I have long wanted to kiss you just like this, in a bed of flowers under the stars," he said in a husky whisper. "I've wanted it ever since I saw you dancing barefoot in the park. Even when we argued, when we were angry and not speaking, I couldn't get that picture from my mind."

As he spoke, his finger traced a path along her décolletage. Her breath caught in her throat. She closed he eyes and shivered as her breasts swelled and hardened. She thrust them upward, begging his attention. Her nipples strained against soft linen, but it failed to give her the release she sought. She swallowed, watching mesmerized as he drew the tip of his finger down the front of her bodice, gently tugging clasps and ribbons.

"Please, Robert, don't tease me."

"But you're like a pretty package, just waiting to be opened. Waiting and teasing are half the fun." He meant what he said. One took a whore to satisfy an urge, but surely a man should take his time to savor his lover or wife. When he took her he wanted her as wild for him as he was for her. Still, a gentleman didn't leave his woman wanting. With a wicked smile he unhooked the clasps of her gown.

Hope felt his gaze like a sensuous caress. Her body felt tender, excited, aching, and her heart beat madly as his finger gently circled her rigid tips. Bolts of pleasure pulsed through her body when he plumped a breast and drew a nipple into his mouth. His teeth bit gently as he teased and nibbled, and stroked her through her soaking chemise with his hot, wet tongue. She moaned and clutched his hair, riding wild sensations that traveled through nerve and skin and sinew to throb at her core.

Entwining one hand in a mass of lustrous curls, he returned his lips to hers, plundering her mouth with lips and tongue as his free hand continued to pinch and fondle until she cried out her pleasure, and then he kissed her some more. They kissed and cuddled through the night, slow and tender, fierce and demanding, playful and teasing, and he brought her to pleasure two times more.

He fell asleep just before dawn, his head resting on her breast, next to her heart. She stroked his hair and bent to kiss the thin white scar that creased his cheek, barely visible beneath his morning's growth of beard. One lone star remained in the sky. It didn't sparkle. It glowed. Wisps of mist drifted through the trees, lingering like the last river spirits of the night. She glowed, too, still enraptured by sweet sensation, though all they'd done was little more than kiss. Last night was a first. A dangerous and delightful new experience. She had been auctioned off, summoned, bargained with and paid for…but she had never been wooed before.

CHAPTER TWENTY-ONE

HOPE FEARED THAT FOR THE first time in her life she might be truly in love. She'd seen it before. It was much like a sickness. It left its victims trembling and broken. Where once they were happy, now they were but shades of themselves; pining, unhappy and insecure. She could count the happy couples she knew on one hand. She had yet to meet a man who could be trusted completely, and Charles had been bad enough. She couldn't imagine how terrible it would be, to truly love a man, and then be betrayed.

But the captain had the trust of his men and servants, people who'd known him for much of his life. Attractive as he was, he was no womanizer, and he had shown honor regarding her funds. His word meant something, even when given to a woman. He paid attention, took notice, made her feel valued. He wooed her where there was no need. Could he be different? She fervently hoped so, because it was too late to go back now. He'd pierced her guard and found her heart and she was thoroughly enjoying being courted.

He took her along with him to visit the village and

see the extent of their lands. He even called them that, as if they were hers, too. He came fishing with her, and today he indulged her when she asked him to teach her how to use a sword. It was a very warm day. He'd removed his shirt and she'd feasted her eyes on his naked torso.

"You must keep your body balanced so you can strike or parry without being hit. Always have your feet shoulder-width and when you move, move so your legs are spread apart. Proper footing is the key." He circled her, regarding her critically. She was wielding a light rapier and dressed in boys' clothes. He came to stand behind her, making adjustments to her arms and shoulders and setting her feet by sliding his hand down her legs.

"There. Much better." He nodded his approval. "The more of your foot planted flat on the ground, the greater your strength when attacking. Slide your feet rather than lifting them and you will be hard to knock off balance. Keeping your posture straight and your chest facing forward will keep you stable as you make your swing."

He adjusted her elbows and placed a hand on her bottom, pushing to straighten her posture. She glared at him through narrowed eyes when he gave it a firm squeeze. He leaned over her shoulder, his breath feathering the hair on the nape of her neck. "It also allows you to escape an enemy's blow with a simple twist…*if* you maintain the proper position."

"Like so?"

He grinned and adjusted her position yet again, pushing her bottom forward to tuck it in, brushing the outer curves of her breasts as he set her arms and shoulders, and sliding his hands from thigh to ankle to set her feet. "So many mistakes. One wonders if it's wise to place pointy objects in your hands."

"I am a fumble-foot," she said. "I expect I shall need lots and lots of practice. Could I ever win a fight? Against someone like you?" Her voice was suddenly serious.

"No, love. I am stronger, faster and have greater speed. I've had a sword in my hand since I could walk and…in my younger days I had a great deal of dedication. Against someone like me you need cunning and guile. A smart fighter is aware of his surroundings at all times. It's better the sun is in your opponent's eyes than yours. Everyone has a weakness. Most opponents will underestimate you, which can be used to your advantage. You don't try to best someone like me. You use your surroundings and watch for weakness and when the moment is right, you escape him. Besides violet eyes and a saucy bottom, what do you think is my weakness?"

"Your size?"

"How? My reach is longer and I'm very fast."

"Would it make you tire quicker?"

"Smart girl! If I didn't practice every day it might." He chuckled and ruffled her hair. "So your best move is a good defense, sliding from side to side until your opponent tires."

"But what if I just wanted to show off? To impress other ladies?"

"Ah! A dilettante I see. Come. I will show you some attack positions and some very pretty flourishes."

Watching his muscles flex and his body move with fluid power as she stood but feet away caused a fluttering feeling inside her that didn't help her concentration. She licked her lips as he whirled his blade, jumping high off the ground and twisting. He landed on one knee with his sword thrust into an invisible body. His sandy hair, almost blond from the sun, hung loose about bronzed shoulders, and his stomach rippled with muscle as, tossing and catching and twirling the sword, he strode toward her. *Dear Lord, how I want him.*

"Enough practice for today?" His eyes watched her with amusement.

He was showing off for me! She grinned her appreciation. "Yes, thank you, Robert."

Her cheeks dimpled when she laughed, which was something she did a lot, and her eyes sparked with mischief. But it was the seductive sway of her hips and the tight fit of her breeches as she walked away that made him decide he ought to give her lessons every day.

CHAPTER TWENTY-TWO

HOPE DIDN'T SEE HER HUSBAND at dinner. He had gone to the village with Sergeant Oakes to discuss building a bridge and new road. It would provide employment to some of those whose fortunes had suffered during and after the war. She didn't doubt it was true, but she knew he did other things, as well. He had men watching the roads from London, and she'd seen suspiciously well-armed laborers with spyglasses tramping the fields and hills. She also had the feeling when she saw him practice that he was preparing for something that lay ahead. *The enemy from London?* There was so much about him she didn't know. She knew what she wanted, though. She waited for him in the upper hall in a blue silk bed gown, amusing Daisy with a ball of yarn.

His eyes smoldered when he saw her. "I have seen that look before, madam. You are bent on seduction."

"And shall I succeed?"

She held out her hand. He took it, and she pulled him down the hall and through her door. He slipped into her room with no hesitation.

She sat on her bed, her heart racing, and he pulled

off his boots and stretched out alongside her, his head resting on his bent arm. He tugged lightly at the loose curls that tumbled down her back, and then he tugged at the shoulder of her gown. With a sibilant sigh the silky garment slipped off her shoulders to pool around her waist. He caught her wrist and pulled gently, and with a soft moan she slid into his waiting arms.

Covering his throat and jaw with steamy kisses, she worked at his shirt until she pulled it free. She trailed her fingers across his rib cage, pressing her palm against his heartbeat, then lightly brushed his waist and hip and bent to kiss his belly. Groaning and twisting he arched against her as her fingernails grazed the front of his breeches. She spread her hand wide, cupping his straining erection, and gave a tight squeeze.

"Christ! Sweetheart," he moaned, jerking against her as his hand joined with hers, hurrying to undo his buttons.

"No," she whispered, flicking his ear with her tongue. "Lie still, sweet Robert, with your hands behind your head, or the play is done."

He took a deep shuddering breath and clasped his hands behind his head as his cock swelled from base to tip. She plucked at his buttons one by one, fiddling and tugging, pulling them this way and that as his helpless erection jumped to her touch. He gritted his teeth as she loosed the last button. Night air swept his skin like a soft caress. She pulled roughly at his breeches and he raised his hips to help her, cursing in a mixture of pleasure, frustration and violent aching.

His eyes flamed with passion as she teased him with her tongue.

"Mmm." She caught his look and arched a brow, smiling seductively as she pointed up.

"Oh, God," he gasped with a weak chuckle, lying back on the bed. She massaged his scrotum with one hand as the other gripped the base of his penis, sliding up and down with the play of her tongue. Still watching in the mirror he combed his fingers through her hair, spreading it out like a dark curtain. Her slim back was arched and the firm buttocks he'd admired were on deliciously rounded display. His fascination was brief, though. Watching in the mirror seemed to put things at a distance, and he was beginning to feel dizzy again.

Growling, he reached for her, hauling her up his body to claim her lips in a burning kiss. He groaned and turned into her, pushing her back against the pillows, throwing one long leg across hers.

Skin burning, aching in every part, Hope thrust her nipples forward and he blazed a trail of kisses along her jaw and down her throat, stopping to nuzzle her neck and shoulders before rasping her peak, kissing and suckling with lips and tongue. She writhed beneath him as his hands roamed her body, petting, soothing, teasing, tweaking, until every nerve quickened, anticipating his touch. Lowering his head, he rested it against the soft curve or her belly, grazing her skin with the stubble of his jaw. She giggled in protest and pushed at his shoulders and he looked up at her and grinned. His smile was dazzling. It stole her breath, and she knew the stranger she'd married had stolen her heart.

"You should smile more often," she whispered, lacing her fingers through his hair.

Instead of answering, he gripped her thighs and parted them, then bent to taste her, stroking her with his tongue. She gasped and gripped his shoulders as wild bursts of pleasure shot through her body, radiating from her center, through skin and nipples and lips and fingers, melting her insides and curling her toes. She bucked against him in a delirium of wild sensation as his fingers joined his tongue. He licked and teased, nibbled and petted, and swirled wet and hot against her nub.

Her life, her future, her very survival had always hinged upon self-control, but this man stripped it from her as easily as he stripped her clothes. She called his name, begging him to take her as wave after wave of pleasure coursed through her body, and when he rose to capture her lips and drive inside her, rocking her hard as her hips rose to meet him, she turned her back on a lifetime of hard-won lessons. Poised on the brink, she willingly let go.

He led her into a full-blown storm that shook her

like a leaf as burst after burst of wild energy exploded inside her, thundering through her body and taking her soaring. It felt like rebirth. It felt like renewal. It felt like a new world was waiting alongside this man. A whimper of fear escaped her. *God help me, I am lost!*

"Elf?" His voice was gentle, soothing, concerned, as he wrapped her in a warm embrace. "I didn't hurt you, did I? God knows I was carried away."

"No," she murmured, touching his cheek. *But you can now. You can hurt me worse than anyone can.* "It was wonderful, Robert." She felt a panicked need to know him better. She needed to know to protect herself, even though it was too late. There was no better time to talk to a man than when his mind and body were unguarded and at ease.

She snuggled against him, resting her chin against his chest, pillowed on her folded hands, and decided to start with something easy.

"Have you had many mistresses, Robert?"

"Are you jealous, wife? Counting you, I've had one."

"But where did you learn that from, then? How did you become so…responsive, to a woman's needs?"

"I am a soldier. I'm not a monk. And as I told you before, a man who fights must learn to be aware and observe. Pleasing a woman is not all that different. Pay attention, respond, gauge the reaction."

Is that all it was to him? A battle, sport, exercise?

"'Tis difficult to do with you, though. I tend to lose myself in the moment. I apologize if I was too rough. I can usually exercise more self-control."

"So can I," she said with a happy grin. "Did you enjoy the mirror?"

"I certainly enjoyed the unfettered view of your delicious bum." He rubbed the object of his admiration with a warm hand as he spoke.

"Ah! But I fear it made you dizzy."

"The novelty was nice, but yes, it did after a while. It made me feel as if I stood outside of things, too. More observer than participant."

"I'll get rid of it. It was a joke really. After you said the only place I might keep one was in my room."

He chuckled and ruffled her hair. "I would say put them in your conservatory, but I fear if you did I'd be constantly walking into them, mistaking them for walkways and pretty paths."

"Mmm. We don't want that.... Robert?"

"Yes?"

"Have you ever been in love?"

"Why all these questions?" His fingers brushed the outer curve of her breast. "Surely, under the circumstances, we have better things to do."

She raised her head to look him in the eyes. "Though my life has been very different from yours, my survival has depended on noticing things, too. There's a sadness in your eyes at times, and something dark. You said you were haunted by memories. I wondered if there was some lost lover, who still has a claim on you."

His hand stopped, and he lifted it away. Her stomach plummeted and she feared she'd made a bad mistake.

"No. There is no lost love for whom I grieve. Just a lost… Never mind. I did have a great admiration for Elizabeth Walters. As a youth I served under her father. She was a sad and lonely child and I enjoyed paying attention to her. It seemed my duty to care for her when her father died…but I was more disgruntled then heartbroken when she chose another."

"Then what—"

"My memories are nothing fit for your ears, Hope." His voice was cold.

She snorted. "Not fit for my ears? From whence do you think I've come, Robert? What do you think I haven't heard or seen?"

"True horror, sweetling. You watch it in your plays."

"You forget. I grew up in the streets of London. I have seen the dead, frozen in place, their arms stretched out for alms. I have seen young girls raped. I have seen men murdered for an accidental insult. I have seen more than you think."

He cocked his head and looked at her strangely. "Yet you seem so innocent, almost pure. How do you manage it?"

She drew herself up, affronted. "I am a great actress I suppose. Perhaps I should have stayed with the stage." Hurt and angry, she got up to leave even though it was her room, but he caught her wrist and drew her back.

"I meant no insult, love. Not at all." His voice was soothing. Warm again. "I merely wondered what magic kept the light within you alive through the dark. It was something I never managed."

"I…" She blinked, shocked that he'd opened a firmly locked door, if only a crack.

"Perhaps because you were a witness, and not a part."

"I lost my maidenhead at auction, Robert. I was a part."

"I've heard the story. Your mother sold you. It was not your doing."

"No. Not then. But after that I sold myself."

"To survive."

"To prosper."

"You weren't very good at it, though, were you?"

"Why must you insult me? Not good enough to please Charles, you mean? Not good enough to please you?"

"Hush, love. It's not an attack." He folded his arms around her, pulling her close. "I watched you the night we married. Your joy and spontaneity were so genuine. You seem to me ill-suited to your role. Lacking the detachment and cold-bloodedness required to keep from being hurt. That's not wise for a courtesan, I would think. "

"No, Robert. You're right. It isn't." She wasn't sure why she was crying. So many hurts, so many disappointments. And it didn't escape her that he hadn't really answered her question.

He pulled a coverlet around them both, and used his discarded shirt to dry her tears.

"Tell me of your life, Hope. I've ofttimes wondered who you are."

Did she really want to remind him of who and what she was? But if she didn't share her past with him, how could she expect him to share his with her?

CHAPTER TWENTY-THREE

"If I tell you of my ghosts, Robert, will you tell me of yours?"

"My memories, my dreams, are ugly things. It's only with you I forget them. That bothered me at first. It seemed somehow…neglectful. But I've grown to like it. Despite…" He waved his hand as if waving something away. "It's been a long time since I've woken in the morning looking forward to the day. Can we leave it be for now? Tonight I'd like to hear about you."

"I'm sure you have already. There's many a story or lampoon about me. I've been called Cinder wench and Cinder whore because of my humble beginnings."

"Hush!" He pressed a finger against her lips. "I want to hear *your* story. Not the words of jealous rivals and spiteful courtiers."

"I was raised in a brothel, Robert. Called the Merry Strumpet. No one made that up. It belonged to my mother, so I was a princess of sorts. I had a pretty kitten and a room of my own. I'm told my father was a captain like you, though he died in debtor's prison, and before my mother became a bawd she was a whore."

"Your father was a military man? That helps explain your combative spirit."

"I am very good-natured when...when my good nature is not being abused!"

"I am but teasing, Hope. Though you rather prove my point. Could it be your mother was once a lady of good circumstance, and misfortune and poverty, rather than depravity, brought her so low? Many were reduced to dire circumstances before and after the war."

"Reduced to being a brandy-soaked bawd who auctioned her daughter's virginity and drowned in a ditch after a drunken ramble about town?"

"Ah... Yes...well..."

"It's no matter to me. I arranged a lovely service for her and placed a monument at St. Martin-in-the-Fields. I'm not ashamed of who I am, Robert."

"How is it you are so accomplished and speak so well, with such humble beginnings? Even a poor accent would have ruined you at court. How have you converted your demons to graces?"

She blushed. She had never been called well-spoken and accomplished before. Nor possessed of graces. "Be careful, Captain, or you will soon be talking like a courtier. It's because I am a good mimic. I try to take all the good I can from the bad, and whenever I've the chance I watch and learn. When my mother sold me, I was still a virgin, but her more lecherous clients sniffed around me from the time I was ten years old. Many were wealthy, aristocratic and traveled. They sent me on errands and told me stories from all over the world. I learned to be comfortable and confident with conversation, and with handling gentlemen from all stations of life."

"You make it sound almost easy."

"I was fourteen when she sold me. He—Sir Charles Edgemont—didn't believe I was untried. He thought my mother cheated him and was very rough and angry at first. It wasn't easy."

"It must have seemed a great betrayal. You must have been frightened and felt very much alone." He thought back to Caroline, and to himself, and his heart felt a sudden stab of pain. "You were so young. I'm sorry, elf." He was at a loss as to what further to say other than offering to kill the man, and he was fairly certain that wasn't the thing to say at this time. But the idea of anyone hurting her angered him.

Hope reached for a flagon of wine from a side table and filled a goblet and tossed most of it back in one swallow. "I hated him at first, though I didn't let it show. I had wanted to escape my life for some time, and I knew he was an opportunity. I used him as much as he used me, but it was her I really hated. I never saw or spoke to her again. The service…when she died. It was a strike at those who mocked me through her. I am glad I did it now, for other reasons. I have come to see her differently since."

Her voice, usually expressive, was a dull monotone. Well used to the art of denial and concealment, he knew by her air of studied indifference it had hurt her far more than she let on. He reached down to scoop up Daisy and deposit her on the bed. Then he scooped up Hope again and gave her a warm hug. She twisted and elbowed him but quickly subsided, leaning back against his chest with a tired sigh.

"It was my lot in life, I suppose, and there was no escaping it. Better to be the plaything of one man then many. I was alone in the world after leaving my mother, and I vowed in the future I'd trust no one but myself. I've not always managed that as well as I might, and whenever I've forgotten I have paid." She thought of Charles and how he'd used her trust to trick her, and she wondered what new hurts trusting Robert might bring. She gave him an assessing look through the mirror but he didn't see.

"I also vowed to take whatever life sent me and use it to my advantage. In the end I had a business relationship of sorts with Edgemont. One that we both honored. It was with him I truly became a courtesan. I learned to manage him, tolerate him, using my charms and his guilt, and in the end he taught me many useful things."

Robert was surprised and a little threatened by

her candor. It seemed a challenge of sorts. *Will she expect the same from me?*

"He felt bad for his initial behavior, of course, and sought to make reparation with gowns and jewelry, some of which I was able to convert to coin and turned into savings. I stayed with him for several years, during which time he introduced me to good manners, good company and good living, and at my insistence hired me a dance master and a tutor who taught me to read and write. We parted when he married. By then the king had returned to London and the theaters had reopened and he left me an entrée though Orange Moll."

"Ow!" Robert snarled as Daisy pounced on his shoulder, digging her claws into his bare chest for purchase, leaving bloody scratch marks as she reached for a loose strand of hair. Wincing, he pried her off him and dropped her in Hope's lap. "Damn it, woman. If Cressly harbors some monstrous being it is this bloodthirsty little thing!"

Hope smiled as the maligned and offended kitten crawled into her arms and bumped her chin with a furry head, then settled down to wash herself in dignified reproach. She hugged her and kissed the top of her head, and Robert did the same to her. She felt a tremendous sense of comfort. She'd never told anyone her story, though people told stories of her. Robert's reaction was reassuring. If he was going to get stiff and judgmental he'd surely have done so by now. It felt good to talk of it with someone else. Like being relieved of a burden, or finding that one was mistaken in thinking themselves alone.

He interrupted her musings by stealing her goblet and downing the rest of her wine. "So you seized the day and launched a career as a great adventuress, by going to work for that famed theater maven and fruit seller, Orange Moll. The one you flattened with your fist."

"Yes! She was freakishly tall, you know."

He smoothed a stray tendril of hair back behind her ear. "I'm sure she seemed so to you."

She looked up, glaring at him in the mirror, and he smiled back smugly, pleased with his joke.

"And so? How did you go from orange girl to hosting parties with His Majesty in Pall Mall?"

Despite her feigned displeasure, her voice grew more animated as she continued her tale. "Moll had a license to sell oranges and sweetmeats and other fruit and candy at the new King's Theater, and I was hired as one of her girls. It paid for rooms at the Cock and Pie tavern just a stone's throw away. It was cramped, but it had a window over the street. I worked six days a week and kept a sixth of my takings, selling oranges in the front row of the pit.

"We also carried messages, paid for by generous tips, between the gallants and actresses backstage. I met many an actor or playwright, and grand lords and ladies, that way. I watched how they dressed. I

listened to their talk and I learned their accent. I discovered that but for their clothes and fancy speech,
they were no better than me, and I teased and joked
and sparred with them that way. It offended some of
the ladies, hiding behind their masks, but it didn't
seem to bother the men. I enjoyed make-believe since
I was a child, and working the pit was an excellent
apprenticeship for the stage."

"It sounds as though you loved it there."

"Oh, yes! I did. I'd never been anyplace so grand.
It was richly appointed and brilliantly lit by chande-
liers, yet very intimate and cozy. Have you been?"

"I have not."

"The pit is taken up with leather benches, and
three galleries rise to the rear. The lowest is for roy-
alty and dignitaries and such, and Charles came there
often. We would stand between the pit and the stage,
with the orchestra behind us, in the center of it all.
It was magical, and of course I saw all the plays. I
imagined taking to the stage as a famous actress.
Buying a fine home, traveling England. It was a wonderful dream."

Robert combed his fingers through her hair as she
talked. It surprised him how easily he slipped into a
comfortable intimacy with this woman. She seemed
to think he judged her, but that was only when he'd
thought her a party to Charles's scheme. The truth
was that he envied her. She could honestly say she
was not ashamed of who she was and he could not.

"And did your realize it? Did you make it to the stage?"

"I did. And the opportunity came sooner than I thought. One of the new actresses failed to appear. It seemed she had caught a lover. And I took her part."

"Did you?" He chuckled and gave her a slight squeeze. "I'm sure you were wonderful."

"I thought so, too," she said with a cocky grin. "Though I had no lines and all I did was hold a torch."

"With great panache, no doubt."

"Of course!" If possible her grin had grown wider. "Enough to secure me another try at it, and then a speaking role. I played a maid who helped her mistress escape an unwanted marriage. We disguised ourselves as two young sparks and I had to wear a waistcoat and breeches. The king started coming more often after that. He's very fond of girls in breeches."

"I can't imagine why."

She shifted position, getting more comfortable, and elbowed him again. "They say he is the first monarch to patronize a public theater. Whenever he came, you could hear the cheers in the streets as his coach rolled up to the door. Everyone in the theater would stand until he took his seat."

"Doubtless he was smitten with your...ah...acting."

"That's kind of you to say but somehow I don't

think so. He always had Castlemaine sticking to him like a burr. I had an admirer in another Charles, though. Charles Hartley, Lord Malcolm." And she had certainly not been prepared for his inflamed and passionate proposition after the curtain came down.

"Lord Malcolm?"

"Yes. He is a court wit and was very charming and—"

"There's no need. I've met the man. He towers close to six feet in his five-inch red heels, writes obnoxious verse and moves from woman to woman like a bee moves from flower to flower. I generally credit women with as much intelligence as a man, except when it comes to languishing, self-important fops with pretty faces and delusions of talent. I swear he's never even learned to use his sword. Please don't tell me you decided to forgo your dream for him."

For several moments the only sound was Daisy's steady purr.

"Hope, I didn't mean—"

"Yes, you did and no, I didn't. I gave up my dream because it soon became apparent that I was not well-suited for dramatic roles. There was an overabundance of comedic actresses, all of them senior to me. It was *then* I decided to take Malcolm's offer. You are right about his character, though. The whole thing lasted less than two months. He did teach me a little about handling my accounts. He found it amusing I had an interest in my own affairs."

"So you picked what he had of a brain in under two months, and then bored with him, you took your leave."

"No!" She laughed in protest. "I went to spend the summer in Epsom with him. He was nice enough, quite charming at first, but though he imagined himself a rake he tried to rule me as a husband, telling me where I might and might not go and what I could and could not do. It led to many arguments and was beginning to wear on my nerves. When he brought home two of his drunken friends and made it clear what they all expected, I packed my bags and left on the morning stage."

"I shall make note not to 'rule you as a husband' and try and ration my store of interesting things for you to learn. Swordplay can take years. Then there is unarmed combat and battle tactics. I know a bit about road building and crop rotation you might find titillating, and can tantalize you for at least a six month with more stories about Sherwood Forest and that foul villain Robin Hood. Once that is exhausted I can teach you to use a pistol."

Hope sighed happily and squeezed his hand. "I think you are neglecting another field of study full of many fruitful lessons I'd like to learn." This was a Robert she was just getting to know, who smiled and joked and comforted. She liked him very much.

He tugged her hair aside and grazed the back of

her neck with his teeth. "That could take years. Now tell me the rest of your story."

She shivered, as if approaching something dangerous, wishing her story began and ended here, lying next to him. "We remained friends, Malcolm and I. He can be very entertaining when he makes the effort, and pleasant when he doesn't think he owns you. He took me to the theater one night to watch from his box, and Charles was in the next one over. He and his brother invited us to dinner at a nearby tavern after the play. When the bill came, neither of them had money to settle it. It seems that royal persons seldom think of such things, so it was I who paid. I told them they were the poorest company I had ever kept, which he seemed to find amusing. He called me to the palace the next day to repay me. From then until the night I met you, we had been together for nearly a year. So…now you know all about me. I am a common whore, but not a common shore."

"You're no whore and you're a most uncommon woman. One can't help what one is born to. Only what one makes of it. You have met adversity and become a fine lady, with a lightness of spirit that warms those around you." His voice turned wistful, husky, and his fingers stroked her shoulders. "I've seen you dancing on May Eve and imagined you a fairy. I've seen you wield a sword, best Mrs. Overton and land a pike as long as my arm. I see the life and beauty you've brought to this sad old house and I'm pleased you're my wife and proud of you."

She smiled, content. He hadn't answered her question, but he said she made him pleased and proud. He said she made him wake up looking forward to the day. He wasn't a glib courtier, or a shallow flatterer. His words held meaning. It would do for now.

CHAPTER TWENTY-FOUR

HOPE NICHOLS WAS A PATIENT WOMAN. And a determined one. As autumn approached and the household began to prepare for winter she acknowledged to herself that much to her surprise, she'd stumbled upon the life she'd always wanted, when and where she'd least expected. Well, almost. She was mistress of a beautiful home and had a handsome husband who stirred her blood with just a glance, but there was still the small matter of the king and her inevitable recall to court. And though she was deeply in love, she wasn't sure what Robert felt for her.

Since the night he'd refused to talk about himself, there'd been a growing darkness about him, as if her questions had pulled something dangerous and all-consuming to the surface. *He came to my rescue several times, though I was often too hurt and angry to notice. He's made me feel welcome, valued, at home, but if he will not let me reach him, how am I to help?*

Responding to the need she saw in his eyes, she did her best to fill their time with happy moments. He moved into her room, and now every night she enjoyed him in their bed. Their lovemaking was hot and fevered. She awoke in the mornings, her hair and bedclothes rumpled, her body ripe and sated, her limbs tangled with his. They talked of Cressly and the household, their likes and dislikes, shared their opinions on matters large and small, and the more they learned about each other the closer they became. But they avoided any mention of her return to court, or anything connected to Robert's past, and it left a gaping hole between them. One Hope had never noticed or minded with other men.

September was a busy month. Whooper swans, ducks and geese came to stay the winter, while swallows and martins rose into the sky to start their journey south. As the first bright leaves began to tumble to the ground the larders were stocked, blankets were mended and on St. Matthew's Day, Nottingham held its justly famous Goose Fair. After five days of shopping and gawking and celebration, Hope returned to Cressly with her husband and retired to her room, exhausted. The night was damp and though it was an extravagance, someone had left a roaring fire. She slipped into a bed gown and settled in with a glass of brandy to enjoy the blaze.

She grinned when she felt the mattress shift behind her, and gasped in delight when cool fingers slipped a lustrous pearl necklace around her neck.

"It was my mother's," he stated simply, but his breath was warm on the back of her neck. "She meant me to give it to my wife." Those few simple words spoke volumes. She threw herself in his arms and tears stained her cheeks.

"It's supposed to make you happy," he said with a rueful smile.

"I know. I am. It's lovely, Robert!" She hastily wiped away her tears on the sleeve of her gown.

"Good!" He stretched out beside her and tugged gently on her hair. "When you cry it's hard to tell. I know you're used to finer, but—"

"No. I've never received a finer gift. A gift that meant so much."

He shifted uncomfortably but didn't deny it. Her good nature and enthusiasm for life had melted much of his reserve, but guardedness remained a deeply ingrained habit. He knew he'd been distant lately, though he felt closer to her than anyone. The necklace was a way to show her how special she was.

"It frightens me to say this, Robert, but I have never been happier."

It startled him to hear her echo his own thoughts. He knew what she meant exactly. "Neither have I. It's like a lovely vision. One is afraid to reach for it or try to hold it, lest it shimmer and disappear."

"Is it that fragile, do you think?"

He kissed her cheek, her nose, her eyelids. "Hope…I am going to have to leave Cressly, for a week, two at most."

"What?" She lifted her head, searching his face,

her dismay clear. "But what if…" What if the thing they refused to discuss should happen? *What if Charles sends for me?* If he meant to recall her to court they might hear from him anytime now. He would want the thing done before winter came and the roads became too difficult for travel. She would hear from him within the next month, or else not before the spring.

"I have important business in the north. It simply cannot wait."

"I see. Might I inquire as to this important business?" Her voice held a definite touch of frost, but underneath she blinked back hot tears. He had promised her that if she was summoned to court he would stand with her. How could he do that if he wasn't going to be there? Did all men forget their promises so soon?

"There is a man I must see in Farnley Wood."

"I had hoped you would be here in case…"

"In case you are summoned. I know. I… It is a matter of grave importance, Hope. An obligation and a duty. One that has weighed heavily on me for a very long time. I would never go otherwise. I will go by horseback and switch mounts on the way. We would have heard from Charles by now if he meant to summon you before spring but I shall do my best to be no more than a week. I *have* to go. I have no choice."

"Why?"

He answered her with silence.

"Your eyes are always sad, even when you smile. You have a door in your mind and heart and it's closed to me. Why won't you let me in?"

"Because some things are best left buried. I've seen things, done things, Hope. Things that are best left unsaid. If you knew who I really was you wouldn't like me much. You might even be afraid."

A shiver traveled up her back. The way he said it. His voice and eyes now so remote. But she was not a timid woman. "Is it worse than what you know of me? Shall I tell you more? My mother sold me, yes, but when I told you I wasn't a good actress I lied. I stayed with a man whose touch made my skin crawl and made him believe I liked it. I didn't have the delicacy or decency to die of shock or heartbreak. I locked my soul in a gilded cage and I laughed, I joked, I thrived! What have you done that is so terrible? What is so much worse than that?"

"You don't want to know. Trust me."

"Can you not take a chance with me as I did with you, Robert? Can you not trust that I would understand? I like you better the *more* I know you. How can I trust you if I don't know who you are?"

He sat up and reached for the bottle of brandy. It had to happen sooner or later. "I have killed men, Hope, and would do so again."

"Of course you have. Along with thousands of

other men. I mean no offense, Robert. But you seem rather squeamish for a soldier."

He gave a short laugh and downed the fiery liquid in one swallow. "I am not squeamish, love. Do you really want to know what my business is in Farnley Wood?"

Something in his tone of voice made her hesitate, suddenly unsure. She snatched the flagon from his hands and poured herself another drink before answering. "Yes. I really want to know."

"I go hunting."

"Hunting? I don't understand. How is that so—"

"I am hunting a man. I've discovered I can find him there. And when I do I will kill him. He is not the first. There have been others." His voice was cold, devoid of emotion. He opened his fist, raising his fingers one at a time and she counted silently, *one...two...three.* "He will be the fourth. There was another, but he escaped me."

Her heart stuttered in her chest and she stared at him, at a loss for words.

"You ask too many questions," he said tiredly. "I have warned you repeatedly." He moved to get up, withdrawing from the bed, the room, the conversation. Withdrawing from her.

She rallied and reached out to grab him, her hand on his arm like a vise. "No, you don't! You don't get to give me that kind of answer and then get up and walk away. You must have a reason and I want to hear it. To kill in battle I understand. Even in a stupid duel. But to hunt a man and kill him, you make it sound like sport. I don't believe it. What would that make you?"

"It makes me someone…something you don't want to know, Hope. Something you should stay away from."

She released his arm and leaned back on her elbows. "But I can't, can I? So you are going to have to tell me who and what you are."

Robert felt so cold inside. As brittle and hollow as the black ice that sometimes coated the river. It was as if the ugly things he kept at bay as he played at house with her had escaped their bonds, stronger than ever. He'd been battling to contain them ever since he'd received the latest missive from de Veres. It was time to act.

"I shouldn't be here, love. I shouldn't be with you," he whispered. "It's something I should never have allowed."

Yet he held her close, his face buried in her hair, and for a moment, she thought he might be crying. Her hand moved to where his neck and shoulder joined, soothing with a soft caress. They lay quiet and still but for their breathing. It took him a while to speak.

"I am so damned tired of being alone with it, Hope, but I've no idea where to begin."

"You don't have to be alone. Just talk to me. Begin by telling me why."

He sighed and rolled over onto his back. "But that, my love, is the hardest part. I have never spoken of it to anyone."

Hope turned on her side, wrapping her body around him, waiting in silence for him to continue, filled with a powerful conviction as her hand rested on his chest. *I love this man. I know this man. He is good and just and honorable. He would never harm me and I have no fear of what he has to say.*

"There were five of them. Younger sons. Drunken soldiers who served the first King Charles. Royal cavaliers. They were bored with their country posting and needed money for liquor, women and cards. They came seeking treasure. The treasure of Cressly. They heard talk of it in the village tavern, and knew from the locals my parents weren't home." He gave an angry laugh. "The treasure of Cressly. It's what my father called my sister. The treasure of Cressly was Caroline."

CHAPTER TWENTY-FIVE

"OH, DEAR GOD!" she gasped in horror.

"I should have been at home to guard her. But it was Valentine's. There was a girl in the village. I… When I got home, Caroline was all alone with them. One of the household guards was murdered, and the other had fled. They were convinced she knew where the treasure was and were trying to beat it out of her. She was crying, begging them…hurt and terrified. I went to get my father's sword."

"That monstrous one with the wolf's head?" Her fingers traced his collarbone and she bent to kiss his throat.

He nodded, his eyes bright with pain and unshed tears. She knew in his mind he was back there. Determined to be with him, she pressed closer, resting her chin against his shoulder and wrapping her arm around his chest. "How old were you?" Her voice was gentle.

"Old enough to wield it. And big for my age. I bided my time, waiting an opportunity. It was the hardest thing I've ever done. But one of them lost patience when she wouldn't answer. They didn't know she couldn't. They…they tore at her clothes. She was kicking and screaming, and one of them decided to silence her with his knife. I charged him and killed him. I don't think any of them were more surprised than I was. It gave me hope, for one sweet moment, and then…" His breath came in deep racking sighs. "Then she called out to me, telling me to run, and one of them, Harris, threw her hard against the wall. God, Hope! I heard her body breaking."

"I'm so sorry, Robert," she murmured, fighting back tears, holding him in a fierce hug.

He took several deep breaths, regaining control. When he spoke his voice was bleak. "I couldn't move or breathe, but she managed to look at me. There was something in her eyes, as if she were pleading, but I was too stunned to understand. Then I ran, Hope. I stopped to look back when I reached the doorway, but her eyes were closed and I knew she was gone. Christ!" He hurled his empty glass against the wall. "My sister died before my eyes and I couldn't save her. I was supposed to be there to protect her but when she needed me I ran. The last thing she saw was my back turned away."

"No, Robert! It wasn't your fault. You were a boy. A grown man could not have saved her from five armed soldiers. You said yourself one of your household guard was dead and the others run away. You *tried* to help her. You even killed one!"

" I should have stayed." It was barely a whisper.

"You would have died."

"Then I should have." His voice rose with anger. "She was my sister. My responsibility. I should have died with her, so at least she would not have died alone. I have done my best to make up for it since. They were cronies of the old king and it was soon clear that justice would never be done. They were called before the court in Westminster Hall where they claimed it was an accident during a stupid drunken ramble. One of them even laughed and suggested she be added to their bill."

She could feel his body vibrating with anger and continued stroking his hair.

"I would have preferred to see them humiliated, hanged, but if there was to be retribution it was clear I needed to see to it myself. I wanted to. I lusted for it. I practiced. I grew. When the war came I joined the parliamentarian cause. It took me years to understand that Cromwell was no better, no worse, than the king. Men are men. No side lays claim to good or evil. War…killing…it's a disguise that allows the monster within us to slip loose and roam unfettered."

"The monster within?"

"From what I've seen we all have one. Well… maybe not you. My view is warped. It's been my life for so many years."

"What monster lurks within you?"

"I wanted more than to kill them. I wanted to make them feel what they did to her. I wanted to make them cry and scream and plead and tremble. It was fierce within me. Jagged."

"And did you?"

He sighed. "No. Other than an extra twist of the sword and telling them they were going to die for Caroline's murder it was not as I imagined. I had no taste for torture and they didn't think I could best them. I was little more than a boy and they were king's cavaliers. They fought and spit and cursed. One laughed in my face before I killed him. We dueled. They died. It was very quick, with a battle raging all around."

He reached for a drink that wasn't there and Hope poured him another. "What is it like? To be a soldier and fight battle after battle?"

"Why do you ask these things?"

"Because they are a part of you. Because I don't want to feel lonely, either, and I do when you lock so much of yourself away from me." *Because I love you.*

"Oh, sweetheart!" He pushed himself up against the pillows and gathered her in his arms, kissing her throat and eyelids. "It's not to shut you out, it's to protect you. I've seen so many things. Chilling, frozen moments. The kind you keep in your head always. It changes a man. My head is crowded with things I can never get rid of. They hound me and haunt me, one image after the next. I've seen women raped, children murdered and people seeking sanctuary in a church be burnt alive. At Naseby…our troops murdered royalist camp followers defending themselves with cooking pots. At Bolton, Prince Rupert's troops killed close to two thousand civilians. I couldn't stop any of it." Now the dam was broken he couldn't stop himself.

"You want to know what it's like? It was shocking at first. One is sickened and horrified, and then one grows accustomed or one dies. Your fellow dies beside you and you're glad it wasn't you. You feel guilty for feeling that, fragile as a candle in the wind, and invincible, too. It's a very strange brew that leaves some men intoxicated, and some…disassembled."

"What do you mean?"

"Unless a fellow puts blind trust and obedience in his leaders, or else stays drunk like many do, one's notions of right and wrong, meaning and what's important, all fall apart. A fellow questions God, his superiors and everything he believes."

"Was that so for you?"

"I wasn't there because I was a believer. I was there seeking retribution. Through it all I hunted. I took my sword and killed them one by one. All but Harris. When the king was defeated he went into exile. But he's back in England now. 'Tis he who waits at Farnley Woods."

"And this has been your business in London."

"Yes. Now you know it all. Is it what you wanted to hear? Is it better now I've told you?"

"I don't know, Robert. Is it?"

"It's not something I ever thought to recount or discuss with a lady."

"But we both know I'm not one."

"To me you are." He was silent for a few moments. He didn't see her smile. "It stirs things I'd rather leave buried, but I'm relieved, I suppose. I expected you to react…with disgust and horror."

"Why? Charles has allowed men to die for him, as his due. He revenged himself upon those who signed his father's death warrant, disguising it as politics. Prince Rupert, I've met him. He's handsome and charming and loved by all. He kills without thinking. To him it's a contest and the casualties are simply part of the score. Buckingham and Jermyn and many others kill each other over women or wounded pride. You killed armed men in battle, seeking justice for your sister. I…I don't know, Robert. Is it worse to kill a man for personal reasons rather than impersonal ones?"

He was silent for a moment. "It's not them, elf, though I feared it might shock you. I don't regret their deaths. I do regret what our forces did at Naseby and in Ireland and Scotland. I hated what we…what the civil war was doing to England. How everywhere we went we seemed to tear her apart. Laying waste to villages, slaughtering civilians. I couldn't have stopped it. I didn't participate and I wouldn't allow it among my men, but in pursuit of my prey I was there."

"So you spent years doing something you didn't believe in and hated, to avenge Caroline. Would she have wanted that? Would you have joined the army if she hadn't died as she did?"

"I don't know. As a child I had dreams of glory. What boy doesn't? My father and his before him were both military men. It was expected, and I had a cool head and a talent for swordplay as a youth. I wouldn't have stayed, though. I would never have followed Cromwell on his Irish campaign."

"And if there'd been no war?"

"I don't know what I would have done." He blinked, looking lost. "What a wretched thing to say. It has swallowed my whole life. If I hadn't married you I'd probably be off fighting as a mercenary right now."

"I'm glad you're not. I don't think you are any more cold-blooded or detached than I am and I don't think that's very good for a mercenary. And now that it's over, there is still plenty of time to discover what you were really meant to do."

"It's not over. Not yet."

"Can you not let it go? Has revenge brought you any peace?"

"No. It hasn't. I go to sleep at night to a woman's weeping, and wake every morning to screaming and fire. But I failed her once and I won't do so again. The thing is almost done. Maybe after Harris I—"

"Robert, you didn't fail her! You showed great courage as a boy. You charged five armed soldiers and slew one. You tried to rescue her against impossible odds. She knew it. She saw it. She called out for you to go. *That* was the last thing she wanted. The last thing she asked of you. She loved you. Did you ever think that you gave her peace and hope? That seeing you leave let her feel you were safe and let her die in peace?"

"Then why do I still hear her weeping? Why does she invade my dreams? Why won't she leave me alone? I told you I don't believe in ghosts, only memories, but at times I feel her presence here. Late at night. In the gardens. Walking the halls. Real or memory, she is restless. I try and bury her again and again but she won't leave me in peace. Sometimes, when the wind sighs in the trees, I imagine it's her. Crying for help. She'll not let me be, Hope. She plagues me unmercifully. She has for years." He looked utterly bereft, as if he were back in the past watching an ancient horror unfold.

Hope shuddered. She, too, had heard similar cries at night, but he had hushed her and told her it was only night owls.

"There are times I almost hate her."

"Oh, Robert, no!" Her heart was breaking for both of them, the brave young lad valiantly trying to do the impossible, to save his sister from five cruel and hardened soldiers, and the lovely golden-haired child who would never grow up, never have children, but whose last thoughts and deeds… She struggled to contain her own tears, and to find words to soothe and comfort.

"It is not the sweet sister that you played with in the garden that plagues you. You torture yourself. She sought to save you just as you sought to save her. I can't believe she wanted you to be unhappy or to spend your life in mourning or seeking revenge. You are trapped in a prison of your own making, my love—" her voice was urgent "—and perhaps… perhaps it is you who refuses to let go. Perhaps it is *you* who traps her."

His startled gaze caught hers. Hurt, intent, but she pressed on, not knowing if he would ever allow her this close again. "If she *is* here in more than memory, perhaps it is you who keeps her. Perhaps she blames herself for your sorrow and grief. Perhaps she cries for you. You must give her leave to go, Robert. If you allow her death to be your life, the only thing about her you remember, then it's you who destroys every good and beautiful thing about her. To think of her should make you smile, not be something you dread. No wonder you've been so unhappy."

"Is that what you did with your mother?" His words were harsh, but he didn't resist when she gathered him warm in her arms.

"I didn't have many good memories of her so I made some up. I told you I gave her a lovely service to strike back at those who would mock me, but it was really to thumb my nose at those who mocked her. I arranged a luxurious funeral procession with torches burning brandy, liveried servants and free beer for all who came to see her on her way. She would have loved it. And now I have a happy memory when I think back on her. I know without a doubt I made her laugh, and it makes me laugh, too. I had to make my own, Robert. You loved your sister and were very close. You must have many good memories. Can you not tell me some?"

He almost gasped aloud. To think of Caroline was to invite a jagged, soul-wrenching pain. To talk of her was unbearable. Hadn't he told her enough? Why did she think he avoided it unless forced? What right had she to pry? To tear open old wounds. If that was the price for her trust...*for her love*... It was too high.

CHAPTER TWENTY-SIX

"I'M SORRY IF I'VE INTRUDED where I oughtn't go,
Robert," she said as if reading his thoughts. "You
said you were tired of being alone with it and I...I
wanted to know you. The dark as well as the light.
You cannot know how much your acceptance has
meant to me. I want to help but I don't know how."
His big body was cold, and she curled herself around
him, passing him her warmth. "But what I want most
is to have you right here, next to me. And I *do* know
you. I know you're a good man. A part of me has
known and trusted this from the first moment we
met. I don't know what this is between us. I told
myself it was lust, loneliness, revenge. I fought it as
a weakness, tried to use it as a tool, but it won't let
me lie. I love you, Robert Nichols, and I don't need to
know anything more than that. I'll stop asking questions if that's what you want."

They lay in silence side by side, in a place halfway between his world and hers. He reached out and
took her hand. It touched him deeply that she could
say those words after all he'd told her. He wished he
could find words of his own. He hoped the necklace

gave her some idea. But he wanted to offer something more. "I remember…" He released his breath on a deep sigh. "I remember how we used to play. We made a grand kite painted orange and black that resembled a butterfly. It almost lifted her off the ground. We clung to it together and had to let it go when it almost toppled us into the river." He wrapped an arm around her waist and rested his head against her breast and her fingers stroked the back of his neck as he spoke.

"I remember, when the rains came heavy, too fierce to venture outdoors, we would go to the little study and make a castle with furniture and blankets. She would say it was Nottingham and she was Robin Hood. She wanted me to be the evil sheriff." He chuckled to himself. "But I was always Richard the Lionheart, of course. She had a merry laugh, you know. It rang through the corridors. 'Tis that I miss the most." His voice was rough with emotion and she could feel his shoulders shaking. There were tears on his face and she kissed them one by one.

"I'm sorry," she whispered.

"For what," he murmured, looking back at her from a time and place he'd been running from for years. What possible trifle could she be sorry for? This shiny bright young soul?

"For your pain." She cupped his jaw in both her hands and drew his mouth to hers, bringing him back with a gentle brush of her lips.

"Hope?"

"Yes?"

"You have come to mean so much to me. I don't know how or why, but even in the midst of anger, even when I've felt sore pressed, almost from the beginning, I have felt an ease with you, and a comfort I feel with none other. When I am with you, I feel I'm home."

She pressed her forehead to his. "I feel the same. In some ways you have always felt familiar to me. You make me feel safe and protected…among other things." She grinned and kissed his cheek. "When I saw you standing in my home, towering over the crowd, my heart almost stopped. It was as if you'd stepped straight from a childhood fantasy. My fierce protector and shining knight. I thought I had met him once before."

"Did you? You didn't tell me that."

"It all seems so silly now. A childish thing."

His hand skimmed her shoulder and arm and rested on her knee. "Tell me."

"I used to have a corner room. Something like a tower. At least to a child. I would pretend it was a castle, and daydream of a handsome prince, a golden-haired knight who climbed its walls to claim me. My very own hero. One September day I woke to ringing bells. Cromwell's army was returning and everyone was hurrying to find a place to watch. I found a spot and spied him straight away. He looked just like my imaginary hero. A dashing knight, tall and handsome, but I couldn't see his eyes because of his hat.

"Well…as you know I'm a fumble-heels. I leaned out as far as I might and over I went, right into the street and the path of the oncoming cavalry. I felt sure I would be trampled. I ought to have been. None of them would stop, and then he, the very man I'd been watching, rescued me, scooping me up and into his saddle. I rode the rest of the parade route in his arms. I tried desperately to find something profound to say but all I could do was bleat a thank-you. When he dropped me off to safety I didn't know his name and still had seen only half his face, but I didn't worry."

She chuckled to herself, remembering. "I was certain he was my own true love, come to my rescue. I knew we were destined to meet again and there would be another chance. But later that day, my mother sold me and I knew I was wrong. My childhood ended in one instant, just like yours did, and I put such silly dreams away. He was just a nice young man who cared enough to help someone in trouble, but he couldn't save me from my life. I realized I was never going to see him again, and if I wanted to be rescued I had best do it for myself."

The silence dragged on for several moments before she became aware of it, still caught up in the one shining memory from her childhood. It was then she noticed his hand had stilled. Perhaps she oughtn't have told him. Even the best of men were prickly about some things. "Robert?"

"And did you buy some new shoes? With the half crown he gave you?"

"No. My friends descended upon me before I was halfway home and we stuffed ourselves with meat pies and tarts. I hid what remained and— But how do you know about that?"

"I was there." His voice sounded amazed. "I...be damned! I should have known you by those violet eyes. It was all I could see of you, other than bare feet and mud."

"That was you?" She felt as though the wind had been knocked out of her. Her hands traced his features and she regarded him with bemusement, but she could see it now. The strong jaw, the smile that had so captivated her. "It *was* you! I should have known you by your smile. I so wanted to see your eyes. It was the same when I saw you standing with the king. I wanted to know what color they were. It seemed so important. Oh, Robert. How can this be? What does it mean? It was *you!*" Laughing and crying she covered his face in frantic kisses. She had been right all along. Here, beside her, was her own true love.

"It means you're right where you're supposed to be," he said with a broad grin. "It seems I am, too. It means you're mine. Beyond that I neither know nor care." He loosed her gown, drawing back its folds so he might see her. Skimming her length, he paused to cup her rose-tipped breasts, feeling the rise and fall of breath, the steady pulse of life, and letting it feed his hunger. His hands, calloused and rough from years of swordplay, thrilled her with their gently rasping touch. His palm slid down, warming the soft swell of her hip, then pressed the downy thatch between her legs. She tossed her head, her body flushed, moving restlessly beneath him.

His lips claimed hers, lush and warm, then his tongue found hers and they thrust and swirled, fierce and heated. She savored the taste of him. She savored his strength and the feel of him, real, alive, with her, not some fantasy consigned to the past but a hot-blooded hard-muscled man, warm against her skin. She arched into his hand like a stroked cat, her body purring, and her hands roamed his sleek form, enjoying the play of taut muscle, marking every part of him. They spoke through sighs and moans, kissing wildly as they both scrambled frantically to loosen his clothing, fingers brushing and working together until he sprang free.

"Christ. I want you, Hope. I need you. You light a fire in me." Painfully engorged, he settled his arousal between her thighs. His lips bruised hers. His bristled jaw rasped her chin and the soft skin of her breasts. He ground against her, whispering endearments in a dance of hands and mouth, thrusting hips and sweet sensation, and then he took her, not as a courtier took his lover, but as a warrior claimed his woman, spreading her, lifting her, holding her, finding her slick heat and plunging inside. Stroking her with hands and tongue and pulsing organ, he lifted her legs above his shoulders and pumped and writhed, harder and harder in a frenzied passionate ride.

He took her higher and higher, approaching peaks of sensation she'd never felt before, and then, just at the brink of exquisite release, he slowed, almost stopped, his smoldering eyes watching hers. She almost cursed him. She twisted and writhed, thrusting against him. Raging with wanting, she raked his shoulders and fisted her hands in his hair. "Do it, Robert. Now. Please."

His teeth grazed her shoulder, his hands gripped her waist and he thrust inside her again and again. An incredible star-burst of white-hot pleasure spread from her center and rippled through her body in blissful waves. Her tight muscles squeezed and held him, owning him, claiming him, as she cried out his name and a slow, deep, beautiful eruption surged from within him, joining them both in a lovers' embrace that was wild celebration and blissful comfort, homecoming and welcome, joy and release.

Spent, they lay in each other's arms, hearts still pounding. "Dear God. I feel as if I have just visited heaven. Each time with you is such a wonder. It was incredible, you beautiful man!" She threw her arms around his neck and gave him a ferocious hug.

He grinned and ruffled her hair. "I think you're beautiful, too."

"Can it be real? Am I dreaming?"

"If you're dreaming than I am, too." He nuzzled the tender skin beneath her ear.

"You really told me about your sister?"

"Yes, love." He felt a familiar pain and a part of him flinched, but it was not quite as sharp as he remembered.

"And it really was you? In London?"

"Unless there was some other grubby shoeless urchin who rode with me that day. Ow! What did you pinch me for?"

"I was just checking," she said with a happy grin. "Making *sure* you are real."

"I believe the accepted practice is to pinch oneself," he grumbled, settling her against his length.

They were both exhausted, mentally, physically, emotionally, in every way a person could be, yet Hope fought to stop the languorous drift toward slumber. She was content where she was right now, safe in the arms of the man she loved, knowing they were meant to be and everything would be all right. Yet a part of her feared what might lie on the other side. What if this *was* a dream, and to sleep would be to wake? *What if he…what if…* A wave of fatigue pulled her under, and a jumble of thoughts followed her down.

Her sleep was crowded with vivid dreams. She

dreamt of Robert as a little boy, a toddler still unsteady on his feet. Laughing, full of joy, he ran on chubby legs, green eyes flashing with excitement and delight. He chased a gold-covered leaf, chortling as he bent to pick it up and the wind plucked it from his fingers. A blond-haired girl ran with him, her dress tucked between her knees. The sky grew dark and stormy, tugging at their hair and clothes as though trying to capture them and carry them away. She shouted and shouted, her heart pinched with fear, but they couldn't hear her and continued blithely on, into the storm.

She dreamt he rode toward her on a gold-caparisoned horse, the sun glinting off his sword and armor, hand outstretched, come to take her home, and then they were walking, hand in hand, laughing and talking companionably as a child danced in front of them, excited by discoveries of oddly shaped stones and colorful shells. The last thing she dreamt was the sound of his voice, faint and fading. *I love you, elf.* When she woke, she was alone.

CHAPTER TWENTY-SEVEN

A BRIEF MOMENT OF PANIC overtook Hope and her hand flew to her chest. Her fingers touched the cool pebbled strands of her necklace and she breathed a sigh of relief. It *was* real. All of it. Last night he had given her the kind of gift a husband gave a valued wife. Last night he had given her the gift of trust, confiding in her regarding his haunted past. And last night she had discovered that the man she had grown to love so quickly and completely was the same man she had dreamt of. The one who had saved her life and she had been so certain she would see again, so many Septembers ago.

She lay back in bed, kicking her heels in giddy delight, no longer worried he wasn't beside her. He was a late sleeper and early riser, and often went off to practice just before dawn. It was a habit she meant to cure him of. He'd be back soon. Hungry for food, hungry for her, and she would give him lessons in the joys of spending a morning lazing in bed. She grinned and stretched, savoring the ache in her muscles, and then went to stand in front of the mirror now gracing the paneled wall.

Her fingers caressed the string of pearls that had once belonged to his mother, and her heart swelled. *One day I shall pass these to my daughter.* The simple necklace, what it represented, made the rest of her jewelry seem tawdry by comparison. She would sell it or give it away. She wanted no gifts touching her skin unless they came from her husband. Turning in a slow circle she smiled in contentment to see where his lovemaking had marked her. The slight imprint of impassioned fingers marked her upper arm and thighs. Here and there…reddened skin where unshaven jaw had rasped tender skin, and along her collarbone and the base of her throat another necklace where deep kisses had left their mark as if to say "This woman is mine."

I have marked him, too. I'll wager he'll not practice shirtless this morning with Oakes, she thought with a mischievous grin, for she knew she'd marked him tooth and nail. If one had little appetite, food and sex both lost most, or all, their pleasure. But when you hungered, craved, she was learning, it could be sublime. She'd never hungered for a man the way she did for him. He had the power to make her forget herself completely and now she understood why. He was her mate. The one man on earth meant for her.

She'd been given a brief glimpse of him years ago but it hadn't yet been their time. Now it was. *He* was what she'd been missing all these years. What she'd needed, wanted, been waiting for. It made her believe in magic, as if she were a child again. And if finding him again wasn't magic enough, what he did to her with his touch certainly was. *And his heart? Have I marked that, too?* She sobered at the thought. He had shared a part of himself she knew he kept hidden from everyone, opened a door into his soul, and what she saw there made her weep. *I don't want to be alone with it,* he'd said. And now he wasn't.

Rose interrupted her musings, entering the room surrounded by the delicious smell of coffee. She carried with her a note on a silver tray. "A messenger has brought this for you, my lady. Mrs. Overton says it looks important and I best bring it to you straight away."

Hope nodded absently. "Put it on my desk. I'll see to it later. Have you seen the captain, Rose? I was hoping he'd join me for coffee."

Rose looked at her in surprise. "Does he know that, my lady? Last I saw he was with Mr. Oakes and looked to be fixing for a ride."

She felt a moment's unease but brushed it aside. Things had changed between them last night. They had talked of his haunted past. They had discovered the connection that bound them to each other. It was still hard to believe. *I would have died that day if not for him. I am where I am supposed to be and he is where he is meant to be.* He had said so himself. He said she was his, and he was a man who took care of his own.... Surely he wouldn't leave her now to

return to the same dark path he'd feared her knowing. He was going for a ride. As he did every morning. Perhaps he would like some company.

"I think perhaps I'll join him, Rose."

"You'll have to be quick, my lady. He looked to
be leaving soon."

"We'd best hurry, then. Fetch my riding coat and
boots if you would. Quick as you can." She picked
up her brush off the dresser and her eyes were drawn
to a flash of silver. The forgotten note still lay on
the tray, sitting on her desk. Anxiety seized her as
if it were a fist, gripping her chest, clutching at her
throat."

"My Lady? Lady Nichols? Is something wrong?"

"No." But her voice came out as a soft gasp.
Charles had written her before and she'd disposed
of his letters unread. But they had borne his personal
seal. This missive bore the royal seal. Her hand trem-
bled as she waved the little maid away. She didn't
need to read it to know what it was. It was a summons from the king.

Robert was in the stables, talking to the sergeant as he waited for Jemmy to saddle his horse.
He greeted her with a wink and a hug that normally
would have warmed her all over if she weren't sick
with fear. *It's too soon!* It was all so fragile yet. So
easily broken.

"You slept well, I hope?"

"Yes, thank you. Very well." Mr. Oakes was

watching her with a big grin and she found to her chagrin that she was still able to blush. "I was wondering if I might speak to you a moment, in private, Robert." She reminded herself everything would be all right. He'd given her his word.

"Certainly. But you'll have to make it quick, love. The morning's well begun and I need to be on my way in an hour."

"On your way?" There was a sharp note of panic in her voice.

"Yes. As I discussed with you yesterday." He looked over his shoulder at his gawking men, then placed a hand on the small of her back and ushered her outside.

"But…I thought…I was certain you had changed your mind!"

"Whatever gave you that idea? I never said so. You eased my heart, love. I swear you are an angel. I dreamt of her last night and it made me smile. I feel years younger and a hundred pounds lighter, but I still have my duty to perform. The man must be dealt with. He's a da—'

"What of your duty to me?" she snapped, handing him the message.

He looked at her carefully, noting her white face and shaking hands, and then he read the letter. His stomach lurched. It was just as he'd feared. *We have run out of time.* Sighing, he handed the parchment back to her. "So…it has come to pass. What do you wish to do?"

"What do *I* wish to do? What happened to *we?* I've told you what I want. I want you to come with me. I don't understand." Her voice sounded hurt, bewildered.

"I've explained to you why I can't. Not right now, elf. Make your excuses and wait for my return." He went to hug her, wanting to soothe her, but she shoved his chest and took two steps back, dismayed at this new betrayal.

"What happened to your promise? You said that if he summoned me you would come, to stand as my husband and bring me back home."

"I know I did. I'm sorry, but I have made other promises, too. If you can only wait for me to—"

"You mean to your dead sister, who has been gone nearly twenty years? Don't blame it on her. You do her no honor. She never asked it from you. 'Tis not a promise you made her but a vow you made to yourself! The sergeant told me once you take care of your own. I can see that *I* am not numbered among them."

"Hope…don't. That's not true! But Harris is the last of them. I've waited years and now there is no choice."

"There is always a choice. You can stop. You can honor a vow to yourself or honor your word to me." She looked over her shoulder to where his mount stood ready. "It appears the decision is an easy one."

She could hardly believe they were having this conversation. How could her world tumble down so quickly, changing completely from night to day? *I am so stupid. Every time I believe or imagine, I end up feeling betrayed. It's my fault. I can't seem to stop making things into something they're not.* First her mother, then Charles and now the one she had allowed herself to love. *Fool! Fool! Fool!*

"Damn it, woman, there is nothing easy about it! But I can't stop yet. This has to be done. This man means us harm. 'Twas he who asked your lover Charles for Cressly, and it's the first real chance I've had at him in years."

She gasped in hurt and outrage. "You throw Charles in my face now?"

He let his breath out on a sharp exhale and clenched his hands behind his head, feeling frustrated and guilty, though he wasn't sure why. When he spoke he did his best to keep his voice soothing. "I apologize. That was uncalled for. But so is your attack on me. I do not go to honor myself, but to take care of unfinished business. He knows who I am, Hope. He knows what I did to his fellows. He has come after me already. The fool still believes there is treasure here. His fear and greed make him dangerous, not only to me, but to you. To everyone here." He spoke to her as if he were calming an overtired child. "Once he is dealt with…"

"Once he is dealt with, what? Once he is gone

you'll have nothing left, Robert. You've built your entire life around him. Clearly nothing else matters. He is the reason you married me, is he not?" It felt as if he'd stabbed her and she was close to tears, but she refused to hold him that way. "Go, then. Seek vengeance. I pray it brings you comfort this time."

"God's blood, woman! Have you not listened to a word I've said. I…have…no…choice!" Sergeants Oakes's words returned to haunt him. *You're not very good with people, are you?* He had thought he'd improved somewhat with Hope, but apparently he was wrong. Be damned if managing a wife wasn't one of the hardest tasks a man could undertake.

"Oh, I've been listening, Robert. I fear it's you who has not been listening to me. You have waited twenty years. Yes. I understand. He is a danger. I understand that, too. Now is the perfect opportunity to act, I assume because he's far from both Cressly and London. I am not a fool. What I also understand is you made me a promise and when I need you, the thing that has waited for twenty years cannot wait a few weeks or even a few months more. You have farmers and shepherds with muskets tramping the fields. Cressly is an armed camp. He would have to come with an army to be a danger to you here."

He spread his hands wide and let them drop to his sides. "Hope I… You don't understand."

"No, Captain, I don't. But you need trouble yourself no further. I will manage perfectly well on my own. In fact, I managed very well by myself before we met."

"And just what is that supposed to mean?"

"I'll be on my own way tomorrow. One doesn't keep the king waiting. I have no more choice than you say you do."

"On your way where?"

"Back to court!"

"Back to him? After the way he treated you? After he betrayed you and allowed his mistress to gloat? After all the fine words you've said to me? You said you were done with him! You *could* await my return. You *could* tell him your husband forbade you traveling alone. Last night you said you wanted me beside you. You claimed to love me. You said you knew we were fated when first we met and were meant to be together."

Hope marveled at the indignation in his voice. *The betrayer acts the betrayed. It is always so.* "Yet you have never claimed to love me in return. Revenge is your mistress and you choose her over me. As for him, he is the *king*. One comes when he summons."

"And last night? It was some game or contest? Did it satisfy your curiosity? Do you know me now?"

"Last night was a dream. If it were real, I would have woken to find you beside me. If it were real, you would not choose to abandon me when I need you most. You are *not* the man I dreamt of, nor the man I thought you were. I am a fool and you… That day, now, it is a meaningless coincidence and nothing more. The kind that happens to people every day."

He spread his arms wide. "Look at me. *I*...am real. *This* is who I am. Last night I told you because you begged to know. I let you see it all. And I warned you, you would not like it. I am no knightly hero, nor have I ever claimed to be. You don't love me. I am not the one you seek. He is but some imaginary fellow you have decorated with my face and form."

"I know." The words escaped as a regretful sigh. Turning her back on him, she walked away.

THAT NIGHT THE WIND picked up off the water, howling through the valley with a dull roar. Trapped within its fury were a thousand eerie voices. Some wailed and whimpered, others shrieked and whispered, and one seemed to breathe her name beneath a low moan. Hope buried her head under pillows and blankets and a nightmare crept in with her. One that had visited her in various guises many times before. The only thing she remembered of it when she woke was that she always ended up alone.

CHAPTER TWENTY-EIGHT

BEFORE THE SUN CRESTED the trees, Hope Nichols was on her way back to court, continuing her journey as it had begun years ago, by herself. Well, not entirely. One had to have a care for highwayman, and apparently marriage made one's husband's enemies one's own. Oakes and a complement of heavily armed men, expertly trained and fiercely loyal, accompanied her.

ROBERT CONTINUED in the opposite direction. Vengeance was a personal business between one man and another. Harris, justice, resolution, lay to the north. How could she expect him to abandon it now? He'd known her less than six months but he'd carried this burden almost all of his life. And why couldn't she understand the danger the man presented? Was his word not good enough? Harris assaulted women… and children, for sport, and he had a grudge to bear.

And what now? Instead of waiting for him so they might face the king's displeasure together as they'd agreed, she had chosen to please her ex-lover by scampering back to London within hours of his summons. He had taken a risk, revealing himself to her. One he had shared with none other. Perhaps, in the light of day, despite her words of comfort and acceptance, the summons had come as a welcome excuse. He had known in his gut it was a mistake to tell her, and that was before she bloody decided he was her toy soldier brought to life.

Well, he was no one's toy. Certainly not Charles's, and certainly no woman's, and a good soldier followed his instincts. He completed his mission. He refused to be distracted. Let Charles deal with her. The man had betrayed and humiliated her and she'd sworn she would never take him back as lover. But what would happen when she was back at court with a charming and charismatic king intent on reclaiming her? How long would she resist? She would be safer at court, though. If Harris had a chance to hurt him through his wife he would, but he would never dare molest one of the king's courtesans.

His jaw tightened. She would be in London by tomorrow. How would Charles greet her? With diamonds and sapphires cut and set to match her eyes. A palace suite now she was a lady. Apologies and blandishments and words to soothe her hurt and anger. Men like Charles and de Veres, they had a talent for such things, but he was unaccustomed to pretty speeches. Try as he might, he never seemed to find the right words. *You have never claimed to love me in return,* she'd said. Well, perhaps he hadn't. Perhaps the words didn't drip from his tongue like honey, but he'd wager no one else had humored her with tales of Robin Hood or indulged her interest in sword fighting or stood patiently for hours while she admired shrubs!

His horse, sensing his mounting fury, grew restive, tossing its head, muscles bunching, fretting to be released. He turned him sideways, holding him in check as he reared and pranced, feeling the power and frustration coiled beneath him. Then he straightened him out, leaned forward and gave him his head, hurtling through the night with the full moon lighting his path and his black cloak billowing behind him like wings. He was vengeance. He was retribution. He rode for Caroline and Harris was his prey.

He approached Gildersome, a village close to Farnley, not quite sure what to expect. The message had been vague and he was wary. A tavern was the best place to mingle, listen to the news, make discreet enquiries and spread a little coin. It usually required a good deal of finesse and even greater quantities of alcohol before suspicious locals actually parted with any useful information, but this night the tavern was abuzz with the goings-on in the nearby woods. It seemed that militant-looking strangers had been making themselves at home with the local farmers and businessmen for several weeks now, and one more stranger was hardly worth a glance.

The heavily forested area was crowded and even easier to infiltrate than the tavern. Over a hundred men milled about, talking and arguing. All of them were Protestant, many of them ex-parliamentarian soldiers, and several of them he recognized, including Joshua Greathead, whom he'd glimpsed in London. What he didn't see was Harris. What he heard shocked him. Not for its content, but its delivery. They spoke of treason, and a more voluble, undisciplined, indiscreet group of conspirators one could not imagine. Perhaps they felt themselves too far distant in Yorkshire to attract attention, but they were blithely out in the open planning an attack on the royalist strongholds in Leeds, with the intent of starting an uprising to overthrow the king. There was even talk that General Fairfax, their old commander, might come to lead them.

It would have been laughable if it weren't so dangerous. He hunched his shoulders to disguise his height, lowered his hat and wrapped his cloak like a scarf to obscure his features, and slipped into the shadows. It was beginning to feel like a trap, though not the kind he'd expected. Any man placed in these woods by witnesses could expect to be hanged, drawn and quartered. He'd overheard enough to make the risk worthwhile, though. It seemed the tavern in nearby Morley had been commandeered by a group of brutal braggarts and bullies. He left the woods as quietly as he entered them, and went elsewhere to hunt his prey.

The King's Arms was at the very edge of the village, backing onto the moor. It might have been a pleasant walk by day, but its isolation made it a perfect gathering spot for men of a certain sort, and a dangerous walk for the uninvited by night. The door burst open on a roar to drunken laughter. A portly older gentleman hurtled from inside, landing face first in the dirt. A voice that had lived too long in his dreams rose above the din.

"Come back when you have the rest, or your wife and daughter will settle the account, you useless piece of dung."

A familiar feeling came over him. Anticipation, exhilaration, a sense of heightened awareness, focused and honed to a deadly, determined calm. His teeth flashed white in the moonlight as his lips drew back in a feral grin. He'd tracked his quarry to his lair. He waited for the uproar to subside, then quietly slipped inside. Only a few of the occupants looked to be locals. The bald man lounged by the hearth, groping the breast of a naked woman who looked to be drunk, asleep or, by the bruises on her face, unconscious. A half-dozen well-armed men were with him. They were all too busy dicing to notice his presence.

He took a seat on a bench near the back of the room and sidled over to rub elbows with a bleary-eyed fellow who looked about ready to slide under the table. "Who's that lot over there, eh?" he asked, sliding his new friend a pint of ale and half a crown. "They don't look to be from around here."

"Neither do you," his drunken companion answered sourly, but he pocketed the coin and reached for the ale. "Too many strangers round here these days." Another commotion drew both their attention. An unkempt, scrawny-looking youth carrying a heavy flagon of beer had done something to earn a string of curses and a cuff that sent him reeling to the floor. The boy picked himself up, expressionless, retrieved another flagon, and continued serving as he'd been doing before.

"That be the mighty war hero Colonel Harris, honoring us small folk with his presence. He's the earl of something or other, or so he claims. He's here and about often these days. Some say too often. Some say it's tied to the doings in the woods, but he ends up here every night cheating at cards and dice. You want to be careful not to draw his attention. If he invites you to play there's no refusing, and no leaving till you're parted from all your coin."

So...the arrogant fool had used his own name. "And that lot with him?"

"Those be his men and the reason none dare complain. The lad is his son, poor bastard, and the woman one of his whores."

"I'm no stranger when it comes to games of chance," Robert said with a slow smile. "Perhaps I'll see what I might take from him."

"They say a fool and his money are soon parted.

Good luck, friend. Beware he doesn't also take your life."

Robert rose and patted the man's shoulder, then tossed him another coin. "Drink to my health at the wake." He moved quietly through the shadows and they moved with him, coalescing into a dark shape that waited, just feet from its prey. Robert's hand caressed his sword hilt. He could see the veins where his enemy's neck met his shoulder, pulsing life in rhythm with his heart. That this thing should live when his sister did not was unbearable. Harris could be dead within two seconds, but he had to recognize and understand. He had to know that his casual slaying of Caroline was what ended his life now.

And so he waited, amazed they could be so complacent. So certain of their invulnerability they never once raised their eyes to scan the room. When at last he did feel a gaze upon him it was the boy's. The lad's eyes met his directly, cool, assessing, and he returned the stare. The boy's cheeks were gaunt, his eyes filled with shadows. They flicked to the sword and Robert lifted his fingers. When he looked back the lad had turned away.

He had waited long enough. He leaned over, clamping Harris's shoulder in a viselike grip. "Excuse me, Colonel, but I was wondering if we might have a quiet word outside."

Harris's grip was as strong as his own. He seized Robert's wrist and threw himself back in the chair, toppling it, dropping the woman and freeing himself, shoving Robert back against the wall as he rose. The men, taken by surprise, watched in stunned silence before erupting into cheers, thinking it a drunken brawl and eager to see their leader break some bones. Holding Robert in a choke hold with only the back of his arm, Harris used his considerable strength to force him up the wall so only his toes touched the floor. "What dog is this come snapping at my table? You'll lick my boots, cur. Or I'll slice you open from belly to throat."

Gripping the man's forearm and using it for leverage, Robert lifted his legs and kicked him in the stomach, knocking him backward and sending him flying over the table, scattering food, drink, and dice and sending his sword sliding across the floor. Leaping up onto the table he unsheathed his own. "A man who mistakes wolf for dog is bound to come to a bad end. Don't you think?"

Harris grinned, spat out a tooth and then spat blood. "Well, well. Young Nichols, is it? I remember you. All grown up, then? Last I saw you, you were running away as your little sister pled for mercy."

"Aye. Her name is Caroline." He jumped to the floor and kicked the sword toward him. "Get up."

Harris reached for the blade and jumped to his feet. "Still squeamish, then, are you, lad? It's a nice gesture, though."

The rest of the men had stepped back, clearing a

space, while the remaining townsfolk had run for the door, fleeing into the night.

"I just want to take my time with it, Colonel. Savor the moment after all these years." He darted forward in a lightning move that left Harris cursing with an inch-wide gash from temple to jaw. "I think it's more fun this way." They were circling each other, eyes locked. Robert was a master swordsman, not a frightened child, and he could see the realization dawning in the other man's eye. "She still thinks of you. She sent me to say goodbye."

He lunged again and Harris gave a shriek of pain and rage as the giant blade pierced his left shoulder, cutting through muscle and tendon. Nerveless fingers opened and his sword clattered to the floor. Laughing and cursing at the same time, Harris pulled himself up against a table and tried to staunch the flow of blood. "As you can see I am unable to wield a weapon. The duel is over. I'll tell you what, Nichols. Why don't you say hello to her for me? Kill him, lads."

CURSING, SHOUTING, SCREAMS and breaking crockery were doubtless viewed as ominous signs to most people, but for Hope and the sergeant they were a godsend. Ever since Hope had decided to turn around and head to Yorkshire instead of London she had been afraid of her husband's greeting, but after searching the deserted Farnley Woods, and the towns of Farnley, Gildersome and Leeds, she began to fear that something might have happened to him on the way. Both she and Mr. Oakes agreed that asking questions might do more harm than good, but that reduced them to wandering from tavern to tavern, inn to inn, hoping to find some trace of him. If Oakes viewed the sounds of battle as promising, then so did she.

"I expect we might find him inside, my lady. Perhaps you should wait here with some of the men."

"I've seen my share of tavern brawls, Oakes. I am not some delicate flower."

They stepped into a chaotic mess. Tables and chairs were overturned. A woman lay unconscious or dead under a table, at least three men lay dead on the floor, and three others were fighting a fourth, who was laying about him with a giant sword that sang as it cut through the air. Robert!

"Why, look, boys! 'Tis one of the king's sluts herself come to call." The words were spoken by a massive bald-headed man covered in blood. She knew him instantly from Robert's description. There was a momentary lull in the battle as the entire room turned to stare. She stared right back. As Robert looked at her, stunned, one of the men rushed him from behind. He raised a gauntleted fist without looking, smashing the man's nose and dropping him like a stone.

Robert heard the snick of metal behind him

and turned just in time to deflect the blade of a wicked-looking *main-gauche,* but he was too slow, catching the man in the thigh instead of through the heart.

"Get the woman, you fools," Harris shouted, and his two remaining attackers rounded on her. Robert turned his back on the man who'd murdered Caroline and plunged his sword through the shoulder blades of one, while Oakes and one of his men did for another. Hope was safe in a corner, surrounded by five more of his men. At least she'd had the sense to bring them. Satisfied, he turned his attention back to the colonel.

"Now…you die."

"I'm not inclined to humor you, Captain." Harris reached behind a wooden pillar, snatching the skinny, battered youth by the hair and pulling him close like a shield. Still able to wield a knife, he held a razor-sharp blade to the lad's jugular. "We'll be leaving now, Nichols, and with no interference or I'll slit the boy's throat."

"No, you won't." Robert's voice sounded cold, disinterested. "He's your son."

Harris grinned and chuckled, shaking the boy's head back and forth by the hair. "You think that will stop me? His mother's a whore and him naught but a little bastard. I've plenty more where he came from."

"Do you think it will stop me?" Robert sounded curious, almost amused. He took a step forward, resting the tip of his sword over the boy's heart. "Beyond this lies your lungs. You took something from me. Why should I cavil at taking something from you?"

"Robert, no!"

"Listen to your bitch, Nichols. You're scaring her."

Robert turned to look at her, the tip of his sword never leaving the boy's chest. What Hope saw horrified her. This was what he'd warned her about. This savage, blood-covered, ferocious man with the snarling voice, sword outstretched and death in his eyes.

"Goddamn it, Oakes!" he snarled. "I'll have your head for bringing her here. Get her out. Now! Take her back to London and the king, where she belongs."

She stared at him in shock. "Robert, please. You can't—"

"Leave. Now," he growled. "You have no business here. Go and don't come back."

CHAPTER TWENTY-NINE

"THAT POOR CHILD!"

"You needn't fear for him, my lady. The captain—"

"Wouldn't hurt him. I know. You told me you'd never seen him harm an innocent and I believe you. But when we left he was holding him at sword point. And to have one's own father use you as a shield. What kind of man does that?"

"The kind who needs killing, I expect, my lady. The captain wouldn't go after a man for no reason."

"No. He had reason enough, no doubt. I am sorry if I have dragged you into trouble with him, Oakes."

"I'm a tough old badger, my lady. I can weather the storm."

"I should not have ordered you to turn back, but we had a terrible argument before I left and I didn't want him going after that man. I was very upset he would not leave it and come with me. At first it was hurt and anger, but the further we got the more convinced I became that he was on a path that would do him far more harm than good. I was a fool to think he needed rescuing. He is clearly a man who can care for himself and all I did was make a mess of things. I have never seen him so angry."

"Neither have I. But the mess was made before we got there, my lady."

"He is quite done with me now, I think."

"Do you, ma'am? I think he was more angry you saw him like that, than he was with you."

She nodded thoughtfully. "There's a name for men who release something savage in battle. It's said they glory in it."

"Aye. A berserker, my lady. The captain, he is a fearsome man in battle. He's good at staying alive and that means he's good at killing. But it doesn't control him. He controls it."

"You told me that at times before battle he had eyes like a shark. You said they looked like ice. I saw that look tonight." She shivered.

"Aye. I noted it, too. But no berserker stays his sword in the midst of battle or stops to see his lady safe. Remember that when you ask yourself what things he holds most dear, or what it is that rules him."

Oakes patted her hand before leaving her to her thoughts, joining Jemmy on the box to ride musket, as the coach took her home to London.

She settled back against the cushions, still haunted by the image of the bruised and hollow-cheeked youth, an innocent trapped between the hatred of two grown men, both whose duty it should have been to protect him. *Oakes is right. Robert wouldn't harm him.* But there were other ways to harm than using sword or fist. His words came back to her over and over, churning to the rumble of the coach. *You don't want to know. I go hunting. If you knew who I really was you wouldn't like me much. You might even be afraid.*

He had told Oakes to take her back to the king, where she belonged. He'd told *her* not to come back, and after seeing him, she was far from sure she wanted to. He had warned her, yes...but some things no words could adequately convey. She wasn't sure she would ever forget the sight of him, blood-covered and snarling with bodies all around. She very much feared it was burned in her memory. It was part of who he was and now it was a part of her.

Oh, God! Just as his sister's death is forever a part of him, and Harris's death will forever be a part of his son. She felt a deep sense of despair. Robert wasn't the pure and shining knight of her dreams, nor the monster of his own. He was honorable and kind and tried to do right, but whether born to it or brought to it by circumstance, he was also a warrior, battered and scarred by wounds so deep they might never heal.

She had said his mistress was revenge and Oakes had called him married to that cold dark bitch called war. Could a man like that ever settle for the kind of life she wanted? As husband, father, lover, friend?

Had it been fair to ask him to choose, or to blame him for following the only path he knew? And did any of it matter anymore when he'd sent her back to Charles?

CHAPTER THIRTY

Oxford Kate's, London

ROBERT NICHOLS WAS FAR MORE comfortable giving help than asking for it, and William de Veres wasn't making it any easier.

"Good God, man! You mean to say you've misplaced her? She's a wee little thing, I'll grant you, but a fellow really should try and remember where last he left his wife."

"And where is Elizabeth?" Robert asked through gritted teeth. "Perhaps she would know where a woman of quality might lodge if not at the palace. I've always found her very resourceful."

"Lizzy? Damned if I know. Probably off in a gambling hell fleecing the life savings from some off-duty footmen. She's very partial to them, you know."

"No...I didn't know."

"You are fond of the girl, then?"

"Of course I am! She is my wife." They paused their conversation as a barmaid came in with bread and beer.

He was more than fond of her. Much more. He'd been struck by an epiphany in the middle of a tavern, with his enemy at his mercy, the tip of his sword at the breast of a lad who looked as lost and angry as he had once been, and the wife he loved walking out the door. She didn't belong to Charles. From the moment she danced in the park he'd known her as his. She had lent him her laughter, her passion, her trust, and for the first time in years, life was worth the living.

She asked but one thing, and look how I repaid her. By abandoning the future, abandoning her, to ride back to a past I hated. She'd stood by him as he relived his darkest hours, and she was right when she said it was his turn to stand by her. And so he'd abandoned his revenge. Hope was more important. The boy was more important. But the decision was not without its dangers.

"Well…Charlie hasn't seen her yet or I would know it. Does she want to be found, Captain?"

"Eh? What? Oh. Perhaps not." Robert shifted uncomfortably. "She has reason to be annoyed with me. I doubt she's expecting me. She was greatly disturbed when I decided to go after Harris rather than accompany her."

"That was not well played, my friend. You have arrived in time to redeem yourself, but what if it's Charlie she wants?"

"It isn't."

"So you have managed to capture the heart of one of London's most charming beauties?"

"Her heart and her hand are both mine." At least he hoped so. "I mean to bring her home."

"Safe from our sovereign's greedy reach. I understand. But what to do about Harris? It's unfortunate you weren't able to finish him off. A wounded beast is a dangerous one."

"I would have had to kill his boy. The lad was innocent."

William nodded. "It wasn't I who sent you the note, by the way."

"I know. I suspected it for a trap immediately, but as I was already there…" He shrugged.

"Fortunately, the trap is not yet sprung. It was baited, of course, to capture larger prey. Harris hoped to lure you there to make you seem a part of it, then play the role of informant and savior in front of his grateful king. You fought for Cromwell. A rumor here and there and next you are a Puritan. An old association found and voilà, a Fifth Monarchist, incensed at a king who would make you a cuckold. People will believe what they hear on very little evidence, because though it may be a sin to believe evil of others, it is seldom a mistake.

"We shall do to him what he meant to do to you. He's already placed himself in Farnley. Several men can claim to see him there, including one of His Majesty's paid informers, Joshua Greathead. It's a simple matter to put him in the midst of the plot. Yes, he was a royalist, but then a parliamentarian, and then back he goes to a royalist once more. Who can trust such a man or guess what he might do? Particularly when the king humiliated him in front of all London, by promising a reward for returning to the fold only to snatch it away to give to a lowly country baronet. A great many people owe him large sums of money. They will be glad to believe it and glad to see him gone."

Robert tilted his head and regarded William through narrowed eyes. "Just what *do* you do for the king? Besides writing scurrilous verse?"

"Oh, a bit of this and a bit of that. Only on occasion and when I'm in the mood, but I've always found it useful to know useful things. Hopefully *you* were circumspect?"

"I am always."

"At the tavern, too?"

"Only Harris is alive, knows who I am and could place me there."

"The boy? He might ask questions."

"A necessary risk. A tolerable one. Leave him out of it."

"None will notice if a minnow escapes the net. It will have to be drawn tight immediately, though, so no one else does. It would be best you were innocently asleep with your wife when it happens. "

The silence that followed was interrupted by a

muffled burst of laughter and the soft strains of a fiddle from the room below.

"It doesn't seem honorable." Robert sighed and unsheathed the longsword, laying it across his lap. It glittered blue and orange, reflecting flames from the hearth. "This was meant for him."

"He is rapist and murderer and I promise you, he *does* dabble at treason. He doesn't deserve any kind of honorable death."

Robert looked him in the eyes, his gaze direct. "He murdered someone I loved, several years ago. I've waited a long time for this. His death should be my responsibility, William."

"Not everything is your responsibility, Captain. This man is also a danger to Charles. He has to be dealt with in any case. If you'll allow someone else to bring him to justice, I can promise you it will be done. A belated wedding gift, if you will. What matters most to you, Robert? Revenge? Pride? Or your woman? It seems to me you have two choices—trust me to handle it with due diligence whilst you see to your lady, or take the risk of losing her and handle it yourself."

"You know the choice is already made."

"Then I have something else to tell you. His Majesty meets with your beloved within the hour."

"Be damned you say! Why didn't you tell me?"

"I have just done so, but I advise you to approach with caution lest you find yourself barking orders at drunken recruits in Tangiers."

CHAPTER THIRTY-ONE

HOPE NICHOLS, LADY NEWPORT, had wandered for three days after her arrival in London, at a loss as to what to do. Her title seemed to act as a disguise. No one recognized this obscure country countess, though she drew several admiring glances from the gentlemen she passed. Her house in Pall Mall was occupied by a diplomat from France, and when she gave her summons to the harried chamberlain at the palace he glanced at it quickly and told her he'd fix an appointment but it might take several days. She took some rooms in an inn facing the park and settled down to wait. Apparently, despite the stress and upheaval it had brought to her life, her summons had been an afterthought to Charles. She had no place to call home, no desire to speak with Charles, and the last she'd seen of her husband he'd had his sword pointed at a young boy's chest. When His Majesty called for her at last her temper was short and her nerves severely frayed.

He rose to greet her the moment she entered the room, arms outstretched and a warm smile on his face. "By God, madam! How is it possible? You are more lovely than I remembered!"

She avoided his hug, stepping in to a proper curtsey. "Your Majesty wished to see me?" She stood stiffly, refusing a proffered chair.

"You are annoyed with me. You feel I left you in the country too long."

"You called me from my home at the busiest time of year, then left me waiting at an inn."

"You never answered my letters."

"Because I had nothing left to say to you, Charles."

"Come now, sweet. I told you it was temporary. You are a lady now. I'll have a suite prepared and—"

"I won't be staying. I don't have feelings for you anymore, other than the honor and respect I owe my king."

"I am certain I can convince you otherwise, sweet—"

The door burst open and a black-clad giant strode through the door with a clutch of armed men scrambling to catch up behind him. He removed his hat and bowed low. "Your pardon, Majesty, for the late arrival. I had a spot of trouble on the road."

Hope felt a thrill of excitement. He was troubled. He was dangerous. He was here!

The king waved his guards away. "Captain Nichols! What a pleasant surprise."

"Surprise? I am confused, Your Majesty. Did you not recently summon my wife and I to court?

Charles lips twisted in annoyance. "So I did. Though it was my understanding you might be too *ill* to make the journey. In future you must not feel obliged to come every time your wife is summoned to court. I will be assigning her duties for my queen, and expect to see her here often."

"Your Majesty is most kind to concern himself with my health, but I assure you it's not necessary. I am of a hardy nature and any afflictions that ail me are only temporary."

"We are most pleased to hear it. Fortuitous news, indeed." The king put a companionable arm around Robert's shoulders. "I've been wanting to talk to you about a commission. You mentioned your interest before. We are growing concerned with these blasted Dutch incursions on our trade routes. Your experience and skills could be most helpful, and present you with some very lucrative opportunities indeed."

At least it's not drilling soldiers in Tangiers. "Again, I must thank you for your thoughtfulness, Majesty. You do me great honor, but surely that is a job best suited to a seaman and I regret to say I've no skill as a mariner, sire. I am content to have served England as a soldier, but now that I am married, I look forward to the life of a quiet country gentleman. Besides, surely a man's place is by his wife's side, particularly when she's as trusting and enticing as mine is."

"You are growing impertinent, sir. I dare say it is not me you have served but yourself. And at my table," the king snapped.

"With all due respect, Majesty, my wife is not your dinner." The challenge echoed through the room.

"No, I am not!" Hope was sick of it. "And I am not yours, either, Captain Nichols. I am tired of others deciding my life for me. Dismissing my concerns. Discussing me as if I were not there. Assuming their wishes must be my own without even bothering to ask. I am quite capable of managing my own life. I am no man's slave. I am a free English woman trapped in a bargain both of you have made. Well, gentlemen, here is some news. The only agreement I'll honor is one agreed to by me, and to the devil with you both!"

She stormed from the room leaving both men openmouthed with surprise behind her.

"Hope! Wait. We need to talk." She flipped an angry hand and kept on walking.

"We are not done here, Lady Nichols! Return at once. I have not given you permission…" Charles's voice trailed off as she rounded a corner and disappeared from sight.

"Well?" The king gave Robert a sharp poke. "You

crow that she is yours. Find her, Captain. And don't think of leaving London without bringing her back."

But quick as that she had disappeared, and he had no idea where to look.

CHAPTER THIRTY-TWO

HOPE WALKED DOWN THE STREET, heading toward the theater district, uncertain of everything except that she was done with Charles. She'd said the words to his face. Beyond annoyance, wariness and mild resentment, the sight of him had stirred no feelings at all, not even friendship. He was her king. That was all. Robert was different. The sight of him brought every nerve in her body pulsing to life. When he'd strode into the king's chamber five days ago like some conqueror of old coming to claim what was his, her heart had skipped several beats and she'd had to remind herself to breathe. He had kept his promise after all.

But what she'd said to both of them was true. All her life other people had tried to manage her, direct her, mold her to their own purpose. She had been claimed and owned, bought and sold, and though her heart and spirit had remained free, it was the decisions of others that had mapped the major turnings of her life. This time she was not going to be pushed. What she wanted, what she dreamed of, was too important. It had to be her decision. There was so much more to Robert than she'd ever imagined. Layer upon layer of dark and light. He'd opened a door and she'd entered, not knowing she stepped into a whirlwind. She needed time to absorb it. She needed time to think.

Unfortunately, deep thinking and paying attention to where she was going had never been her strong suit and as she rounded the corner she quite literally bumped into an old friend, the redheaded, gap-toothed actress Peg Hughes.

"Watch the bloody hell where you're going with that aristocratic arse! You're as blind as my granny and smell like… 'Od's fish! Hope? Hope Mathews, is that you?" Peg gave her a hug that almost crushed her ribs, and then hauled her into the King's Tavern for beef pies and beer.

"Well, ain't you looking the fine lady now! We all wondered where you disappeared."

"I got married, Peg. And went to live in the country."

"Lost the king but gained a husband, did you? Now that's a very nice play indeed. Keep you secure in your old age, that will. Is he poor but young and handsome, or a rich old toad?"

"He is rich enough and devilish handsome, Peg. Taller than the king. As tall as Prince Rupert. The kind who makes girls swoon."

"Pah!" Peg spit on the floor. "What's got into your head? You never marry one like that. Soon as they've gambled away all your money they're out running after whores."

"Not my husband. The only whore he wants is me. He leaves the rest alone." They both broke into laughter and Peg reached over to pinch her cheek. "Yep. You're real. And still making up fairy tales, you are. I swear you left the stage too soon. There's two companies of royal players now. The kings and the dukes. They'd be glad to have you back. People will always come to see one of Charlie's girls."

"I'm done with him, Peg."

"But if he sent you away and now he's brought you back it seems he's not done with you."

They chatted and drank Rhenish for the rest of the afternoon. Hope hadn't realized how lonely she was until she'd run into Peg. She missed Rose and Daisy, even Mrs. Overton. But most of all she missed the man whose touch sent shivers to every part of her body, whose warm voice soothed and excited at the same time. Who told her stories when she was hurting and taught her how to use a sword. Their last night together, before he'd left for Yorkshire, had introduced her to pleasures her body still ached for and—

"Hope?" Peg banged the table with her mug until she was sure she had her attention. "There you are, back again. You certainly can't hold your liquor like your mum." Peg filled her in on all the London gossip. Most of it centered on the usual protagonists—the king, his friends and now his little queen.

Bored, her thoughts drifted back to Robert. Did you leave a man like that, knowing that you loved him? Did you stay, knowing the dark thing that claimed him? Knowing how dangerous it was? Knowing it might always mean more to him than you? *But he came! He kept his promise.*

"Now the talk from everyone is that she's barren," Peg continued with breathless excitement.

"But she's only been married five months!" Hope protested. They talked a while longer and Peg invited her to come to the Duke's Theater, where she was performing that night. It would be a chance to make connections and renew old acquaintances, but she was lonely for something else this night. Peg gave her a hug and promised to visit soon, and then took the boat that traveled along the river to the new spring gardens in Vauxhall. It would be closed for the season by the end of the week, and she needed to feel as though she were back in the country this night.

The boat bumped gently to a halt by the river gate. There was laughter and gaiety beyond the stairs, and the gentle swell of music. She entered into an enchanted world of shopkeepers, courtiers and families with their children. They jostled in an excited mix, dancing and flirting, listening to harpists and fiddlers, enjoying cakes and powdered beef, or dining on white-draped tables. Hope smiled as she moved among them, determined to put her worries behind her and let this beautifully crafted fantasy soften her night.

She wandered until she discovered a quiet alcove next to a burbling fountain, and there she passed a glade filled with dancing and light. A thrush sang sweetly in a hidden bower with the sky above a glittering dome. Roman temples, magicians and jugglers, magical, beautiful, and she felt so very alone.

A strong arm suddenly encircled her waist and a rough hand covered her mouth, cutting off her scream. She bit it, drawing blood as her cursing captor dragged her kicking and clawing through the bushes into a secluded grotto.

"God's blood, Hope! Sheath your claws and loosen your fangs. You're worse than your bloodthirsty kitten. Where in hell have you been? I've been searching for you for four bloody days! I'd begun to think some harm had befallen you."

"Robert?" She looked up at him, stunned. It was as if her thoughts had conjured him from the air.

He growled in response, examining his injuries as best he could in the moonlight. "You've left me with more scars in this one night than in all my years of fighting. It stings like the very devil."

"Well, you shouldn't have snuck up and grabbed me like that!" Her body shook with shock and fear, anger and excitement, but she didn't forget to send a quick thank-you to whomever had answered her prayer.

They stood, awkward and silent, just inches apart, both of them chests heaving.

"You shouldn't have been standing on a darkened path at nighttime. It's dangerous. Any fool walking by might mistake you for a common strumpet."

"Perhaps that's why I'm here."

His lips twisted with annoyance. "I understand I've made you angry. I know I've disappointed you. But we're both well past pretending to be something we're not."

"You mean brave when I'm frightened? Cold when my heart is breaking? What choice do I have? It's my only armor. What do you pretend?"

"I pretend…" He drew a deep breath. "I pretend the very same."

"I saw you, Robert. I saw what you can do. What could possibly frighten you?"

"Oh, Hope, *you* do. I've been frightened from the moment I told Charles that I would marry you. I was watching you from the trees as you danced. I was so entranced I didn't hear his approach. As soon as I said it I knew I would love you, and I feared what might happen if you really knew me. I never wanted you to, but you kept insisting. God, Hope. I never wanted you to see me like that. I should have listened. I never should have left." His voice was barely a whisper.

"But you came. When I needed you, you were there."

He reached out to tuck a stray lock of hair behind her ear and she was in his arms. He moaned and pulled her tight against his length, plunging his hands in her hair, cupping her head and covering her face with feverish kisses.

"I want you to love me, Robert," she breathed against his lips.

"I do love you, elf. I've been cold and alone so long it's become a habit. And then you came into my life and warmed me like the sun but I didn't know how to show you or tell you. Sometimes I think I dream you. You've brought me back to life and I can't let you go. Charles can't have you. No one can have you. You're mine."

He sank to his knees, pulling her down with him, kissing her belly, her breasts, her lips and throat.

"I imagined your coming, Robert, ever since I was a child. I could feel you when it stormed. You're not some little girl's fantasy. But you *are* my man. I wished for you tonight and here you are."

They fumbled at their clothing, tugging and pulling, hungry and impatient as he pressed her to the ground. "I've missed you. Your feel, your taste, your hot smooth skin. It's been over a week you've been missing from my bed." His hands roamed her surface, rough and demanding, tugging at her skirts, bunching the material and rasping it across her belly as he bent to cool the throbbing heat between her thighs with a lush wet kiss.

She gasped and arched against him, threading her fingers through his hair, moaning in pleasure as his agile tongue swirled lazy patterns, sending throbbing waves of liquid pleasure from her heated center through limbs and muscles and skin. Every part of her wanted him. Wild thrills ran the length of her even when his fingers brushed her hair. "I want to feel you deep inside me, Robert. I want you to fill me as you fill my heart."

He kissed her belly and pinched a nipple whose peak demanded attention through linen and lace and velvet bodice. She gasped and jerked against him and he tugged her clasps open, peeling back lace and linen to lash her with his tongue. She whimpered and shifted, pulling his head closer as he bit her gently. Pressing her everywhere with hot sweet kisses, he traveled slowly up her body to claim her burning lips, dragging his mouth gently back and forth across hers as he teased her to open with his tongue. Her lips parted with a sigh and he stroked and tasted, his kiss an act of possession and wild caress.

Moaning and tangled they rolled in the grass until he straddled her, his naked skin opalescent in the silvery wash of moonlight. Her eyes were luminous like the sky above them, seeming to mirror all the mystery and magic of wild glades and soft nights.

She reached out a hand and laid it flat on his chest,

feeling the steady pulse of life beneath. "You are no dream," she whispered. "But you bring my dreams to life."

He gathered her warmth beneath him, his rampant arousal straining hard against the juncture of her thighs. And then he entered, slow and deliberate, savoring the moment, not as conqueror or supplicant, rescuer or rescued, but as someone who, after years in the wilderness, had finally found his way home.

She bucked against him, urging him deeper, each movement pulling him further into a sensual, soul-searing embrace. Never had the sky blazed with such majesty. No bed had been warmer, softer, more welcoming than the grass beneath her. No birdsong had ever sounded as sweet. Never had she felt so warm and safe. She held power and life and love in her arms and the world throbbed with color and everything pulsed with life.

Robert ground against her, his tongue thrusting with the same urgent rhythm that powered his hips. She squeezed him tight inside her as spasms of pleasure rocked her, melding with his and joining them in a blissful floating ancient bond. With a final sigh they fell back together as one, in a sated tangled heap.

"Well!" he said when he'd caught his breath, "We ought to do that more often. Every night, I should think, don't you?" His voice was hopeful.

Cuddled in his arms, she gave his ear a playful

nip. "Every time is new with you. I feel things I'd never imagined before. You take me places, Robert that... I've no words to describe it."

"Have I redeemed myself, then?" he asked as he combed his fingers through her hair.

"For being such a blockhead?" She could have said more but she didn't. "Yes, you have. But I've yet to forgive you for giving me such a scare."

He held out his mangled hand for her inspection. "Look at how it's swollen. I expect it's all infected now. I pray I don't lose my sword hand."

She gasped in horror, taking it gently, and gave it several little kisses. "We'll see a surgeon straight away. I'm sorry, Robert! I had no idea it was you."

He reached for his discarded coat and tucked it around her like a blanket. "I'm teasing you. I've survived many an injury worse than this. With the proper wifely care and attention I'm sure that I'll be fine."

"How on earth did you find me?"

"It wasn't easy. I remembered your fascination with gardens and flowers. I have been to Hyde Park, St. James Park, the gardens at Whitehall, to every damned garden I could find, asking strangers if they'd seen an elfin beauty with midnight hair and violet eyes. Did you know there are two gardens here? An old one and a new one, though this is deemed the better. I was offered blondes, brunettes, redheads of every talent and description, but no one had seen you. It's sheer luck I found you tonight. Were you hiding?"

"No. Yes. I needed time to think."

"It's over. With Harris."

"You killed him?"

"No. I couldn't without harming the boy. I couldn't after seeing you. I hated that you saw me that way and suddenly it all seemed so senseless and stupid. It wasn't going to bring Caroline back but it might cost me you. I don't want to live in the past, Hope. I want to have a life and future with you. My life had little meaning until you came along and I knew if I lost you it never would again."

He took her hand and kissed her fingers, then held up a tiny band of woven grass. "Hope Mathews, I've never been in love before. I'm likely to make lots of mistakes. I expect if you agree to stay with me you'll have to be very patient. Oakes knows me well and he says I'm not very good with people. But I do try and listen and I want to learn. So if you cannot feel free or happy with me, then I will do my best to help you to wherever you wish to be. But you know me now, and I know you, and I would ask you first, given free heart and free will…would you marry me?"

Laughing through her tears she shoved him over onto his back and held out her hand. "I am *exactly* where I wish to be, foolish man. I want to see my ring."

He slipped it on her finger and pulled her in to a

tender kiss. Hope nuzzled the sensitive spot behind his ear. "What does Oakes know? A good deal less than you, I expect. He has eyes for Mrs. Overton and doesn't even realize it. Trust me, Robert." She folded her arms on his chest and rested her chin on her hands. "You are very, very, *very* good with women."

CHAPTER THIRTY-THREE

LORD AND LADY NICHOLS WANDERED through a stately bedchamber crowded with books and paper, curiosities and ticking clocks.

"So this is his room?"

"Yes."

Hope blushed furiously but she needn't have worried. Robert never felt intimidated or doubted his prowess in any arena when it came to other men.

She watched as he fiddled with a telescope. His fascination with it made her smile. Perhaps she would present him with one at New Year's. She could picture him using it on dark summer nights on the terrace. It struck her that she didn't even know when his birthday was. There was so much about him to learn. She knew what was important, though. When she needed him, he was there.

"Look you here, Hope!" He was standing over a mechanical automaton of otters catching fish.

She came over and leaned against his shoulder, nodding her head, trying to look suitably impressed while wondering why such silly toys made grown men act like boys. "Does it ever seem strange to you how we were brought together?"

"You mean the parade?"

"That and other things."

"Well, the whole night at Pall Mall seemed strange to me, starting with your hall of mirrors."

"But think of it, Robert. I was hardly likely to ever go to Nottingham, or you to come backstage at the theater."

"Ah! I see what you say. You wonder how fate conspired to join us a second time."

"Exactly!"

"Well," he mused, "if one thinks of you as Cinderella, then Charles would be your fairy godmother. He clothed you for the ball and settled you in a fine coach, though you lost both slippers." They broke into helpless laughter.

"His scepter is a magic wand!" she cried.

"And Castlemaine an evil stepsister!"

"Let's hope he's not annoyed and turns us both back into pumpkins."

"Why don't you ask him yourselves, my dears. He is standing right behind you. I believe you mean country bumpkin, Captain."

Hope's face looked almost comical in its surprise while Robert's was merely assessing. Charles couldn't help a grin. "Your husband is very big, Lady Nichols. One notices more when he stands behind you. Are you still angry with me for choosing him?"

"*I* have chosen him, Charles." She held out her hand, proudly showing off her woven ring. "In the end that's all that matters."

"And if I strip your handsome giant of his lands?"

"We are a talented pair, Your Majesty." Robert stepped in. "I'll still have my sword, and my wife will design gardens."

"Gardens, you say!" The king barked with laughter. "Charles. Call me Charles. 'Od's fish! Fairy godmother indeed! You've a sharp tongue on you, Captain Nichols. Come. Sit. We'll share some wine. To your health, my dears, and a very happy marriage."

"You're not angry?" Hope asked.

Charles shrugged. "I'm not known for being jealous. While some dreamed of jewels, pensions, favors, you wanted to go fishing. You wanted a possessive, glowering husband. You wanted to be in love. Apparently you wanted shrubbery, too. If he was man enough to fight for you, you'd have your knight in shining armor. If he wasn't, then you'd be better off with me. I'll admit I had hopes for the latter outcome, but I'm pleased to see you happy and I'll not deny it out of spite."

NOT LONG AFTER they left, a moody Charles Stuart tossed back a glass of wine. A gloating, spiteful mistress, a weeping, homesick wife, deserted by his pretty country miss—what did her towering husband call her? Ah, yes, elf. It suited her. He had promised to see her taken care of. She was a lady by title now, with a husband who loved her. It wasn't the usual reward, but she was an unusual woman. *I shall miss her. Who will I fish with? Who will I sail with? Who will come to the races and swig brandy and beer?*

Castlemaine he loved the most, though it was cold and cynical. His wife Catherine he owed the most, though she'd yet to conceive and half her dowry had not been paid. But it was Hope who he liked the most. *Her husband is a lucky man indeed.* He made note to have his gardener send her a selection of bushes and roses, and some trees for her orangery come the spring.

One of his gentlemen came to whisper in his ear and he nodded. "Yes, by all means. Send them in." He rose from his seat, his arms outstretched to greet them. "William! Elizabeth! What a pleasant surprise. Come, sit, have some tea. It is a favorite of my wife's and I am growing fond of it myself."

They joined him at a table by the window. "I am indebted to you, William. For warning us of Harris. He was caught with nearly thirty other conspirators, badly wounded while trying to escape. Will we ever see the end to these ridiculous plots? Sit, please, and tell me why you came."

"Charles, we have come to say goodbye. Lizzy and I are going home."

"No! Everyone I trust and enjoy is going home.

The place is barely recognizable anymore. I need you here."

"We shall return to visit often, Charles. And of course you are welcome in our home anytime."

"*Et tu,* Elizabeth? After all my kindness to your latest charity?"

She rose and came around the table to kiss him. "Thank you, Charlie. I am grateful to you once again."

The king rose, too, and kissed her back. "Do you see, de Veres? I just kissed your wife. I could take her from you anytime I want."

"My wife *let* you kiss her, much like she lets her puppy do. I find it sloppy and somewhat off-putting, but she doesn't wish to hurt its feelings."

Charles grinned and chucked Elizabeth under her chin. "I need my poet. Particularly in these bitter times. Give us a poem, Will."

"'Our Romish bondage breaker Harry
Espoused half a dozen wives;
Charles only one resolved to marry…'"

"Enough!" Charles said wearily. "I see where this goes."

William bowed low. "I haven't rusticated so long in the country that I warble pretty tunes, Your Majesty. Let me go, Charles. The gaiety rings false. I can't do it anymore, unless I am drunk. If you force me to stay I will maul you. And I love you too well to enjoy doing that."

Charles sighed. "I can see this is going to be one of those days. Go, then, if you must. Back to milking cows and planting potatoes. I've had enough of leave takings for one day. A black mood calls for the theater."

THE KING SAT WITH BUCKINGHAM in his box. The curtain opened to wild applause and gasps of delight as a beautiful girl in a gold helmet with purple plumes descended from on high with golden sword and shield. She set foot on the stage in a pair of high-heeled gold boots and but for those and the shield, she was completely naked underneath. Breaking into full-throated song she twirled around the stage revealing a pert, naked bottom.

"George? Who is she?"

"That, my lord, is the newest comedic actress. Her name is Eleanor Gwynn."

CHAPTER THIRTY-FOUR

Sherwood Forest, Nottinghamshire

UNDER A CANOPY of gently rustling leaves, Robert leaned against the bark of the greenwood tree, a majestic yew with widespread arms that grew in Sherwood Forest. Hope nestled quiet in his arms. Well over one thousand years old, one could almost feel the life and warmth flowing through its ancient veins. One had but to close one's eyes to imagine a time when ordinary men and women had done extraordinary things, defying great lords and braving great odds to keep their freedom.

What wonders had this monarch of the forest seen as it bore witness to the fleeting lives of men? It was not so much one tree as two, with roots entwined and trunks grown so close together they had, in a far distant past, melded into one. Some folk called them marriage trees. Some said Robin and his Marian had been joined beneath this very one. He smiled and kissed the top of his pretty wife's head. It certainly pleased her to think so. And so they had married again, on this first day of May exactly one year from the day she had first stepped into his life, joyfully and freely, in a place of their own choosing, for themselves this time.

Hope stirred and put a sleepy arm around his waist. Exhausted from the revelry, they watched contentedly as friends and servants and the Derbyshire pastor made merry in the distant courtyard. The sounds of flute, fiddle, laughter and song came to them in quiet bursts, carried by a dulcet breeze.

"Do you remember, Hope? When you told me that if I let go of the past, I might find what I was meant to do?"

"Mmm, yes. I remember."

"I have discovered it, the thing I was really meant to do. I was meant to love you."

"Of course you were, silly man. I am very wise. You should always listen."

He tickled her and she elbowed him and shifted, settling now with her head resting in the crook of his arm.

"I love you, Hope Nichols, lady of the forest glades and my own sweet elf."

"And I love you, Captain Nichols. I am thankful every day that you stepped out of my dreams and carried me away." Something caught her eye, a movement through the trees that drew her attention to the top of a grassy hill. She saw a beautiful young girl with sweetly rounded features and flowing gold locks, flying a brightly colored kite. The child turned to look at her with a brilliant smile, then waved her hand. The sound of happy laughter followed her as she disappeared over the hill.

EPILOGUE

GULLS SCREECHED OVERHEAD and flags snapped in the stiff breeze. The creak of straining rope and shifting wood rode atop the thunder of the waves. The boy watched from the shadows. Now the shouts of rough men, the crack of whips and the dull jangle of chains and iron shackles. A ragged line of broken men stumbled toward the fretting ship, bound for Jamaica. One of them was his father. Nothing but a slave now. If he survived the voyage. No pity stirred within his breast. He stayed, watching, as the ship left the dock, sails billowing. He didn't turn away until it dipped below the horizon. When it was gone he looked to the ground and spat, before hefting the fat purse his father's would-be killer had given him. He still didn't know what to make of that, but he knew what he was going to do with the money.

* * * * *

AFTERWORD

AN AFTERWORD provides the opportunity to share a few tidbits one finds interesting but might have slowed the pace of the story, a chance to acknowledge the contribution of others to one's story and a chance to address things one could have missed. Some readers might have recognized that the character of Hope Mathews is loosely based on Nell Gwyn, the orange girl and actress who became an enduring mistress of King Charles II, giving birth to the Earl of Burford, later Duke of St. Albans. Hope and Nell share some similar adventures, including three lovers named Charles, and according to Charles Beauclerk, a direct descendant and Nell's biographer, the moniker of Cinder wench and Cinder whore. These seem to have been more a term of endearment on the part of Londoners who were delighted to see one of their own risen from the gutter to grace the bed of a king. Charles had a penchant for actresses from Drury Lane, and Nell was not his first or last, but from the moment she became Charles Stuart's mistress, she never loved another man. She was, however, content to share him with Lady Castlemaine, his wife and several mistresses, and remained with him until his death, something Hope would never have done. Readers who would like to know more about Nell

Gwyn and Charles would enjoy Charles Beauclerk's biography, which includes stories and private papers passed down through the family.

Many people believe stories such as *Cinderella* are inventions of the Brothers Grimm, but as noted in the afterword of *Libertine's Kiss,* Mother Goose was well-known at the time. Some say she was a real figure, the wife of a fifteenth-century monarch, but by the seventeenth century *a Mother Goose tale* was a common phrase. Charles Perrault (12 January 1628–16 May 1703) was a French author whose best-known tales, derived from preexisting folk tales, include *Le Petit Chaperon Rouge (Little Red Riding Hood), La Belle au Bois Dormant (Sleeping Beauty), Le Maître Chat ou le Chat Botté (Puss in Boots)* and *Cendrillon ou la Petite Pantoufle de Verre (Cinderella and the Glass Slipper)* complete with pumpkin, glass slippers and stepsisters.

May Day and Valentine's Day were both celebrated with a good deal more passion than they are today. According to Samuel Pepys, one's Valentine was the first person of the opposite sex one encountered that day. In his diary he grumbles about being caught by a maid before he sees his wife. One assumes he had to give them both presents. May Day celebrations were raunchy, uproarious and decidedly pagan. They were banned during Cromwell's reign, but made a triumphant return with the Restoration. May Day celebrations generally included traditional

Morris Dancers (who are still present in May Day parades and celebrations today), the choosing of a May King and, more important, Queen, dancing around the maypole, and jack-in-the-greens—men loaded with so many garlands they ended up resembling trees. Different guilds would often compete to see who could provide the most elaborate celebrations. They are still a part of May Day festivities in Britain to this day.

The Restoration and termination of the civil war did not end all divisions in England at the time. The king was a suspected Catholic, his brother James a professed one, and there were many lingering plots to remove them both. The foolish and ill-planned treason at Farnley Wood was one of the first attempts. Undermined by informers, it came to nothing but resulted in the arrest and charges of treason against twenty-six men.

Poetry, music, literature and plays were an integral part of seventeenth-century life. Those who read *Libertine's Kiss* are already familiar with William's penchant for conversing at times in verse, and that the words are actually those of John Wilmot, the Earl of Rochester, on whom the character was based. None of the poetry in *The King's Courtesan* is my own. Some of course belongs to Wilmot. Some include his translation of verses that were originally Ovid's, and the Robin Hood poem comes from *Robin Hood: a collection of all the ancient poems, songs and bal-*

lads, now extant, relative to that celebrated English outlaw, which was first printed in 1795.

If you go to Sherwood Forest today you can still visit the major Oak, where legend has it Robin Hood and his men often stayed.

Hope's interest in gardening was not unusual at the time. The English loved their gardens, and during the seventeenth century there was an explosion of exotic plants available from all over the world. John Rose, King Charles's gardener, is credited as the first to introduce the pineapple to English gardeners, but it was the Tradescants, father and son (1570–1662), botanists, explorers, adventurers, horticulturalists and garden planners, who introduced many exotic plants to England that remain staples of English gardens to this day. Amongst many other plants and flowers these included magnolias, yucca plants, asters and Virginia creepers.

I'd like to thank my copy editor, John Oberholtzer, whom I missed in the initial acknowledgments, but whose contribution, insights and sharp eyes were of tremendous value. I'd also very much like to thank my readers. Your encouragement and kind words mean more than you can know. I hope you enjoyed *The King's Courtesan.* Having read it, you have, I suspect, a very good idea of what's coming next.

All the best,
Judith James

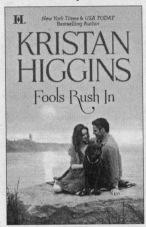

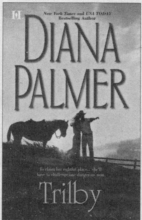

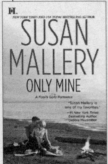
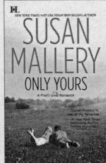
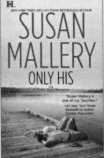